Praise for

DARK
BLADE

'This has everything you want from an epic fantasy adventure –
devious Gods, hideous monsters, a portal to another
dimension and a hero with an enchanted blade. Great stuff'
Charlie Higson, author of the Young Bond series

'Fans of Rick Riordan and John Flanagan have a whole
new world of dark magic, mysterious gods and brave
heroes waiting for them'
Sebastien de Castell, author of the Spellslinger series

'A razor-sharp, spellbinding read full of intrigue and magic.
This tale truly takes the crown as the young heir to the
likes of *A Game of Thrones* and *Throne of Glass*'
Chris Bradford, author of the Young Samurai series

'The world of Strom is rich with peril, political intrigue,
conspiracies and betrayals … Why aren't you reading this already?'
Sarwat Chadda, author of the Ash Mistry Chronicles series

'An epic dark fantasy set in an arcane world where kings
are murdered, monsters roam and ordinary boys are
given extraordinary gifts'
Mark Walden, author of the H.I.V.E series

'A powerful, compelling story in a world that stays with you'
Angie Sage, author of the Septimus Heap series

Books by Steve Feasey

Mutant City
Mutant Rising

Dark Blade

DARK BLADE

STEVE FEASEY

BLOOMSBURY
LONDON OXFORD NEW YORK NEW DELHI SYDNEY

BLOOMSBURY YA
Bloomsbury Publishing Plc
50 Bedford Square, London WC1B 3DP, UK
29 Earlsfort Terrace, Dublin 2, Ireland

BLOOMSBURY, BLOOMSBURY YA and the Diana logo
are trademarks of Bloomsbury Publishing Plc

First published in Great Britain in 2019 by Bloomsbury Publishing Plc

A catalogue record for this book is available from the British Library

ISBN: PB: 978-1-4088-7339-7; eBook: 978-1-4088-7340-3

4 6 8 10 9 7 5 3

Typeset by RefineCatch Limited, Bungay, Suffolk
Printed and bound in Great Britain by CPI Group (UK) Ltd, Croydon CR0 4YY

To find out more about our authors and books visit www.bloomsbury.com
and sign up for our newsletters

To Zoe.
Here's to a new adventure.
But without the swords, I hope!

Fair Forest · Eshk

Scoodale · Feclanger Farm

N e s h

CORLNE

Kuss

the Great Marsh

BANCUSZ

to the Southern Kingdoms

STROM
and the Surrounding Kingdoms

Prologue
A Gift

Lae Fetlanger awoke with a start. Sitting up, she looked around the room, trying to work out what had pulled her from the deep sleep she'd been in. The remaining embers in the fire still glowed enough to suggest there were a few hours until dawn. Even so, she could make out little in the darkness of her bedroom. Lae turned her head towards the shadowy shape of her husband lying beside her, wondering if his snoring had caused her sudden awakening, but Gord's breathing was shallow and even.

A noise outside – a cry – made her pulse quicken, the sound rekindling fragments of the dream she'd been having. Living on a remote cattle farm, Lae was used to the noises of wild animals beyond the safety of her wooden walls, and on any other occasion she might have dismissed this as just that: the screech of a mating fox or a winter owl perhaps. But not tonight.

She wrapped a blanket about herself, the rough wool itchy against her skin, and made her way through the farmhouse. The front door groaned in protest as she pushed it open into the darkness, and she caught her breath as the icy air rushed in.

She'd no sooner set foot outside when she heard the cry again. There was no doubt in her mind now that it was the plaintive call of a baby, and she hurried in the direction of the barn where the noise was coming from, ignoring the harsh bite of the cold ground beneath her bare feet.

Leaving the barn door open behind her, she looked about frantically until her eyes fell upon the little bundle laid on the straw pile inside one of the stalls. The baby was well wrapped up so that only its face was exposed to the night air, and she instinctively bent down and picked it up. There was colour in the child's cheeks and the skin was warm to the touch; he could not have been out here long. Lae pressed the tiny child close to her body, tucking the blanket around them both. As she did so, the baby stopped crying.

She hurried back to the house, crying out for Gord. As she re-entered the farmhouse, her husband was on his feet standing in the doorway to their room, hastily trying to pull on his boots. In his left hand was a long hunting knife. His eyes grew wide when he saw what it was his wife was clutching to her breast.

'It's a child, a little boy. We're keeping him,' she said.

'But—'

'He's a gift. From the gods.'

'Lae …'

The look she gave him stopped further protest. Gord had not seen that look often but he knew what it meant; there would be no changing his wife's mind. She had waited long enough for a child, and now it appeared one had been gifted to her.

'We're keeping him,' she repeated.

The Maiden's Fingers

1

The year Lannigon Fetlanger turned thirteen, almost a man in the eyes of his people, was an unhappy one. It was the year that Horst Rivengeld, their beloved king, was killed in battle. But it was also the year Lann was to experience personal tragedy of the worst kind, when his mother died trying to give birth to what would have been his brother or sister had the child survived.

Lae's death coincided with the night of the great storm, a storm that would be spoken of in the Six Kingdoms for many years to come. Even the witch Fleya, armed with her majik and her potions, was unable to save the mother or her unborn child.

Lann would never forget that night for the rest of his life. Banished from the bedroom, he had stood looking out of the kitchen window at the fields outside, doing his best not to get too upset by the sounds of his mother's cries.

Tiny fists of rain beat on the roof overhead, a persistent cacophony that did nothing to ease the tension inside the house, and he prayed to the gods, both the old and the new, that they might ease her suffering. His father, who had been pacing about the house, came into the kitchen demanding Lann close the shutters against the foul weather. It was as he reached through the opening to do so that a dazzling knife of light struck the big elm tree in the yard, forcing Lann to snap his eyes shut against the glare. When he opened them again he could see how a great fissure had opened up down the length of the trunk, as if the thing had been struck with the giant axe wielded by the first god, Og, himself.

It was a portent, he had little doubt about that, but what it symbolised was a mystery. Unlike the witch across the hall in his parents' room, he had no skill in interpreting such things.

The boy was still standing like that, wet from the rain being blown in at him and staring out at the tree, when a loud sobbing noise behind made him turn around. His father was standing in the bedroom doorway, his face streaked with tears. It was only then that he realised that his mother's cries had stopped. And just as the elm had been split by the lightning bolt, Lann knew his own world had also been torn in two.

* * *

5

Amidst all the grief and confusion of that night, one other memory was etched into Lann's memory. As the witch, Fleya, was leaving their farmhouse, she stopped in front of him. She was a tall woman with piercing blue eyes that shone with intelligence. Were she not a witch, Lann guessed that men would find her beautiful. She cast those eyes over him, taking in his face before giving a little smile.

'You've grown,' she said, her voice not unkind. 'How long until your sixteenth year?'

He hesitated before answering; he knew the Volken people around these parts were scared of the woman, even though her midwifery and healing skills had helped so many of them. Rumours about her were rife, and it was difficult to know which were fact and which were fiction. Despite this, Lann lifted his chin and met her blue eyes with his own. She was younger than his mother had been, he realised.

'A little under three years,' he answered, struggling to get the words out under her intense scrutiny.

She leaned in close to him and he caught a whiff of lavender and sage. When she spoke, her voice was little more than a whisper.

'Hear me, Lannigon Fetlanger, and mark my words well. One day, not too far from now, you will see a star with a serpent's tail. Beware that moment. Run when you see that heavenly sign. Run for all you are worth. And trust

6

your instincts on where to find safety, or those three years will never come to pass.' She held his gaze for an instant longer, then turned, pulling the hood of her cape up over her head and sweeping out of the house into the rain and wind before he had a chance to ask her what she had meant.

The boy watched her leave; she strode past the smoking elm tree without giving it so much as a second glance.

Gord Fetlanger never recovered from his wife's death; the following months saw him reduced to a shadow of his former self. He took to sitting about the farmhouse, staring into space and disregarding his work. Even when a wolf pack came on to his lands and killed some of his cattle, Gord could not be persuaded to set off in pursuit of the beasts. Instead, it was the young Fetlanger who joined Orlof, the head cattleman, and the others, camping out overnight in the cold and the rain in an effort to kill the predators.

Lann and his father had never been close, but now it seemed the boy could do no right in his father's eyes, and when the pair were together in the house, the older man would ignore him completely, even leaving the room when the youngster entered. He drank more and more, the alcohol causing wild mood swings. Silent apathy would give way to fury in which he would tear the farmhouse apart, resisting Lann's efforts to calm him down. 'My wife and son are dead!' he would howl. The boy knew better than to answer back when he was like this. But the words stung, and Lann wanted nothing more than to point out that he was still alive, that he was missing his mother and that he was in need of a father, now more than ever.

Two months after Lae's death, things finally came to a head. His father, drunk on strong spirits, sat by the fire all day staring into the flames. Lann went about his chores as he did every evening, and when he'd finished, announced he was off to bed.

'Wait,' Gord muttered. He gestured for Lann to come over to him.

Lann did as he was bid and walked over to where his father sat, slumped by the fire. Gord said nothing, but there was an odd look in his eyes as he glowered back up at the boy.

'What is it, Father?' Lann asked.

'Don't call me that,' the man spat back, slurring his words. 'You have no right to call me that. Just as I have no wish to call you my "son".'

Lann stared down at the man, not sure if he had heard him correctly. His father's words made no sense, but the cruel expression on Gord's face caused a frisson of fear to snake its way through the boy.

'What do you mean?' Lann asked.

Gord waved the question away and returned his attention to the fire.

His heart thumping, Lann stepped between the man and the flames, forcing the farmer to look at him. 'Tell me.'

And Gord told him. Told him how Lann had been found that night, a little bundle wrapped in blankets, abandoned in the barn. How Lae had insisted on keeping him, even though Gord knew he would only bring the family heartbreak and bad luck.

'A foundling, that's what you are!' Gord finished, sneering back at the boy. 'A curse, left by evil spirits to bring us misery!'

Unable to bear any more, Lann ran from the house. The night was dark and he stumbled in the darkness, hot and angry tears falling from his eyes as Gord's words replayed in his head over and over again. Not wishing to return to the house, he spent a sleepless night in the same barn his mother had first discovered him in all those years ago.

The next day, Gord had given a brief, muttered apology. 'Just the drink talking,' he had said. But his eyes told a different story and they told Lann he'd been speaking the truth.

Everything changed for Lannigon from that night onwards. The farmhouse felt different, and Lann made a point of spending as little time there as possible, choosing instead to roam the lands that made up Gord Fetlanger's considerable holding. He liked nothing more than to climb the craggy hills known as the Maiden's Fingers or ride his pony down to the river where his mother had come to wash their clothes when she was still alive. That was his favourite place. He would sit on the bank and relive memories of her singing to him as she rinsed the garments, her voice mingling with the river's own song as it tumbled across the stones and rocks.

He yearned to travel, to get away from this cold place and explore lands he'd heard whispers of. Places that could only be accessed by days afloat on vast bodies of water, or by crossing huge mountain ranges that made the Maiden's Fingers look like little more than the ancient burial mounds to the east of Gord's lands.

Little did Lann know that, all too soon, he would leave these lands; and that the far-flung places of his dreams would become reality.

Stromgard

2

Kelewulf stared at the king's dead body. Horst Rivengeld had been laid out in his finest armour: the studded black leather ensemble he had died in. The gaping hole where an enemy warrior had thrust a spear through it had been neatly repaired. The blood had been cleared up from his hair and beard, and, were it not for the ghastly grey colour of his skin, Kelewulf might have believed Horst Rivengeld were merely sleeping on the cold stone plinth.

The boy shifted his attention to his father's lifeless face. He felt no swell of emotion, no remorse at this man's passing.

I'm glad you're dead, old man, he thought. *My only regret is that I was not there to hear you cry out as the spear pierced your side. I would have liked to have seen the look on your face when you gazed into your killer's eyes.*

Kelewulf's relationship with his father had never been a happy one. They were too different. Horst Rivengeld, like so many of the Volken people, believed in the way of the warrior. So when it became clear to the king that his son had no interest in the art of war, the man had become desperate, trying everything in his power to change the boy's nature. When words and admonishments failed to have the desired effect, Horst had resorted to more physical methods. But the beatings, intended to 'toughen up' his son, had merely turned Kelewulf even further away from him. The simple truth was that the boy was too much like his mother.

Queen Elenor's marriage to the king had not been for love. Instead it had been a political match, intended to mend the historical rift between the Bantusz of the south and the Strom kingdom Horst ruled. As a foreigner, she had little regard for the ways of a people she considered to be barbaric and backward. Rather than aiding her husband in trying to mould Kelewulf into the type of son the king wanted, she turned her son's mind to books and the power contained in them. She told him about the majik her people had learned, and how they had used it to defeat barbarous invaders like the Stromgardians. She taught him about history and geography. She taught him that true power lies not just in the sword, but in knowledge.

As far as the king was concerned, Elenor's actions were not driven by a mother's love. Instead, he believed she was using the boy as a means to defy him. Whatever her true motives were, they had ultimately cost the queen her life.

It was when Kelewulf turned twelve that the madness took hold of his mother. Her sickness, Kelewulf was convinced, had been brought on by his father's mistreatment of them both. And the madness had robbed Kelewulf of the one person he'd ever loved when she'd taken her own life in Vissergott.

And now the man was dead.

Sensing someone entering the great hall behind him, Kelewulf was careful to wipe away the sneer on his lips, replacing it with a look more becoming of a grieving son.

His cousin Erik joined him, standing respectfully at Kelewulf's side as they stared down at the dead king. 'He died a good Volken warrior's death,' he said.

'Whatever that means.'

'In battle. With his axe in one hand and his shield in the other. He will enter the Great Halls and meet the gods as a hero.'

'And that is a *good death*, is it?' Kelewulf said, unable to hide the sarcasm in his voice.

'As good a one as any of us could hope for.'

'If that is the case, then I'm afraid my own death will not be considered "a good one".'

The silence that followed was uncomfortably long. Erik, like so many of the Volken people, felt uneasy around the pale-faced scholar. The Volken way was the warrior's way, and Kel was anything but a warrior.

'I'm glad I managed to find you on your own, cousin,' Erik eventually said.

'Oh?'

'I … I wanted to know how things sit with you … regarding my father's claim to the throne. While the decision was voted for by the high council, I suspect there might be some who disagree with it. I would like to know if you are one of them. After all, the throne could just as easily have gone to you.'

Kelewulf smiled inwardly. His uncle, Mirvar Rivengeld, had ascended the throne and this had all but ruled out Kelewulf's chance of ever taking that role. There had been rumours at court he was unhappy about this. What nobody in this or any of the neighbouring kingdoms could possibly know was that Kelewulf had never harboured any wish to rule over these … savages. No, let his cousin Erik and other oafish axe-swingers like him rule Stromgard; Kelewulf had other, grander ideas.

Seeing that Erik was watching him, Kelewulf forced his lips into a humble smile. 'It is the right of the council to vote that the crown can pass from brother to brother if they think it is for the good of the people. The crown is in safe hands with your father. He is a just man and a great warrior, perhaps even greater than my father.' When Erik put a consoling arm across his shoulders, Kelewulf cringed. He hated to be touched and he wanted nothing more than to peel himself away from the unsolicited contact.

'Shall I go?' Erik asked. 'I came to pay my respects before the funeral, but I can come back ...'

'No, stay. I was just going.' Kelewulf stepped to one side, relieved at having broken the physical connection between the two of them. 'I will be in my rooms if you need me. I have a particularly interesting book I'm reading at the moment, and I wish to get back to it.' He caught the disapproval in his cousin's face. 'I find that reading helps me forget my loss,' he quickly added, twisting his face into what he hoped was a reasonable semblance of grief.

'Of course. We must all find our own solace at a time like this. Perhaps we can talk again soon? When your pain is not so raw?'

'Yes, perhaps. Excuse me, cousin.'

Erik watched Kelewulf leave before turning to look down at his dead uncle again, his mind awhirl. He felt sorrow for his cousin's loss, and also relief that the throne would pass unchallenged to his own father. As a warrior, his uncle was unsurpassed. He'd used his military might to bring the kingdoms together when they might have fallen into civil war. But his rule had been one largely of fear. Mirvar Rivengeld would be a good king to the Volken people, a people whom Erik secretly suspected Kelewulf held in low esteem. He frowned, silently reproaching himself for these unkind thoughts. He and Kel had grown up together. Back when they were little they played well together; friends as well as cousins. But when Kel's mother killed herself the younger boy changed. He had always refused to learn to wield a weapon. Instead, he found refuge in the hundreds of books he'd surrounded himself with. And while there was no harm in that, it had—

A movement to his left caused Erik to spin around, his hand already on the hilt of his sword.

'Calm down, brother.'

His younger sister, Astrid, stepped out from behind the pillar. She approached him but was looking off in the direction Kelewulf had just left in, an odd expression on her face.

'It's not nice to spy on people, Astrid.'

'I wasn't spying. I was in here on my own when Kelewulf came in. I didn't want to be seen by him, so I hid behind the pillar.'

'Why hide? You should have spoken to him. He is grieving.'

She gave him a sceptical look. Astrid had never been keen on Kel; he was arrogant, she said, and contemptuous of their ways. Erik on the other hand had always defended him.

'Did you buy all that guff?' she asked.

'Guff?'

'About our father, and how the crown was now in good hands.'

'He seemed genuine enough to me.' Astrid snorted, and Erik sighed. 'You are being unfair. Kel has never expressed any interest in ruling, you know that.'

His sister met his gaze and held it. 'On that we agree, brother. He has no wish to rule over the Volken people, and do you know why?'

'Enlighten me.'

'Because he sees us as … beneath him. He has no love of these lands or its people.'

'You don't know that, Astrid.'

'I do, brother. And I think you know it too.'

Erik shook his head. 'Regardless, he is family. We must do our duty by him.'

She gave him a crooked smile and set her head to one side. It was a mannerism their father Mirvar used whenever he thought someone was being foolish. 'I doubt our cousin

17

will ask me for any help, but if he does I'll be sure to give it to him. In return I ask that you do something for me.'

'And what might that be?'

'Don't trust him, Erik. He is not the person you think he is.'

The Maiden's Fingers

3

It was early in the evening and Lann was almost back at the farm, having been out all day tending to the cattle. The pony beneath him was tired and he needed to let her feed and drink soon. At the edge of the world, the sun was doing its best to cling on to remains of the day, and as Lann looked up to take in the changing colours of the sky, he witnessed the star streaking through the firmament. A gasp escaped him at the sight: a bright pinpoint of light trailing a white tail in its wake as it raced towards the sinking sun.

There were three days before his fourteenth birthday, and the witch's words from the previous year came back to him: *One day, not too far from now, you will see a star with a serpent's tale. Beware that moment.*

With difficulty he tore his eyes away from the heavenly sight and looked towards the farmhouse.

His father's horse was dead in the front yard, its flanks wet with blood where it had been clawed and bitten. The front door to his childhood home was open. The icy fingers of fear gripped him and he sat in the saddle staring at the poor creature, desperately trying to work out what he should do.

'*Run for all you are worth,*' the witch had told him, and he knew he should pull the pony about and set it off in the opposite direction as fast as he could. But his father was in the farmhouse …

Just then, a naked, blood-covered man emerged from the house and caught sight of the boy and his pony. What followed was the stuff of horror. The man let out a strangled cry and dropped down on to all fours, his entire body taut and rigid as if a terrible pain coursed through him. And right there, before Lann's eyes, the man transformed into a hellish wolf. The thing was far bigger than any wolf he'd ever seen before, and when it lifted its head, it stared back at him through black, hate-filled eyes. The creature had no place in this world. It was a thing of fable, from the days when the gods still walked across this world. The foul chimera opened its gore-covered jaws and let out a howl of rage. With that, it launched itself off the front porch towards Lann, taking great, leaping bounds on powerful legs and halving the distance separating them within a few heartbeats. For a moment, both the boy and his mount froze, terror turning their bodies to stone. Then Lann pulled the pony's head around and set his heels into the beast's flanks, loudly urging it forward.

The pony was hardy and well suited to the rocky terrain at the bottom of the Maiden's Fingers. Spurred on by its own fear and that of its rider, it quickly opened up a gap again between them and the hellish wyre-creature. Even so, Lann knew they couldn't hope to keep their pursuer at bay for long. The pony was too tired to keep up her pace for much longer and the creature would then be upon them.

The witch's words came to him then: '*Trust your instincts on where to find safety.*'

An idea occurred to him, a crazy idea of where they could hide. Desperately he steered his mount in the direction of the Dark Wood at the western edge of his father's land.

Leaning forward over the animal's neck, Lann urged it to greater efforts. It was then that he caught a flash of something black at the edge of his vision. Allowing himself a brief sideways glance, he saw a crow perfectly matching his speed. The bird let out a caw and flew out ahead, arrowing in the direction of the forest as if leading the way for him.

The woods were as old as time itself. It was said a great battle had been fought there and each tree represented a fallen warrior. It was also said that a curse hung over the place. Even during the brightest days light struggled to make it through the thick overhead canopy to the forest floor, and now, as he approached it in the gloom of the evening, the place appeared to Lann as a sea of blackness. The idea of entering that inky nothingness filled him with dread.

They were no more than fifty strides from the treeline when the pony's foot found a rabbit hole and the creature tumbled forward, its front leg breaking with a sickening snap. Thrown from the saddle, Lann hit the ground hard, the air knocked out of him. The pony had been given to him as a gift on his tenth birthday, and his heart sank to hear her stricken cries. Fighting the impulse to go to her aid and forcing himself to his feet, he turned his back on the poor injured beast and took off at a sprint in the direction of the murky gloom created by the forest's canopy.

He was close enough to smell the damp, musty rot of the forest floor when he glanced over his shoulder.

The wolf-thing was level with the stricken pony. But it paid no attention to the injured animal. Its eyes, black as the woods ahead, were fixed on Lann.

Plunging into the thicket, he ran, stumbling over rotting wood and living roots that grabbed as his feet and ankles. A sob of fear escaped him, the noise echoing back at him from the trees all around, as he imagined death at the jaws of the beast.

No more than twenty strides into the forest and the darkness was complete for Lann. The wolf would not think so. Its eyes were perfectly adapted to hunting in the dark. He could hear it, crashing through the undergrowth behind him.

In choosing this desolate place to hide, he had chosen death.

He was running with his arms out in front of him, a long wailing moan coming from his mouth as terror took complete control of him. He would die here, alone in the darkness. And he would not be found. What was left of his body would remain here among the mud and mildew of the forest floor until even his bones were swallowed up. Without a Volken funeral where his physical body would be burned, his soul would be trapped here on earth as a rordnuk – a shade cursed to forever roam the shadow worlds. He offered up desperate prayers to the old gods, asking each and any of them for their help.

In his mind he could almost feel the wolf's teeth sink into his flesh from behind. He would fall and …

The caw of a crow made him turn his head. There, ahead of him, was an oasis of silvery light. A hole in the canopy of leaves allowed the moonlight through, illuminating the one thing that might save him: a tree much smaller than the giants surrounding it, with branches low enough to climb – if only he could reach it in time. He sprinted, forcing his legs forward as he gasped for breath. The wolf was almost upon him; he leaped up towards the lowest branch just as the creature's teeth raked the flesh of his foot, wrenching the shoe from it.

Lann scrambled up into the arms of the tree, pulling himself up out of the way of the predator. Belly down on a branch, the boy looked back down into the black, dead eyes of the creature. The wolf seemed to be contemplating its options as it prowled back and forth. Stopping directly below him, the beast sunk down as low as it could, and, as Lann watched in horrified disbelief, leaped high into the air.

Lann jerked backwards. The wolf's teeth snapped shut inches away from his face, close enough for him to smell the fetid stink of its breath. The enormity of the leap, coupled with the near-success of the attack caused Lann to pull away too quickly. His bare foot slipped on the mossy branch he was on, and, with his hands desperately clawing at nothing, he fell backwards out of the tree.

When the back of his head connected with an old tree stump jutting out of the ground, the world went black. He was not unconscious, but the silvery moonlight and shadowy half-light of the forest were replaced by an inky void.

Getting to his hands and knees he tried to stand, but the swirling in his head and his blindness made it impossible, and he collapsed back down again.

Lann sensed the beast moving in for the kill. Consumed with fear, he let out a despairing moan, knowing that death at the jaws of the creature was inevitable.

It was then that he heard the harsh caw of the crow again, followed by the fluttering noise of its wings as it landed close to his side. There was a moment's pause, and the boy had the distinct impression that the bird was no longer a bird. A thing much larger was standing over him now. There was a snarl, followed by the sound of leaves moving as the wolf pounced, and then an intense feeling of heat, so hot it made the boy cry out.

Something large fell to the floor a short distance away and the air was filled with the rank smell of burnt flesh and fur.

The leafy carpet close to his head stirred again and Lann threw out an arm in the direction of the sound, his fingers grasping hold of the hem of a heavy woollen cloak. 'Help me,' he managed.

The sounds of the forest changed then. What had been the brushing of leaves and wind in the branches overhead was replaced with whispering noises. Words in a tongue so alien it made him shiver to hear them come from all directions at once. They were angry, those whispers, angry that death had been allowed to come to this forest again.

'Please ... help me,' he croaked.

The last thing he remembered was a woman's voice. The voice was strained, as if it were only with immense effort that the stranger was able to talk.

'I must go,' the voice said. 'You will be safe here now. The Spirits of the Forest have spoken to me. They will ensure you are not harmed, but I am not welcome in this place.'

'No,' gasped the boy. 'Don't leave me. My eyes! I'm ... I'm blind!'

There was a flapping of wings and he was alone.

Unable to fight it any longer, Lann slipped into unconsciousness.

When he woke again, the smell of the meadows and the distant sound of birdsong told him it was daytime, but to his eyes it was still featureless night. Fighting the panic that threatened to engulf him again, he cocked his head and listened. If the leaves up there were stirred by the wind, the sound never made it down as far as the forest floor.

On all fours, he groped around until his hand brushed against the corpse of the wolf that had pursued him. He jerked his fingers back from the charred flesh in horror. Despite his fears, Lann couldn't help but wonder what powerful majik might have been unleashed on the beast and by whom.

Terror still gripped him, but he knew he couldn't stay here beneath the ancient trees. Managing to get to his feet, he stood as still as he could. Without the ability to see, he was forced to trust his other senses to provide him with a sense of where he was and which way he should go. A slight breeze brushed his face from the right, and as he turned in that direction he fancied he caught the distant call of a redthroat warning other birds away from its territory. 'Redthroats are meadow birds,' he mumbled to himself. He couldn't recall ever seeing one in a forest. Hands held out before him, he slowly made his way in the direction of the birdsong.

It was hours later that Orlof, the head cattleman from Gord's farm, spotted the boy, his face and hands cut and bruised from the many falls he'd taken, stumbling among the foothills. When he called out to the boy, Lann's head swung round in the direction of the sound, and the older man fancied he caught a faint groan of relief. He called out again, and as he did so, it was as if all the strength and fight suddenly fled the youngster's body and he crumpled to the floor, where he lay, unmoving.

With the help of some of the other workers, Orlof got the boy safely inside the farmhouse. The men were already in a fearful state. They had found Gord Fetlanger's mangled body earlier in the day, and now here was his son in a condition that suggested he'd almost come to the same end. There was talk among the men of leaving the place before whatever it was that had killed their former employer returned, but Orlof quickly put a stop to that, pointing out that the young boy, not their own safety, had to be their main concern right now. But the cattlemen were more used to caring for calves than boys, and they exchanged worried looks, wondering what would be the best thing to do for the lad. Their concern increased when the boy stirred, crying out that he had seen a man-wolf with death in its eyes that chased him into the Dark Wood, where a crow that was a fire-wielding woman had killed it.

'He's delirious,' reasoned Orlof, noting the rising panic in the men. Eventually, with no other recourse open to him, he sent one of the men to fetch Fleya the witch.

'You did well to come across him when you did,' Fleya said to the rancher after he'd recounted his side of the tale. She stood in the doorway of the bedroom, looking down at the figure of the boy lying on the pallet.

'I was looking for a lost calf.'

'And you found one,' she replied.

At the sound of their voices, the boy stirred from his sleep. They watched as he opened his eyes, a tear falling from them when he realised the world was still hidden from him.

'Will his sight come back? Can you heal him?' Orlof asked, his voice low so as not to upset the boy too much. The woman was silent for a long moment. When she asked to be alone with the boy, the cattlehand left, but not before reassuring Lann that he would only be in the next room and that he should call out if he needed him.

The witch sat unspeaking beside Lann. When the silence was finally broken it was the boy, not the witch, who spoke, his voice little more than a whisper.

'He's dead, isn't he?'

'Gord? Yes, child. He is dead.'

'I knew it. I should have—'

'Hush now,' Fleya said, placing a hand on his. 'You could not have saved him.'

'How can you know?'

'I have the gift of future sight, Lannigon Fetlanger. Do you think it beyond me to peek into the past too?'

'What was it, that terrible creature? Not man or wolf, but something of both.' He sensed her stand up and move across the room to where the window was.

'Do you believe in the monsters of old? The creatures from the Void that roamed this world when the gods did?'

29

'I … I thought they were just stories.' He remembered the moment when the blood-covered man had transformed into the wolf-creature before his eyes. 'But now … I don't know.'

'There are very few, it's true. Most were banished back to the place they truly belong when Trogir vanquished the dark god, Lorgukk. But some of those terrible creatures still exist. It was one of these you saw today.' She placed a hand on his arm. 'We will talk more of these things in good time, Lann. You are safe and I will do all I can to keep you that way. That is all that should concern you right now.' She sighed. 'The cattleman in the next room, Orlof – he's a good man, no?'

'He's been part of this farm for as long as I can remember.' He waited for her to say something, then added: 'Yes, he's a good man. He's my friend.'

'Could a friend like that be trusted to run this place if you were not here?'

'Why would I not be here?'

'Because you are coming to live with me.' The smell of lavender and sage filled his head again. 'That is, if you would like to, of course.'

Fleya ordered the men to put the boy's things on to her wagon. When she told them that she was taking the boy away to live with her too, they mumbled something under their breaths, but nobody dared question the decision.

Only Orlof summoned up the courage, though he still would not look the witch in the eye as he did so. In response, Fleya took the man to one side and spoke quietly with him, and when they came back, whatever it was she'd said seemed to have satisfied his fears.

With everything on board, the witch set the ponies into a walk, taking Lann away from the Fetlanger farmstead for the last time.

Faun Forest

4

Fleya proved to be precisely what Lannigon needed during the first months of his blindness. Kind when she needed to be, severe during the times when he began to wallow in self-pity and doubt, she made him understand that his new life without sight didn't have to be as terrifying as he'd first believed it would. He found himself inspired by her enthusiasm, and threw himself into the things she suggested, learning to develop a greater sense of the world about him through smell and touch and sound.

While Fleya was a positive presence in Lann's life, it was the garden that was the saving of him. One day, Fleya asked him to help her plant some seeds at the start of the growing season. Reluctant and grumbling to start with, she noticed that he soon began to enjoy the task; feeling the earth beneath his fingers and putting the small grains into the soil sparked something in him, something she'd thought had almost been lost for good. Later the same day, when she suggested he take over the running of the plot of land, the enthusiasm he'd shown for the idea had filled both of them with hope.

Over the next few days and weeks, he suggested plants they might cultivate, pressing her for information and greedy for the knowledge she possessed. She passed on as much of her considerable botanical expertise as she could, and what she didn't know she looked up for him in one of the many books she had on the subject.

They had a bumper crop of fruits and vegetables at the end of the growing year, not to mention the herbs and plants Fleya needed to make her medicines and treatments, a process which now fascinated Lann.

One evening, after a busy day in the garden, the pair found themselves sitting across from each other at the table in the kitchen. More than nine months had passed since Lann had discovered his love of gardening.

'I'm glad you have found something that interests you so much, Lann. It makes me happy to see you among your plants.' She paused and reached over to collect his plate. 'Tell me, what is it about the growing you like?'

He sat, considering his response for a moment.

'The plants and the cycles they go through,' he said. 'I guess … in a strange way, they remind me of myself.'

'Go on,' she said.

He hesitated, trying to put his feeling into words. 'The seeds are taken from plants that have spent their lives in the light, stretching up to Mother Sun for her life-giving energy. Then we put them into the darkness of the earth where they sit until it's time to become that thing in the daylight again. I was taken from a world of light and plunged into darkness too.'

'You wish a similar rebirth for yourself.'

'I do.' He shrugged. 'But if I cannot have it, I like the idea that I can give it to other things, even if they're just plants.'

She sat looking at him. He no longer appeared to be consumed by the sadness that had so blighted him during the first few months of his blindness, but she knew it would not take much to plunge him into unhappiness again. She tried to imagine what it must be like to have seen the world in all its splendour, only to have that ability taken away.

'What ... what will I do when you're gone?' he asked. The question took her a little by surprise.

'Why do you ask that?'

'Without you, I would not have made it through this difficult time. But ...' He paused, trying to find the right words. 'You're not going to be around forever, Fleya.'

'And exactly how old do you think I am, Lannigon Fetlanger?'

'I didn't mean to be rude.' She gave a little snort of amusement and he relaxed, knowing that she was merely teasing him. 'But you told me you were born during a time of terror, when the necromancer Yirgan was at the height of his powers as an agent of the dark god Lorgukk. Later that week, when you were teaching me history, you mentioned that Yirgan was killed by the gods over a hundred years ago.' He paused, not quite knowing how to go on. 'So, what I'm trying to say is … you've lived a long time.' He could feel her gaze on him and he squirmed a little, wishing he'd never brought the question up.

'Well, if that is indeed the case, and I'm not saying it is, how can you possibly know how much longer I might still be around for, hmm? Come on,' she said, standing up and offering him a hand by resting it on his sleeve. 'Time for bed. This old lady needs her rest.'

Lann didn't know it, but his speculations were pretty close and the witch had already lived for more than a hundred and twenty years, despite looking exactly as she did now for most of that time.

5

Their days followed a regular and easy pattern; they would rise early to feed the goat and chickens, and after his chores Lannigon would work the garden until Fleya called him in for dinner. Having cleaned the soil from his hands he would sit at the table and eat whatever she put before him, usually a hearty stew. At the end of the day they would sit by the fire, where Fleya would read to him from one of her many books. Growing up on the farm, Lann had never really been exposed to books, but Fleya was determined he know as much as she could impart about the world he lived in, and her schooling covered a whole host of subjects. She taught him the history of these lands and those beyond the Six Kingdoms, describing to him the places she'd seen, both in person and by using a form of majik that allowed her to leave her body and travel vast distances for a short period of time. He wondered at this, but whenever he pressed her on her use of majik she would change the subject.

She taught him about the Volken people and other peoples that came before them, their beliefs and folklore – stories of the gods and the heroes that fought for and against them. And she taught him about the darker side of the world: how monstrous creatures had gained access to this world from their own, a place called the Void. These last lessons were always delivered in a low voice, as though she believed merely speaking of them might lead to these creatures appearing again. Whenever she did so, he would remember the man who had been transformed into a wolf on that fateful day when he'd lost his sight.

The dull thump of the book being closed indicated the end of the lessons. It was usually the signal that they should also go to sleep; but one night Lann took the opportunity to ask Fleya about her own childhood. It was not the first time he had done so, but in the past the witch had always found some excuse not to answer, telling him she was tired or had too much to do to talk about such matters.

Tonight, however, was different. 'What would you have me tell you?' she asked.

'Anything.'

She gave a small laugh. It was the laughter of a girl much younger than he guessed the witch's age to be. Then she took a deep breath and began to tell him how her mother had encouraged both Fleya and her sister to take up majik under the tutelage of a local woman. She spoke haltingly at first, as though the memories were hard for her to recount. She told him how they had both had to leave home in order to do so, and how reluctant they'd been to leave their mother, despite knowing what a great honour had been bestowed on them both by being chosen to learn the Art. 'If we had known it was to be the last time we'd ever see our family or the village again, we would not have gone.'

'What happened?'

'The place was attacked by raiders the very next day – the invaders destroyed the settlement.'

Lann felt his chest grow tight with sadness when he realised Fleya had lost a family too. 'If you had not gone, you and your sister would have died with the others.'

'Yes. But at the time I found it hard to accept. We both did. Family is precious, and we should do everything we can to protect it. Even if that means making hard decisions sometimes.'

He was aware of her eyes on him. Sitting up in his chair, he summoned the courage to ask the question he'd kept to himself since the day the witch had come to get him from the farm. A question that had been brewing inside of him since Gord Fetlanger had told him he was a foundling.

He was nervous and excited at the same time, so much

so that he stumbled over the words as he finally plucked up the courage to utter them.

'Fleya, I … I need to know something, but I don't know how to …' He paused and took a deep breath. 'Are you … are you my *mother*?'

The silence that followed seemed to go on forever.

'Why do you think that?' she eventually responded. Her voice had a curious quality to it, as if she were struggling to control her emotions. 'Lannigon, a witch cannot lie with a man. If she does, she will lose her majik. I have told you this.'

The boy pressed on desperately. 'But you know who my real parents are, don't you?'

The fire spat and Lann imagined the fiery ember landing on the stone hearth, glowing brightly for a second before finally going out.

Finally the witch spoke, her voice little more than a whisper. 'I know who your mother is, Lannigon. But not your father.'

'Who is she?'

'She was my sister. She is no longer with us.'

The boy waited.

When she spoke again, Fleya's voice was full of emotion, the love she still felt for her sister clear to be heard in every word. 'Your mother was beautiful. A woman who would have challenged the goddess Niaffar for her beauty. But like me, she was a witch, and was chaste.'

Fleya continued, and Lann fancied he could hear the smile in her voice. 'I adored her with all my heart, and we shared many special moments together as only sisters can. You know I have lived on this earth for a long time, and for most of it my sister was a constant presence. And then, about sixteen years ago, she ... changed. She became secretive and I suspected she was in love. She denied it, but I could always tell when Lette was lying. I told myself it was none of my business, and that she was free to choose the path of her life. Even so, I was worried for her and what she might be considering.

'When she told me she was pregnant I was devastated. Lette was so happy, but all I could think of at that time was what she had sacrificed. We argued – something we had never done before – and I said some things I had no right to say. I asked her over and over who the father was, but she refused to tell me. All she would say was that he was unlike any man she had ever met, and that losing her powers was a price she was willing to pay if it meant she could have his child.'

'What happened?'

'With the loss of her powers Lette also lost the ability to stay youthful. That day she told me she was carrying you inside her, she looked much the same age as I do now. By the end of the pregnancy she was an old woman. She fought with all her strength to give life to you, Lann. But once she had done so, there was nothing left.'

Lann swallowed, trying to hold back the tears. His mind was a frenzied turmoil of conflicting thoughts and emotions. 'You are my aunt,' he said, forcing the words out.

'Yes.'

'We share the same blood.'

'We do.'

'Then why did you give me away to the Fetlangers? You did, didn't you? Everything Gord told me was true. You left me there in that barn, to be discovered as a foundling. Why?'

The witch paused before answering.

'I am a witch, Lannigon. I use my powers to help the people of this community and the kingdom in which it resides. I *deliver* babies, I do not bring them up. And for good reason. Being a witch carries certain dangers, dangers that it would not be right to expose a young child to. There are things in this world that would prey on such an inno-cent, and I would not have the son of my sister imperilled by such dark creatures.' She paused, and he heard her give a little sigh. 'And if I am being honest, I think I was … resentful of you, and that deep down I somehow blamed you for what happened to Lette. That was wrong of me. I hope that someday you will forgive me for harbouring those feelings. I knew Lae Fetlanger had failed to conceive on a number of occasions, and I also knew she was a good woman. I knew she would care for you.'

'So you gave me away.'

'I put you in a safe place.'

'You gave me away!'

Fleya laid a hand on his arm but he pulled away. She didn't try to follow when he struggled to his feet and felt his way to his room at the back of the cabin.

Sitting alone by the embers of the dying fire, she thought about what she had done to protect him – and what she must continue to do.

6

Lann and Fleya barely spoke to one another in the three weeks following the revelations about his past. Lann spent all his time in the garden, only replying in the briefest terms whenever his aunt spoke to him.

Fleya knew better than to push the matter. Even so, the boy's hostility stung her in a way she found surprising.

For his part, Lann couldn't shake his sense of betrayal. He felt strongly that Fleya was still not telling him all she knew about his birth, and this fuelled the anger and sense of frustration he felt towards her. Yet at the same time he missed their fireside chats and the mealtimes that they'd always shared. He could sense how much his behaviour, walking away whenever she tried to speak to him, bothered her, but he couldn't help himself. He was hurting and confused, and he saw no reason why she should not be feeling the same way.

It was a cool morning in March and he'd just placed a young snowtear seedling in the ground, gently covering the fragile stem with a fine soil, when he became aware of his aunt standing at his side. Despite his acute hearing, she could still creep up on him like this at times, and he felt his annoyance rise at this unheralded interruption.

'I have to go into the village of Bjoven to help a sick girl,' Fleya told him. 'If the child is as sick as I fear, I doubt I will be back until the morning. I might even be gone until this time tomorrow.' She paused, waiting for a response that never came. 'There is fresh bread, and I have left some cheese and butter next to it. Slide the bolt across when I have gone and wait for my return. I don't need to tell you not to open up for anyone else.' She sighed, but when she spoke again her voice was softer. 'I want us to be friends again, Lann. I care a great deal for you. I know you may not believe that right now, but it is the truth.' There was another pause and he heard her give another little sigh before she turned and walked away.

When the sound of the wagon had faded away, Lann got up and groped his way over to the cabin. Inside, he leaned his weight against the door and slid the heavy bolt across. Fleya often left him to go off to help the people in the lands surrounding Faun Forest, and she always made a fuss about him being left alone. But right now, he welcomed the solitude.

After supper, he sat beside the fire that he'd fed from the pile of logs his aunt had left for him. The words she said before she left – about how much she cared for him and wanted to be friends again – came back to him. In truth, his anger had subsided over the last week, and he realised it was his stubbornness that was stopping him from making up with her. He resolved to fix that when she returned: they would talk and try to get back to the way things were before. Half snoozing in the chair, he listened to the fire's music as it popped and sighed and crackled until, eventually, feeling himself drifting off, he took himself to bed.

His sleep was haunted by a strange dream in which he was not himself but a dark-haired boy a few years older in age. He was standing before a great shimmering wall of blackness, a darkness so complete it was unsettling to look at. He was chanting in a language that was harsh and alien. There was something in each of his hands, and when he looked down at the thing he was holding in his left, he was amazed to see it was burning. The black flames flickered up towards him, but there was no heat. The thing pulsated between his fingers, the unmistakeable rhythm telling him it could only be a heart he held. In his other hand was a staff, and he slowly raised both items up in the direction of the inky void, his voice increasing in volume as he did so. There were ornate carvings on the wooden staff; strange symbols that, although completely unfamiliar, managed to convey a sense of fear and abhorrence. He also noted the tattoo on the top of his left hand: a star design with an eye at the centre. The heart's metronomic contractions increased in intensity, as did the flames licking up from the thing, and he struggled to hold on to it. At the same time he saw something stirring in the blackness: something ancient and evil that was being drawn into this world from another …

Lann sat up in his bed with a start. When he opened his eyes, he could only think he was still dreaming because he could *see*. He cried out as happiness flooded every cell of his body. *He could see again!*

And the first thing he saw – there, sitting at the end of his bed – was a man.

His heart hammered away inside him, reminding him of the flaming black thing of his nightmare. He knew he must still be asleep, but everything – the cold of the room, the feel of the rough blanket between his tightly clenched fingers, the noise of the trees rustling beyond the window – felt real.

The man was staring out of the window at the shadowy woods beyond. He was surrounded by a dim aura of light, and Lann could see that his hair was shoulder length and of an extraordinary golden colour. As if becoming aware he was being observed for the first time, the man turned to face him. As he did so, Lann's breath caught in his throat. The man's eyes were of the same bright gold as his hair.

'Lannigon Fetlanger,' the man said with the hint of a nod in the boy's direction. 'I shall call you by that name for now, at least until you ask your aunt for your real one.'

'Wh-who are you? How can I see you?' He managed to force the words out despite his fear. 'What do you want? Am I still dreaming?'

'Which of your questions would you like me to answer first?' the man said, his face breaking into a smile. 'Very well. I will take the questions in reverse. No, this is not a dream, although I fancy you might wish it were by the time we are finished here tonight. As to what I want? Nothing. No, I am here to offer *you* something: a chance to change your life … again. A change you may or may not wish to accept. But we will come to that, Lannigon.' He paused. 'You can see me because I *will* it. In the same way that I will it, you see me in this particular form at this particular time.'

Lann frowned, only half taking in everything the man was saying; it was too wonderful to be able to see again after living in the world of darkness for so long.

'As for who I am … I have many names in many different worlds. To your people I am known as Rakur.'

It was as if the world ground to an abrupt halt in that moment. The idea that the being sitting at the end of his bed might be a god was not impossible for Lann to imagine, but what the immortal was doing here was a mystery to him. To those who worshipped him, Rakur was considered both malign and benevolent in equal measure. A trickster not to be trusted because the gifts offered by him always came at a price.

'Are you here to see my aunt?' the boy asked in a whisper.

'Your aunt?' The god seemed to find this amusing and chuckled to himself. 'No, Lannigon, I am here for you. Tell me, boy, what do you know about your birth?'

The question took Lann by surprise and it must have showed on his face because Rakur mirrored the expression, a mocking look in his eyes.

'Nothing? You know nothing about who and what you are?'

Excitement and trepidation built up in Lann at the thought that he might finally discover the whole truth about his birth. 'My mother was Fleya's sister, and her name was Lette. I know she, too, used to be a witch but that she gave up her powers to give birth to me. I know that my aunt left me at the Fetlangers for protection.'

'Protection from what?'

'I'm sorry?'

'What is it that you needed protection from? And why?'

'I don't know.'

48

The god gave a sniff, as if he were less than impressed with the boy's sketchy knowledge. 'Lette was a great witch, did your aunt tell you that? Fleya is powerful and wise now, but it was her sister who most fascinated those who knew them both. Her grasp of majik and the control she had over it was matched only by her beauty.'

'That is what Fleya told me.'

'Powerful and beautiful. What kind of man could tempt such a woman to give everything up, hmm? Since discovering these things, have you stopped to wonder that? Or maybe you have considered that it might not have been a man at all. Maybe only a god could woo such a woman?' That mocking look was in the god's eye again, and the smile he gave Lann sent a shiver running through the youngster.

'Enough of such things,' the god said, waving the matter away. 'Right now they are unimportant. I promised I would return to the reason I am here, so let us do so. Tell me, Lannigon, how did you come to be blind?'

The boy's head was still spinning from the god's words, and he wanted nothing more than to return to the matter of who his father might be. Despite this, he answered the god's question. 'I … I fell from a tree. When I hit my head I lost the ability to see.'

'And what were you doing up this tree?'

'I was trying to get away from something.'

'Something?'

'A creature, a thing that was at the same time both man and a wolf.'

'But it was neither of those things really, was it?'

'No.'

'Then what was it?' A long, uncomfortable silence followed, the god sitting perfectly still as he studied the boy. 'What do you know about the one your people call Lorgukk?'

'He is the dark god who rules over the Void – the place he was banished to after he lost the great battle with Trogir. He created a multitude of monsters that he unleashed on earth until they were all driven out following the same battle. He is all powerful in his own realm but, despite attempts to return here, he has always failed to do so.' Images of the dream he'd been having came back to Lann: the gateway with the impossible blackness at its heart, and the thing that threatened to emerge from it. 'It is said he will return with his dark legions one day and that the gods will fight one last great battle to decide who rules the human realm.'

A short silence followed until it was eventually broken by the god.

'It is a good tale, is it not? One guaranteed to keep children terrified in their beds at night. Especially that last part. But what if it were true? What if Lorgukk were massing

50

his apocalyptic army right now, and that he was on the verge of finding a way to bring them across into this realm. Imagine if the monsters of old – giants, wraiths, griffins, harpies, draugr and all manner of hellish creatures – were returned to wreak havoc on the human race that replaced them.' The deity stared at the boy. 'Who could stop the dark god and his foul legion if he were successful in returning?'

'You?'

The god's laughter – a musical sound – filled the room. 'You still have faith in the old deities of this world. That is good. But alas, your gods grow weak, Lannigon Fetlanger. The Volken people of this realm hold little faith in their immortals any longer. New religions have sprung up, and as you humans turn your backs on the old gods, so our powers wane. That is why Lorgukk is chancing his hand now. He sees this as his last chance to bring chaos to this world.'

'What happens if people stop believing in the old gods completely?'

Rakur sniffed. 'We disappear altogether. From this world, at least.'

Lann sat silently remembering the cruel eyes of the thing that pursued him into the Dark Wood. 'So that is what I saw on the day I was blinded? One of Lorgukk's legion? A wyrewolf?'

'The dark god's army is largely confined to the Void. Some of the ancient creatures managed to stay here when the rest were driven out. A small number manage to creep across, even now.' He paused, noticing the confused look on the boy's face. 'Occasionally there are rifts created between the two worlds that allow certain opportunistic individuals to creep through, and these fissures become more common as Lorgukk's might increases in his dominion and this world becomes less stable.' The immortal studied the boy for a few moments before speaking again. 'How much would you like to be able to see again?'

Lann stared, startled by the abrupt change of subject.

'More than anything,' he whispered, hardly able to get the words out.

With a nod, Rakur patted an item laying across his legs. Lann eyed the thing suspiciously. It had not been there when he'd first woken to find the god in his room.

Pulling back the layers of cloth it was wrapped in, the god revealed a long sword, the scabbard of which was made of a dull black material that appeared more like stone than metal. There were no intricate designs on it; it looked ordinary, in fact, but something told Lann that it was anything but. There was something about it that caused conflicting emotions inside of him: a mixture of fascination and fear that had come on in a rush as soon as the deity had revealed it.

'What is it?' he asked, unable to take his eyes off the weapon.

'It is one of the Swords of Destiny. Like me, it has had many names, but in this world it is known as the Dreadblade.' He paused, turning to stare unblinkingly at the boy with those golden eyes. 'The four swords were forged by the god Og when the world was new and an altogether different place from the one it is now. The Dreadblade was wielded by Trogir in the great battle with Lorgukk. It defeated him. But after the battle the god and his blade were separated. It has stayed hidden for a long time, but now it has woken from its torpor and desires to go about its work again.'

'Where are the other swords?'

'Lost. Or destroyed. But the Dreadblade survived.'

'You talk about it as if it were a living thing.'

'Indeed. The blade, once accepted, becomes one with the wielder. It has needs ... hungers that must be fed. In return it imbues the owner with powers. It could return your sight.'

'You mean to give me this thing? Why? If it is as special as you say, why do *you* not wield it?'

'That is a question I cannot answer for you right now, boy. But know this. The blade will let you see again, but not the world you once knew. No, the world revealed to you will be one in which the things wishing to remain hidden will no longer be able to do so. In the same way that you can see me now, you will see the creatures and wonders of a world that is both alien and familiar to you at the same time.'

Lann stared at the object, unable to believe he was being offered this chance. 'What must I do?' he whispered.

'You must simply agree to take the blade.'

The god raised a hand to halt the youth. 'There is no going back once you choose to do so, Lannigon. The sword and owner become one, feeding and aiding each other until the bond is severed by death or destruction. The blade is well named and not just for the fear it strikes in its enemies.'

Lann noticed how the deity kept his own hands well clear of the weapon, and it occurred to him that it must be a powerful thing indeed to instil fear in a being as powerful as Rakur.

'Before I make my choice, I have a question for you.'

The deity raised an eyebrow. 'Ask it.'

'Are you … my father?'

The god seemed genuinely surprised at being asked such a thing. The laugh that escaped him had a harsh quality to it. 'A strange notion, young one. If I *were* your father, what would that make you? A demigod?' The deity shook his head, but the look on his face was impossible to read. 'Such a thing would have no place in this or any other world. A *halfling* of that kind would be abhorrent not only to the gods, but to mankind.'

'You have not answered my question.'

'Mother, father, brother – I could be one or all of those things to you. These terms mean nothing to the gods. We are. You are. That is all there is. That is all there has ever been.'

'You talk in riddles, god.'

'I do. It is my way. But riddles are there to be solved, are they not? And the riddler is there to pose the question, not provide the answer.'

'And will the sword help me to solve the puzzle of who I am?'

'It may help you to discover such a thing, if that is what you truly want. But mark my words, Lannigon Fetlanger, the answers to some questions are best left undiscovered.'

There was a moment of silence between them, then Lann leaned forward and took the Dreadblade from the god's lap.

As his fingers curled around the grip of the sword, a wave of energy rushed through Lann's body, making him cry out in a mixture of joy and pain. In the same instant, the god Rakur disappeared.

Lifting the weapon up before him, Lann pulled the sword free of the scabbard, staring down at the black metal of the blade. He could see. He could see the world again, and the realisation filled him with a happiness that was so great, tears immediately obscured his newly returned vision. Wiping them away, he lifted the blade up towards his face, holding the thing point up. A noise, a long-drawn-out sigh, filled his ears and he was forced to clamp his eyes shut as a thousand images flashed through his mind so quickly they became a blur. The sword showed him glimpses of battles it had been used in, armour it had rent, blood it had spilt, souls it had drunk. The terrible images tainted Lann's happiness with fear as the weight of responsibility and power he'd accepted finally dawned on him.

Along with the images came a voice, and Lann had little doubt it was the voice of the blade; a deep and sinister whisper in an alien language that had long since disappeared from the earth.

Ish'nukk rahhg.

He shuddered at that sound. At some deep and barely understood level he was aware the weapon was itself satisfied to be once more in the hands of a living, breathing being. He also sensed the longing it felt; a hunger to return to the thing it was forged to do – to reap the lives of the dread creatures for which it was named, creatures who had no right being in this world.

Forcing himself to calm down, he hefted the weapon in

his hand, feeling its weight. It seemed to him there were strange symbols set into the dark matter of that blade, symbols that could almost be made out as he turned it this way and that in the dim light, but which always remained just too faint and indistinct.

Lannigon had no idea how long he'd stayed like that, sitting at the edge of the bed staring down at the black blade in wonder and fear, but with the first stirrings of the birds in the forest it slowly occurred to him that dawn must be approaching. He couldn't imagine anything he would like to see more, his newly seeing eyes filling with tears at the mere thought of witnessing a dawn again.

Returning the blade to its scabbard, he strapped the thing to his waist and made his way through the dark house so he might watch the waking of the world.

Night still had a tentative hold: the shadows thrown to the ground by the trees, the intricate design of the leaves, the patterns of the bark, glimpses of the starry sky through the overhead canopy, the movement of some creature scurrying into the bushes. He was overwhelmed at the sight of even the smallest and most insignificant thing after so much time in darkness, and it was as much as he could do not to cry out with the joy of it.

A thought occurred to him. He reluctantly unbuckled the sword belt and carefully laid it on the ground. Taking a step away from it, he was relieved to find he could still see.

Perhaps he only had to be close to the sword for it to lend him its powers. He took another step away, then another. It was as he took his fourth step that suddenly he heard the voice of the sword again, low and urgent. He noted too how his hands had begun to shake and a thin film of sweat beaded his forehead, so great was his physical yearning to have the sword at his side again.

Hurrying over to the black scabbard, something at the edge of his vision caught his attention. Turning to look back in the direction of the cabin, he saw the figure of a girl standing at the window looking back at him. He blinked and the figure was gone. Lann was on the verge of returning inside to investigate when he heard the sound of the wagon coming down the path towards him.

Fleya was driving the wagon too fast and there was a sheen on the ponies' flanks that suggested she'd sped all the way back through the woods. Pulling to a halt, she leaned forward on the seat, scanning him quickly as if to satisfy herself that her nephew was not injured in some way. When her eyes settled on the sword in his hand the colour drained from her face.

'What have you done?' she said, her voice barely audible.

'I can see again,' Lann said by way of an answer. 'The blade, it ...' He stopped, confused and a little scared by what he saw before him. Sitting atop the wagon, the reins clutched in her hands, was the Fleya he knew, forever young and beautiful, but at the same time another vision of the witch presented itself, the two images superimposed on top of each other so he could also see the ancient woman his aunt would be if she were not a creature of majik. The vision reminded Lann of what his aunt had told him about his mother's rapid deterioration when she'd relinquished her witchhood to give birth to him. He screwed his eyes shut and shook his head, willing himself not to see the unmasked version of the witch. To his relief, when he opened them again he was faced with the Fleya he knew.

'Do you have any idea what that thing you hold is?' Fleya's voice, usually so calm, was laced with fear.

'It's the Dreadblade.' He lifted the scabbarded sword in her direction, and gasped as he felt it hum – a galvanising force that knifed its way through him, filling him with alarm and wonder. The Dreadblade recognised Fleya as a creature of majik like itself, and wanted her to marvel at its majesty and power. Unlike its wielder, the blade revelled in the fright Fleya exhibited at having seen it.

Us'dith orgh, the blade's voice inside his head hissed, and although Lann didn't understand the words, he knew what the sword wanted. It wanted to be freed from the scabbard it was housed in, freed so the witch could see it and be cowed by its power. Without knowing he'd done so, Lann noticed how his hand had wrapped around the hilt and how he'd already unwittingly pulled free a small amount of the dark blade.

If you bend to its will now, the sword, not its wielder, will forever be in control, a warning voice inside him said. *And nothing, not even your precious sight, is worth being a slave to this thing.*

Summoning up all his will, Lann forced his fingers to unfurl themselves from the sword's grip, he placed his hand instead on the large round pommel at the top of the weapon and gently but firmly pushed it down.

He lifted his chin in the witch's direction. When he spoke again, it was in a voice that sounded much older than his years. 'It is the Dreadblade. Fashioned by Og to maintain balance in this world by ridding it of creatures from the Void. I am its bearer and its master, and it will do you no harm, Aunt. This I swear on my mother's soul.' As the words left his lips, he felt the sword's influence slowly diminish.

Fleya, too, appeared to sense how, in those moments, her nephew had managed to establish a degree of control over the thing he held in his hands. Her eyes never leaving the black scabbard, she slowly climbed down from the wagon and gestured to the cabin.

They sat across the table from each other, Fleya sipping from a cup of hot chae that Lann had made her. The recipe was one she'd taught him and was supposed to help calm the nerves. Strong daylight poured in from the door and windows at the front of the cabin, illuminating dust motes dancing in the early morning air.

It had been strange for Lann to see the house for the first time when they'd both come inside. He'd learned to navigate his way about the place in complete darkness, and in his mind he'd painted a picture of how it might look. In many ways his mental image was fairly close, but there were still things, like how colourfully Fleya had painted the walls and the furniture, that surprised him.

His aunt did not want the weapon in the same room as her, and at her insistence Lann had taken the sword to his bedroom. Despite it only being a short distance away, he could sense the weapon's desire to be reunited, and he did his best to shut out his own disquiet over the separation.

Eventually his aunt put down her cup and sighed. 'This is my fault. There are charms and wards built into the very stones of this house to keep out all manner of creatures that might try to enter it. But even my considerable powers are of nothing compared to that of an Ancient One. Tell me, what form did Rakur take when he came to you?'

'A man. A man with golden hair and eyes.'

Fleya snorted. 'A rat would have been more appropriate! Or a dog. A lying, treacherous dog.'

'I hoped you might be happier for me, Aunt. I have been

living in the darkness all this time, and now I am in the light again.'

She looked thoughtfully at him, considering her words before going on. 'I am sorry, Lann. Of course I am happy that you have had your vision returned. But I fear the price you may have to pay for your sight will prove to be a high one. Your golden-haired god knew this, and yet he still gave that … thing to you.'

'Rakur didn't lie or try to trick me, Fleya. He told me that accepting the blade would come at personal cost. How it would demand to be put to use against the creatures it was forged to eliminate.' He paused as something occurred to him. 'If anything, he seemed almost reluctant to offer the thing to me.'

'Such a weapon coming back into this world will not go unnoticed. Why do you think I came hurrying back from the village? The universe let out a warning cry, a cry that was heard by all creatures of majik. Many will seek out, not only the blade, but its bearer. They will long to steal it or destroy it, and they will not care it is only a young Volken boy who wields it. Did your reluctant deity tell you that?'

'No.'

'No. Of course he did not. That is his way – to play with the lives of people as if we were amusing playthings for him.' She pushed the cup away from her with her fingers. 'What else did he say to you?'

62

Lann looked levelly at his aunt, remembering the first words the god had said to him. 'He told me I should ask you what my real name is. With everything else that happened, I'd almost forgotten that.'

'Your name is Fetlanger,' Fleya said. There was a challenging tone to her voice.

Lann shook his head. 'No. That is the name of the people who raised me. As much as I loved Lae for the devotion she showed me through the years, she is not my blood. And Gord was nothing like a father to me. His name is not my name.' He paused, and continued in a softer tone. 'As you claim not to know who my father is, maybe I should take my mother's name, as the northern tribes of the Ice People sometimes do.' He saw a hint of a smile play on the edge of her lips; she had taught him that from one of her books. 'What is your family name, Fleya?'

The witch paused for a moment before replying quietly. 'Gudbrandr.'

Gudbrandr. God sword.

The pair sat across from each other, neither wishing to be the first to break the silence, but inside Lann felt a strong galvanising current flowing through every inch of his body as he took in what his aunt had said. It was as if another piece of the puzzle that was his life had dropped into place.

'God Sword?' Lann said, giving a snort and a shake of

his head. 'You, of all people, with your visions and portents, must see this is no mere coincidence.' He frowned, his words stirring something in his memory. 'Fleya … Before Rakur came to me last night, I had a dream.'

Her eyes met his. 'What kind of dream?'

'In it, I inhabited the body of a young man – a boy, really. He was a person of majik, but … not like you.' He paused, gathering his thoughts. 'The Art for him was fairly new, and he intended to use it for evil. I could sense that. On the back of one hand was a tattoo – a five-sided star with an eye at the centre of it.' He stopped again, allowing more of the dream to come to him. 'In the other was … something burning.' He shook his head as the memory escaped him. 'There was a wall of blackness before me, and at its heart was a terrifying force. Something terrible and ancient.'

He looked up to see the colour had drained from Fleya's face for the second time that morning.

'The tattoo. A pentagonal star with an eye at the centre? You're sure?'

He nodded. 'You know who he is, don't you?'

'No. But I know *what* he is. Or at least what he is becoming. A necromancer. That tattoo is worn by all practitioners of that form of dark majik.'

'They raise the dead?'

'Or the spirits of the dead.'

64

'I think I have been given the sword to find him and stop him. Rakur spoke of the god Lorgukk, and how his armies are stirring in the Void. How our defences are weak, because we no longer cherish our gods. I think this boy is trying to bring the god Lorgukk back to this realm.'

Fleya stood up quickly, walking to the window. Her back to the boy, she stood looking down at her shaking hands for what felt like an age until she finally seemed to come to a decision.

'My sister once told me that we must all be free to choose the path our lives will take, even if those choices appear foolish to those around us. I argued with her at the time, and I said things to her that I have regretted ever since. But she was right. Her decision resulted in you, and, even if she paid the ultimate price for it, I now know her choice was the right one.' She turned to face him. 'Your decision to ally yourself to that blade spells danger for you … for us both. But the deed is done and there is no going back now. You have made your choice and I will do everything in my power to protect and help you, nephew.' When she offered him a smile the mood in the cabin seemed to change. 'Lannigon Gudbrandr. It has a certain ring to it, doesn't it?'

Lann smiled back at her. He was about to reply when something at the edge of his vision caught his eye and caused him to turn. There, in the dark corner of the kitchen, shadows were coalescing, forming into a human shape. The thing was looking back in his direction, and when it started to move towards him, Lann shoved himself back in his chair, almost falling backwards as a result. Alarmed, he turned to Fleya and saw she looked, not frightened, but amused.

The shade drifted towards them and stopped beside the table.

'That's Halbe,' his aunt said, nodding in the thing's direction. 'It's not her real name. I'm not sure house wights have names as such, but that's what I call her. She doesn't speak.'

'A house wight?' Lann stared at the thing. It seemed to have more substance to it now, and even though he could still see the details of the room through it, so too could he make out features on the ghostly face. She looked young, perhaps the same age as him. The wight stared back at him blankly. Suddenly he was sure it was the same creature he'd seen in the window earlier.

'A spirit that's attached to a building. She's always been here. Og knows, I've been here long enough, but I'm guessing she chose to inhabit the place when it was first built.'

'She's a ghost?'

Fleya paused. 'Yes and no. She's not a shade in the trad-itional sense – more a spirit that has chosen to set up residence in a particular place. She and the cabin are one and the same thing. She is the reason why this house is a calm and happy one, I think.'

Lann thought about the times he'd been in the house on his own, and how relaxed and peaceful he had always felt. He wasn't sure he'd have felt the same had he known the wight had been a constant presence.

'She doesn't like arguments or disputes,' his aunt continued, 'so she hid from view earlier on. That you can see her at all is because of the majik you've inherited from the blade.'

As though stirring at the mention, a voice from the blade began to call Lann. Sensing the boy's unease, his aunt nodded her head in the direction of his room. 'Go. I know it calls to you.'

'Are you sure?'

'You and the sword are bound together by fate, Lannigon. I have to learn to accept that, even if I do not like it.' She gave a little sigh. 'I am tired from my time healing in the village and I would like to sleep now. Later I will use my majik and see what I can find out about the young necromancer you encountered in your dream.'

'The ritual I witnessed him performing … I do not think the dream was showing me the here and now. It didn't … feel like that.'

'Your vision was of a possible future, a view of things

that will come to be unless we can stop it.' She paused, her head at an angle as she studied him. 'You have much of your mother's Art in you. Go now, strap your sword to your side again and build a fire while I rest.'

Lann watched her walk across the room in the direction of her bedroom. 'Thank you, Fleya,' he said.

She paused and looked at him with affection in her cool gaze. 'For what?'

'For rescuing me. For keeping me going. For teaching me about this world and the world of the gods. For your love and your understanding during our time together. For … for understanding that this is something that I have to do, even if I myself don't know why.'

Fleya nodded back at him. 'And thank you, Lann. For reminding me what courage and love can create in this world. I fear we will face many dark times in the coming weeks and months, but we will do so together. You, me … and the Dreadblade.'

Stromgard

7

Kelewulf stared out of the window of his living quarters. Below him, in a large sand-filled square, a dozen or so people were engaged in combat training. The sound of their weapons making contact against each other, mixed with their grunts and shouts, hardly registered with him and he paid the combatants the same attention he would a colony of insects. If he was honest, they meant about as much to him.

No, he had other, more pressing matters on his mind.

In the room behind him, on a small table, was the book he'd sought for so long. And yet, now that it was finally in his possession, he felt afraid. He'd spent the morning trying to summon the courage to unlock the brass clasp that held it shut, but he had not been able to.

Kelewulf walked over to the grimoire, staring down at it for what must have been the hundredth time that day. It was thought to be the only one in existence, and it was much smaller than he'd imagined. Surely something containing such ancient knowledge and power should look more impressive? He shivered. He had shed blood to lay his hands upon this book, and now he was too frightened to open the thing and look inside. Why?

Because there's no going back. Once chosen, the path you'll follow leads one way, with no return.

He shook his head angrily. The price would be high, yes; but it would be worth it to show this barbaric world he inhabited what it meant to be truly powerful. Real power wasn't shown by wielding a length of sharpened metal or by beating your wife and child while sycophants stood by and did nothing, but through creating fear in the hearts and minds of people.

And I could wield that power. But first I must open the damned book!

He turned away from the window, closing the shutters to block out the light. The door to his room was already barred but he couldn't help but check it again. And, finally, Kelewulf stood over the Book of Roth'gurd. Taking a deep breath, he reached out and twisted the latch of the brass clasp.

The blunted axe crashed into Astrid's shield and she swivelled on her left foot, twisting around to give herself a view of her opponent's exposed flank. Thrusting forward in a short but firm motion, she allowed herself a small smile at the loud exclamation Matulda made as the rounded tip of the wooden training sword smacked painfully into her ribs.

'You're dead,' Astrid said. 'Four or five inches of cold Volken steel have just slid between your ribs and punctured your right lung.'

'You don't have to sound so happy about it,' Matulda replied, rubbing her side.

'You went too hard in that last attack and lost your form. You must strike a balance between aggression and patience.'

'I saw an opening.'

'An opening I *wanted* you to see. Your opponent will often offer up what appears to be a perfect attacking opportunity, when all they are really doing is baiting you.'

The younger girl nodded. 'Thank you for the lesson, Sister Astrid,' she said, using the term all shield maidens addressed each other with. The stoical response was typical Volken, and was one that Astrid knew all too well from her own early training days. It made her like the younger girl all the more.

'You are getting better each time we fight, Sister Matulda. It won't be long before you're beating me and leaving *me* with bruised ribs.'

The two embraced for a moment, and as they separated Astrid heard someone call her name out. Turning towards the source of the noise, she groaned. Brant Skifrmunn stood waving at her. He was a tall, well-built young man. A great warrior from an established family, her father had almost promised him her hand in marriage. Astrid, however, had other ideas. Even if she had it in mind to wed, which she most certainly did not, Brant was the dullest man she'd ever met. His entire conversational skills involved talk of fighting and swordsmanship. Knowing he would not leave unless she at least spoke to him, she walked over.

'Brant.' She nodded.

'I was watching you teach that youngster. Very fine sword-work.'

'Coming from the finest sword in these lands, that is high praise.'

Brant beamed back at her, the colour rising in his cheeks. He took a deep breath, gathering himself. 'I wondered if I could take you for a walk by the shore this evening?' He paused, then added, 'It will be a full moon.'

'I'm afraid I'm washing my hair.'

He looked at her short locks and frowned. 'All evening?'

'It's very dirty.' She watched the frown lines deepen as he tried to take this in. 'Another night? The next full moon, perhaps?'

'Yes. Right.' He nodded his head, as if trying to commit this to memory. 'Next full moon.'

She watched him walk off. As she herself turned to go, she glanced up to see her cousin Kelewulf standing at the window of the building he occupied, looking down on them all. *How apt*, she thought. Nearly two years had passed since Kelewulf's father had been killed and her own had taken the throne. The kingdom was flourishing; Mirvar was much loved by his people, including, it would seem, his young nephew, who made a point of always appearing deferential and cheerful in his uncle's presence. Astrid, however, could not bring herself to trust her cousin. She had seen how the smile dropped from his face whenever he thought nobody was watching, the look replaced with one of disdain. One evening last summer she'd been out by the stables when she heard someone talking in a low voice. Intrigued, she'd crept closer to one of the stalls. Kelewulf was there grooming his horse, brushing the creature's flanks and muttering to himself. She couldn't catch most of what he was saying, but she distinctly heard the words 'Volken savages', 'brutes' and 'worthless thugs'. She'd moved away as silently as she could. Disturbed by what had happened, she'd gone to speak to her father. But Mirvar had waved away her concerns, telling her she must have misheard her cousin and how she should not eavesdrop on people.

He's a snake with two heads, she told herself. *One head that he shows to my father, brother and the other people of Stromgard, and another that he keeps hidden. And that other side is the true Kelewulf Rivengeld. He's … dangerous.*

Her brother Erik was too good, too innocent to see it. He still thought of Kelewulf as the innocent boy he'd grown up with.

'Why does he go on those long journeys alone,' she would ask him, 'without a guard or anyone to accompany him? What is he hiding? Where does he go?'

'He's still grieving,' Erik would say. 'It's his way of dealing with his loss.'

Loss! She remembered the day of Horst's funeral, when the former king's body had been sent out to sea in his long-ship, surrounded by his riches. As the burning arrows were fired out into the wooden boat, Kel had turned his head away and raised a hand to hide his face, the movement causing Astrid to look in his direction. She doubted anyone else had seen it, but in the instant before her cousin's hand obscured his features, she could swear he'd been smiling. She'd resolved to keep a vigilant eye on her dark-haired cousin ever since.

As she watched him now, he turned away from the window. Not for the first time, she wondered what her cousin was up to.

* * *

74

Kelewulf obeyed the instructions carefully, knowing even the slightest error would prove fatal to him. A large circle of salt was laid out on the floor. At its centre was a golden cup containing the dark blood of a hen. Alongside this was the thigh bone of a dog and an earthenware bowl containing uncooked pig flesh, the smell of which was making his stomach lurch each time he caught a whiff of it. The final item was the most important of them all. Like the grimoire, it had taken Kelewulf an awfully long time to find. The phylactery was a small, ornate wooden box that did little to suggest the power of the thing it contained.

The grimoire itself, the Book of Roth'gurd, lay open on the small table at his side.

Satisfied everything was in place, he stared down at the elaborately scripted page. Eight words in an ancient tongue. Words which, once uttered, would change his life forever …

What are you waiting for? Are you scared? It was his father's voice he imagined in this moment, and the harsh, mocking tone – a tone he'd heard all too often during his life – stirred Kelewulf in a way nothing else could.

He approached the edge of the circle, careful not to step too close. His hands were shaking uncontrollably now and he clasped them together. There was, however, nothing he could do to calm his heart, which hammered away almost painfully inside him. Drawing a deep, shuddery breath, he threw his arms open and intoned the words, taking the utmost care with both the pronunciation and the metre of the spell.

The air inside the salt circle seemed to change. It was subtle to begin with, a tiny shift in the quality of the light, as if something had momentarily passed in front of a window. But as he watched, black swirling smoke emanated from the phylactery and filled the space – a slowly churning cylinder of darkness that stretched from floor to ceiling. Slowly it began to coalesce, gathering together and solidifying until it finally formed the terrible thing he'd dreamed of summoning all these years.

With torn and rotted clothing, flesh hanging from a skeletal figure, this spectral corpse, the lich of Yirgan, the last great mage, was nothing short of terrifying. It floated in the air before him, taking in the young human through baleful eyes set into a face that had completely decayed on one side, revealing the skull beneath. More than a hundred and twenty years had passed since the sorcerer had died, and the sight of him now filled Kelewulf with both fascination and revulsion. Except this was not really Yirgan. This was his soul, his spirit, that he'd carefully hidden inside the phylactery after his death, waiting and hoping for a moment like this to come along – when some mage, drunk on the possibility of power, would free him.

Trying to look braver than he felt, Kelewulf lifted his chin and dared to look back at the lich.

'I have summoned you,' he said, doing his best to mask the fear in his voice.

The sound that filled his head was like a long and drawn-out groan. 'Why?'

'I desire knowledge. Knowledge of the sort you possessed during your time on this earth.'

'Such knowledge is power.'

'I know.'

'But ...' The lich seemed to grow, the smoke that gave it its form darkening further until a huge figure loomed over the youngster. 'Knowledge alone, when it comes to majik, is not enough. To use it I must have a physical form here, and as you can see, that I do not have.' The lich gave him a knowing look. 'How are we to resolve that?'

It was the question Kelewulf had been expecting. He knew what the lich desired above all other things. The words he chose to use now were critical; the slightest slip would result in his undoing. Swallowing hard, he summoned up his courage.

'I ... I will give you physical form again in this world.' He gestured down at himself. 'You will inhabit this body. It is strong and young, and would be a fine vessel for your powers, but –' he held his finger up, stressing the rest of the sentence – 'you cannot inhabit it as a controlling force. You will be a partner, not a possessor. You will protect this corporeal form in every way you can. This must be our covenant. You might have cheated death once, Yirgan, but I doubt that the same opportunity will be afforded to me if you misuse this human body.'

The lich stared down at him through long-dead eyes, and Kelewulf fancied he caught the hint of a smile form on the creature's lips, or at least what was left of them. 'What would you do with such knowledge?'

'Make this world tremble.'

The lich tilted its head. 'How?'

'By completing your work. I wish to return the god Lorgukk to this world and show its pathetic inhabitants what real power is.'

The wraith shook its head. 'If I could do such a thing, do you not think I would have done so at the height of my powers? When I had this world trembling at my feet?'

'The tales say that you tried, that you were close to achieving your goal, before you were killed by the gods for doing so …'

'I was close, yes.'

'Then now is the chance for you – for us – to try again. New religions are springing up, and with them the belief in the old gods is on the wane. So are their powers. This time we will succeed.'

'You are bold, young mage.' The spirit seemed to be thinking. 'My return to this world will not go unnoticed. There will be those who will try to stop us.'

'We will wreak havoc on the Volken people and anyone else who seeks to stop us. Together with Lorgukk, we will usher in a new age. A new power.'

A sound, like a wave pulling back from a pebble-strewn shore, filled Kelewulf's head, and it took him a moment to realise the lich was laughing.

'You have a dark heart, boy. Perhaps as dark as mine once was – when I had one.' It looked down through its own smoky body at the wooden phylactery. When the lich looked back at Kelewulf, it seemed to have come to a decision. 'I have been trapped for too long, in a place so terrible that the human mind would tear itself apart trying to imagine it.' It paused, but Kelewulf could tell it had already made up its mind. 'Very well, young necromancer-to-be, I agree to the conditions of our covenant. Let us join together and create the havoc you seek. Let us rule these petty humans with a reign of terror.'

Kelewulf hesitated for a second; he knew that Yirgan, while living, was famed for his trickery and his cunning mind. 'Be aware, lich. I have read the Book of Roth'gurd well, and I have learned the Spell of Revocation. If I believe you have reneged on this agreement in any way, I will use it to return you to that terrible place you spoke of. There will be no third coming for you, Yirgan. If I send you back again, your dark soul will remain in hell forever.'

'Naturally. I would expect nothing less from as formidable a partner as you.'

Kelewulf could not tell if the lich was mocking him or not.

'Well?' the lich asked.

Steeling himself, Kelewulf stretched out with a foot, placing it inside the salt boundary before dragging his heel back to break the salt circle. As he did so, a wave of icy cold struck him like a slap. Opening his mouth to gasp, he almost managed a scream as the smoky creature poured through that hole and entered him, filling him with a terrifying coldness that permeated first his lungs, then his blood, and then every part of him.

The boy wobbled on the spot, but managed to stay upright.

Where shall we start? asked the voice inside his head.

'With the seat of power,' he answered. 'I have business with the rest of the Rivengeld family. They have taken what was rightfully mine, and even though I had no wish to rule, I will nevertheless have them pay.'

Faun Forest

8

Fleya sat in a small clearing in the woods. It was two hours before dawn and the ground was sodden with the night dew, the moisture soaking into her woollen garments and boots. The witch, deep in a trance-like state, hardly noticed. Her senses were all turned inwards to the bright thing at the centre of her being: her majik.

It was by no mere chance she had chosen this forest to live in, and she allowed the power that resided in the place to enter her soul, revelling in the beauty of the woods, and the wider world. Other similar forests were revealed to her, and she understood that she was being given glimpses, not of other worlds exactly, but of alternatives to this one where other Fleyas existed. She might have stopped to marvel at this, but she could not allow herself to become distracted. She was at her most vulnerable now, in a place

81

between this realm and the one she was trying to reach, her mind open to attack.

She allowed her psyche to fly out, up and up, beyond the physical, out beyond the stars and galaxies to a place of pure energy. In her mind's eye she pictured it as some vast and swirling cloud of colours and sounds. All of majik was here. And danger – that was here in abundance, too.

Infinitesimally small. After all these years practising majik, that was still how she felt. Like nothing more than a fleck of desert sand before a wild and frenetic storm that threatened to pick her up and toss her away. She wondered at its might, its power, knowing, too, that it would engulf and destroy her if she did not proceed with the utmost caution. Because a part of her wanted to surrender, to throw herself into that beautiful storm and be one with it.

This was the Art. To avoid being devoured and destroyed by it was what set apart apprentices from the true masters. Not that Fleya considered herself a master; nobody should think they were ever in complete control of majik. That way lay madness and ruination.

Fleya blindly reached down for the article at her side. She unravelled the scroll, holding the blank parchment in front of her.

'Show me,' she whispered, concentrating her will on the thing in her hand. At first the scroll remained blank; then, slowly, an image formed on the surface. Fleya dipped her head, her milky white eyes taking in what was shown there.

The young sorcerer of Lann's vision was before her. One look at his face was enough to identify him as a Rivengeld. She racked her brains until it came to her: Kelewulf. The son of the former king. They had met, a year or so ago, when the new king, Mirvar, had summoned her to discuss a disease that was sweeping through Stromgard. During her brief visit, she was aware that the boy had done his best to keep his distance from her. When they were finally introduced, she fancied she understood why: he was fascinated by the Art, but did his best to keep this interest concealed from those around him. She'd felt him reach out into her, probing her mind for what knowledge and abilities she possessed.

It was not unusual for practitioners of the Art to do this when they met, but it was usually done with a form of mutual psychic consent. Instead, Kelewulf had bullied his way into her in a way that was not just clumsy, but ill-mannered. Blocking any further attempts, she felt perfectly entitled to reciprocate the act, and reached into the young-ster in the same way. That brief encounter had left her unsettled. There was something dark in the boy, something he kept well hidden from those around him. But it was there to see for anyone with the ability to do so. Kelewulf desired more power. This, in itself, was not unusual among those who studied the Art. What alarmed Fleya was the impression that he had begun to seek it in areas of majik that were best avoided. Going down that road – into the darker realms of the Art – was fraught with danger.

After her meeting with the king and his advisors, she'd had it in mind to talk to Kelewulf about his interest in majik and to warn him away from the darker forms of the Art. But he had left the city on an expedition from which nobody knew when he might return. Her encounter with the young sorcerer had left her with a bad taste in her mouth that she'd done her best to forget. Until now.

Now it appeared that her foreboding about the young man and the risks he was taking had been well founded. For the boy she could see was not alone. A dark spirit had invaded his body. An icy shiver of fear snaked through her and she almost lost her control. Kelewulf had somehow summoned a lich, the undead spirit of a powerful sorcerer – and not just any sorcerer. The boy had brought the necromancer Yirgan back! The young fool had willingly allowed the lich to possess his physical body, giving the thing a presence in this world again. How could he have been so stupid? To invoke the necromancer who had almost brought this world to its knees; a man who had made the gods themselves tremble and quake until they were forced to intervene and kill him. It was … lunacy.

Allowing the scroll to slip from her fingers, she hurriedly

sought out Stromgard with her mind. The city was in a state of mourning. Anger and sorrow were powerful emotions, and it felt to Fleya as if the place were awash with both right now.

Visions flashed before her – appalling visions. The cold, dead body of the benevolent king, Mirvar Rivengeld, lying in state. His son, Erik, being dragged away by guards, accused of his murder. And a girl, Mirvar's youngest child Astrid, fearful and sitting atop the throne in a reign that had already courted controversy. Stromgard was never short of people who would happily take power, and Fleya saw members of the royal court already plotting against the young queen.

All of this, she was sure, could be laid at Kelewulf's door. But she could not see where the necromancer was now.

Feeling her strength abandoning her, Fleya let out a sigh and withdrew back to her own body, struggling against the waves of nausea that swept over her as she did so. Exhausted from her efforts, and wanting nothing more than to return to her cabin to sleep and reflect on what she'd learned, she slowly and unsteadily got to her feet.

A crescent moon provided meagre light to the dark and foreboding woods around her, but she liked the way its silvery glow gilded the canopy of leaves above her head. She froze when she heard the unmistakeable sound of a snake in the branches of a nearby tree. When she turned to look in the direction of the noise, she saw an old woman standing beneath the creature, looking back at her. Dressed in dishevelled clothing, her face obscured by the tattered hood of a cloak she wore about her shoulders, the woman leaned heavily on the staff she grasped in her gnarled hand, as if she might fall to the ground if the thing were not there.

Anger ignited inside Fleya. 'What? No golden-haired, golden-eyed idol for me? Or do you just use that particular manifestation to trick young boys into making terrible choices?'

The old woman chuckled and straightened up a little. Pushing the hood back, she revealed a wizened face. The snake stretched out towards her from the tree and she lifted a hand, lowering the thing down on to her shoulders, where it, too, stared back at Fleya, its tongue testing the air between them.

'I thought *this* would be more to your liking, witch. After all, if you strip away the majik, you and I would look remarkably similar.' The old woman's cruel laugh turned into a nasty, wet, coughing noise, and she spat on the ground before her.

'What do you want, Rakur?'

'To help.'

Fleya gave a humourless snort. 'Help? Like you helped Lann? No, thank you. I think he and I have had enough of your meddling to last us a lifetime.'

The haggard old woman seemed to consider this for a moment. When she spoke again her voice was low and Fleya had to strain to make out the words.

'You seek a young necromancer. You know what he and the foul lich did before leaving the place you call Stromgard. The fate of the Rivengelds, the capital, the Volken people and maybe the world lies in the balance right now. So I suggest you be careful when refusing help that is offered.'

Fleya forced herself to forget her anger and pride. 'I'm listening,' she said.

'The other Rivengeld boy, the prince who is now a king – albeit one in chains – is accused of murdering his father.'

'He didn't do it.'

'Many believe he did. And there are others who would, despite his innocence, like to see him blamed for the deed. His sister cannot protect him for much longer. She herself is in danger.' The god lifted a hand to stroke the snake. 'Unless something is done to help them, neither has more than five days to live.'

A cold wind blew in through the trees, stirring the overhead leaves and sending a small shiver through the witch.

'Kelewulf and Yirgan's lich – where are they?' she asked.

'The imprisoned boy Erik knows the whereabouts of the necromancer. The young sorcerer and he spent time there as small boys.'

The witch was silent for a moment as she took this information in. Eventually she shook her head and gave the god a stony look. 'Why did you do it?'

'Do what?'

'Why did you give the devil sword to Lannigon?'

'Because he needs it for what lies ahead.' A smile played at the edge of the god's mouth. 'Who knows? You yourself might need it in the not too distant future. Perhaps all our destinies are now tied to that sword and the young man who wields it.'

Fleya glared at the god, who laughed.

'You don't trust me, do you, witch? That is a sensible position to take. I am not to be trusted … most of the time. But ask yourself this: if I am the villain of this piece, why would I intervene at all? Why not let Lorgukk and his creatures from the Void simply enter this world unhindered?'

'I despise you gods and your meddling.'

'Then you must be glad that our time in this realm is coming to an end. Perhaps, however, some of us are unwilling to leave this world in the hands of a creature as vile as Lorgukk. Perhaps some of us have come to admire the chaos and madness that is human life, and want it to continue in order to see what they are truly capable of. Who knows what they might achieve if they are left alone to explore their own fates? They might build cities in the skies, fly inside the carcasses of giant silver birds. They might even travel to the very stars.' The god smiled at her, revealing a toothless mouth. 'But none of that will come to pass if the dark god is allowed back. Humankind will be crushed and enslaved. You know this to be true, Fleya. Just as your sister knew it.'

Fleya studied the ground at her feet, lost in thought. When she looked up again, the god was gone.

Away from the small clearing, the forest was dark, but Fleya could have found her way back home with her eyes closed. Her encounter with the god had dispelled some of the fatigue she'd felt, and she replayed their conversation as she walked, considering everything she'd been told. She still didn't trust Rakur, but she had no choice but to listen to him now. One thing was for sure: she and Lann must journey to the coast, to the city of Stromgard. There, they would have to get an audience with an imprisoned prince. And they must do so in less than five days.

Lost in her thoughts, she was not aware of the creatures lying in wait to attack her until it was too late.

Lann was in a deep sleep when he woke suddenly to the sight of the house wight looming over him. Halbe's shadowy face was so close it was almost touching his own, but no breath came from her open mouth. When he cried out in alarm, the wight momentarily disappeared, winking out of existence before reappearing again almost as quickly. Lann started to mumble an apology, stopping when he saw the extreme distress on the spectre's face.

'What's wrong?' Lann said, throwing back the covers. He stopped, staring down at the sword in his hand, his heart beating furiously in his chest.

He hadn't taken the blade into bed with him. He distinctly remembered putting it next to the nightstand in its scabbard. Now here it was, unsheathed, in his grip. Maybe Halbe hadn't woken him after all, maybe it had been the sword. Because it was talking – a haunting, urgent whisper repeated over and over.

Nir-akuu. Monsters.

The house wight raised a hand in the direction of the door at the rear of the cabin.

Fleya.

Throwing a cloak about him, Lann hurried through the cabin and out into the gloom of the woods beyond.

Long, thin clouds raced across a moon that briefly painted their edges with its silvery light. It was cold, but the temperature hardly registered with the boy as he ran through the trees. The sword was more than a weapon now. It was a thing of energy, and the power coursing through his body excited and scared him in equal measure. It was also his guide, and he knew the blade sensed where and what the danger was.

Nir-akuu, it continued to repeat in that eerie voice.

A cry, unmistakeably Fleya, caused him to take off in the direction of the noise, ducking branches that whipped at his face and skin. A tiny part of him told him it was foolish to rush headlong into danger like this, but his aunt needed him.

He stumbled into the clearing and stopped in horror. Two creatures were attacking Fleya. They were twisted and misshapen things, with large bulbous heads and grotesquely bulging eyes. One had grabbed Fleya from behind, its left arm wrapped around her throat in a grip that was choking the breath from her. The other was standing before the witch, its hands clamped on either side of her face so she was forced to look straight into its wide-open mouth. White, smoke-like stuff, was being drawn out of his aunt into that mouth, the extraction accompanied by a sound, like a lover's sigh. Whatever the creature was attempting to take by force was weakening her so much, she seemed on the point of collapse.

Lann took all this in, in a heartbeat. Roaring with anger, he leaped forward, lifting the black blade over his head as he did so and swinging it at the nearest monster.

The blade sang as it cleaved the air, a low, thrumming noise that caused the creature to stop and look back over its shoulder just as the edge bit into the flesh of its neck. Time seemed to slow almost to a halt for Lann. He watched as the blade cut easily through flesh and bone before it emerged again on the other side, droplets of inky black ichor flying from its tip and out into the night air. There was a surprised expression on the foul creature's face as its head toppled to the floor.

The second creature let out a terrible scream of fear and rage. Fleya was momentarily forgotten, thrown to the ground, as her tormentor leaped towards Lann, clawed hands outstretched to rake flesh and tendon. But Lann, empowered by the magical sword, moved like a shadow. Swiftly stepping to his right, he twisted his torso so the black talons missed him by inches, while simultaneously reversing the swing of the sword, pulling it up and across, so that a huge diagonal gash opened the creature from hip to shoulder. As he delivered that dreadful slashing wound, Lann bellowed a war cry in a long-dead language, becoming, in that instant, one with the Dreadblade.

A terrible screech filled the air, and the creature stumbled to a halt, looking down in surprise as its entrails tumbled out into the night. The monster grabbed at the steaming, grisly mess as if trying to put its innards back where they rightfully belonged, before crumbling and joining its dead partner on the forest floor.

Plunging the blade into the ground, Lann hurried over to his aunt, dropping to his knees by her side. Tears fell from his eyes at the thought that she might be dead, but he hurriedly cuffed them away and forced himself to think straight. With shaking hands he sought out a pulse.

'Please be alive. Please be …'

His heart soared from the depths it had been in seconds before and he let out a loud sob of relief. He silently thanked the gods: she was unconscious but still breathing. Still fuelled by both his own adrenalin and the power provided him by the Dreadblade, he easily picked Fleya up. Pausing only to retrieve the sword, he carried her back to the cabin.

Stromgard

9

The young queen was beautiful. Sitting atop the throne in the great longhouse, dressed in all her finery, she looked every inch a ruler, despite her sixteen summers. It was hard to imagine this was the shield maiden who had, until recently, been swinging axe and sword as leader of the kingdom's most elite fighters.

In truth, Astrid felt anything but a queen. *It's not for long*, she told herself over and over. *Just until Erik is freed. Remember that. Be strong. Be fierce if you need to, but most of all, make everyone remember you are Mirvar Rivengeld's daughter and that you intend to rule as long as it takes to prove your brother's innocence.* She shifted on the great chair, adjusting her ridiculous clothing.

Her father had always called her his little 'svartrsvanr' – black swan – and it was true that she possessed the grace and elegance of that animal. But that was not the reason

Mirvar had given her the nickname. The sable-feathered birds that lived in the waters around Stromgard were also famed for their courage, and it was this quality above all others that the young queen knew she needed right now.

Because Astrid was a warrior, not a ruler.

Stromgard had suffered its fair share of raids from neighbouring kingdoms over the years, and because of this, all Volken people, regardless of status, were schooled in combat skills. Astrid Rivengeld was no exception to this rule. What had surprised many, however, including Astrid herself, was what an apt pupil she'd turned out to be. When her compulsory training was finished, she'd begged her father to allow her to try and enrol as a shield maiden. Mirvar had baulked at the idea at first, but eventually he'd given his consent.

Astrid was no fool. She knew her father had only agreed because he thought she would fail, and that her disappointment would put an end to what he considered foolishness. After all, no king's daughter had ever become a shield maiden. Only the fiercest women combatants were chosen for the role. So when the small, sable-haired princess turned up for the selection process, her fellow students had looked at her with thinly disguised contempt. Those looks were not worn for very long. Like the black swan, Astrid proved to be fearless when faced with opponents much bigger and stronger than she was. She quickly won

95

the respect of those around her, who no longer addressed her as 'Princess' but as 'Sister', in the tradition of their kind. She was good with shield, axe and sword, but it was with the horn bow that she excelled, and she'd bested the kingdom's finest archers in competition with the weapon. She had proven to everyone, including Mirvar himself, that she was a warrior every bit as good, if not better, than the male defenders of Stromgard.

Her faith in her shield-maiden sisters was the reason a number of them, including her beloved friend Maarika, were stationed around the longhouse interior instead of the traditional guard her father had used. She thought the great Mirvar Rivengeld would have been proud that she'd inherited his famed caution when it came to matters of security: nobody could doubt the maidens' commitment and fervour when it came to protecting one of their own.

Thinking of him as she sat on his throne brought a terrible sadness, like a dark cloud, down on her. She would never again hear her father use her pet name, never walk into this place to find him poring over a map or sitting with his counsellors to peacefully resolve an argument between two of his jarls. He was gone. She'd watched him set out on his final journey, floating off into the harbour on a boat laden with firewood and oil, his body laid atop it as if he were merely sleeping. As the flaming arrows set it ablaze, Astrid found herself thinking how she would quite happily have gone on that last great trip with him. Instead, she was now sitting where he should be, dressed in these ridiculous clothes, listening to these boring men prattle on about things she struggled to understand, let alone make decisions upon.

'My Queen?' The chancellor looked at the young ruler, a perplexed expression on his face. She had not been listening to him. 'These matters? They need your approval.'

Astrid glanced about her at the other nobles present in the longhouse. Men who'd sworn allegiance to Mirvar Rivengeld, not just because of his leadership in battle, but because he made Stromgard the place it was today: a jewel in the Volken kingdoms. One look at them told her how many of these same men doubted her ability to reign. She couldn't blame them; she felt the same way. But she had no choice. Abdication wasn't an option. Relinquishing the crown would also mean relinquishing the ability to protect her brother, and Astrid would die before she did that.

She did not believe for one second that her brother was capable of the terrible deed he was accused of, despite the evidence against him. And on the face of it, the weight of that evidence was damning.

Erik had been seen in the market buying the ingredients necessary to poison Mirvar, and signs of potion-making were found in his private rooms. Her brother had denied this furiously, swearing to Astrid on everything he held sacred that he was not the murderer. His defence, however, was not helped by the fact that he had no recollection of anything in the build-up to the murder. She believed him. Something smelt bad about the whole affair, but she couldn't put her finger on what it was. Kelewulf was nowhere to be found. Her cousin, on hearing of Mirvar's illness, had set off on an expedition to find a cure and not returned. To top things off, an expert in poisons she had sent for, from the kingdom of Nesh, also seemed to have disappeared.

The chancellor coughed, the sound bringing Astrid from her reverie for a second time. She looked across at the man still waiting patiently for her response.

'My apologies, Jarl Glaeverssun,' she said, offering him a small smile. 'But these matters you and your fellow jarls have brought before me seem small in comparison to other things weighing on my mind right now.'

'If you would rather we come back, we could do so. Maybe in an hour?'

Astrid felt a terrible sinking feeling. She wanted nothing more than to throw off the crown and the stupid furs she'd been made to wear, and ride out into the forests to fish and hunt.

'An hour would be fine,' she said in a small voice.

Glaeverssun nodded and began to leave, stopping after a few steps. He turned to his queen, giving her a sad smile. 'I wonder ... If I may be so bold as to make a suggestion?'

'What is it?'

'You are surrounded by your father's men. Jarls and elders whom Mirvar Rivengeld hand-picked for their advice and counsel. At a time such as this, maybe it would be an idea to *use* their knowledge and expertise?' He looked around at the others gathered in the room. 'Why not allow us, on your behalf, to make decisions on some of these more wearisome matters?' When Astrid shot a sceptical look back at the jarl, he continued, 'We all swore oaths to the Volken king. Blood oaths that bound us to him. We swore to defend his realm and do everything we could to keep law and order in this kingdom. Let us take some of this burden from your shoulders, as we did for your father.'

The sudden wave of emotion Astrid felt at hearing this offer took the young queen by surprise, and it was all she could do to hold back the tears that began to well up. She imagined what her father would have said at hearing that the ruler of his kingdom had openly cried while sat upon the ancient River Throne, and she forced herself to sit up straight, lifting her chin and fixing Jarl Glaeverssun in the eye.

'Let it be so. You and the other jarls here will pass judgement on those matters you deem fit. You will, of course, include me in anything that represents a threat to the people of Stromgard or the Volken lands that fall under this city's protection.' She studied the faces of the men around her. These men were loyal to Mirvar, and she believed they would prove to be the same to her. 'Most importantly, you will ensure all of our efforts are directed towards finding the Neshian expert on poisons. He alone might be the key to proving my brother's innocence.'

'Of course, my Queen.'

'Good. That will be all.'

As he turned away, Astrid thought she saw a look of triumph cross Glaeverssun's face. She dismissed it, though; since her father's murder she'd had trouble sleeping and she must be seeing things. Only that morning she'd woken to the vision of an old woman, a snake draped around her shoulders, standing at the bottom of her bed; a mere blink of Astrid's eyes had made the old crone disappear. She watched the men file out until only she and her shield maidens were left.

A cough a short distance from the throne made her turn in that direction. 'Was that wise?' Maarika said, stepping forward. Astrid and the girl were the closest of friends. They had grown up together, cried and laughed and stuck together through the best and worst of times. Astrid had been overjoyed when Maarika had become a shield maiden at almost the same time as her. 'Jarl Glaeverssun is already a powerful man. You have just made him more so.'

Perhaps it was the lack of sleep and the stress she'd been under, but her friend's comment lit an angry spark in Astrid that made her snap back at Maarika. 'Are you the Queen of Stromgard? Are you? No. It is I who must carry that burden, I who must try to investigate my father's murder and exonerate my brother, all the while ruling my people and keeping them safe. So allow me to find help where I can!'

'I'm sorry Astr—' The shield maiden stopped and corrected herself. 'I'm sorry, my Queen.' She began to step back, but the hurt was clear to see on her face.

What am I doing? Astrid asked herself. *This is Maarika. If I cannot trust her to tell me the truth, then who?*

'Wait,' she said, halting her friend's retreat and reaching out a hand in Maarika's direction. 'Please. It is I who should be sorry.' She sighed. 'You are my most beloved friend, and you have always done your best to give me good advice.' She tapped the arm of the great throne with a ringed finger, the sound punctuating her thoughts. 'But right now, I am unable to concentrate on farmers' land disputes or the theft of a pig. My father trusted these men to think for him, and I don't see why I should not do the same. For now, at least.' She gave a sly smile. 'Besides, I am not as trusting as you think. It's like the Fool's Guard we learned in sword-play: you allow yourself to look weak and vulnerable, inviting the attack, when all the time you are the one

101

in control. This will show me who is truly loyal and who is not.'

'That sounds like something your father would have said.'

Her friend's words made her pause for a moment. It was true. She'd clearly learned more listening to the old king than she allowed herself to admit.

'I miss him so very much.'

'We all do.'

Astrid gave her friend a sad nod. Then, forcing a smile on to her face, she pushed herself upright in that damnable chair. 'I would like to go hunting, Maarika. I feel the need to ride and shoot. Perhaps bag one of those troublesome wild boars we saw in the southern forests last month?'

'Brant Skifrmunn is hoping for an audience with you. He's waiting outside.'

Astrid sagged back down, a groan of despair escaping her at the same time. Brant had been good enough to leave her be for a short time following the death of her father. Now, having decided her mourning was at an end, the great warrior was pursuing her hand in marriage even more fervently than he had before. The man seemed incapable of taking the many hints she'd given to him that she was not interested. 'I could go out the back way.'

When her friend began to protest, the queen interrupted.

'Please, Sister, I need to get away from this place for a few hours or I truly will go mad.'

'Are you issuing a royal order, my Queen?' Maarika looked back at her with a blank expression for a moment before the spell broke and a broad smile lit up the blonde shield maiden's face.

'Yes, if that's what it takes, I am *ordering* you.'

'Then I have no choice but to obey. The queen might want to think about changing her clothes, though. That fine coat might get caught up in one of the boars' tusks!'

Astrid was already on her feet. 'Give me an hour. I will see Erik, then meet you at the Four Mounds by the edge of the Western Woods.'

Faun Forest

10

It took Fleya two days to recover from the attack; it would have been longer were it not for the healing potions Lann prepared for her, using the very skills she'd taught him.

It was odd being able to see, rather than merely smell and touch, the herbs he collected. Everything he knew about herblore and medicines had been learned in the darkness of the period he'd been blind, when he'd had to rely on his other senses to identify the oils, salves and lotions his aunt kept on the shelves. Oddly, he found his restored vision was more of a hindrance than a help when it came to the task. A red-knot mushroom *looked* almost identical to the blastcap toadstool, and his aunt had already taught him how they often grew next to each other. One was used as a means of quickly bringing down a fever; the other was deadly if ingested, killing in a matter of hours.

When he came across a group of almost identical-looking fungi growing beneath an old log at the back of the house, he'd been forced to close his eyes and smell them. Like that, it had been easy to separate the red-knot from the blastcap.

He made a poultice that he applied to Fleya's neck and throat, both of which were a livid purple colour where the creature had held her in its deadly embrace. Having done this, he bade her drink a strong tonic that would help her to sleep and heal.

At the end of the second day, she was shushing his orders to stay in bed, insisting she was strong enough to get up. He built up the fire so the heat from it poured into the room and they sat in their old familiar positions, Fleya sipping on grudnflower chae while he read to her from a book. The irony of the situation was lost on neither of them.

Finishing her drink, she smiled at him. 'Thank you, Lann. For everything.' Her voice still sounded strained, and he guessed it must hurt her to speak. As if reading his thoughts, she shook her head. 'I'm fine. You are a good healer, Lannigon Gudbrandr.'

'You taught me well.' He leaned forward. 'Those creatures in the forest … What were they?' he asked.

'Kurgyres. They seek to take the thing most precious to each and every one of us living in this realm: our essence …

souls, if you prefer. And if they had taken much more of mine, I would have surely died. It was fortunate you came when you did.'

'Thanks to Halbe,' he said, looking about him to see if the house wight was lurking in the shadows somewhere.

'Kurgyres are not usually so bold,' she said. 'And I have never heard of them working together as they did against me. They are usually sneak-thieves, creeping up unexpectedly on their victim while they sleep.' She shook her head.

The fire spat a small ember on to the hearth. 'Before I was attacked I saw your god,' she told him.

'Rakur?'

The witch nodded, but seemed reluctant to continue.

'What happened?' he prompted.

'He told me I would have need of the black blade in the near future. He was right. No ordinary weapon could have saved me from those monsters.'

She stared into the fire.

'How did they come to be in the woods? I thought this place was protected by powerful majik.'

'That is a good question.' She leaned forward and placed her cup on the hearth. 'The young necromancer you saw in your dream? His name is Kelewulf, and he is the son of our former king, Horst Rivengeld. The boy is possessed by a lich.' She paused when it was clear her nephew had

106

never heard the term before. 'The undead soul of a powerful sorcerer,' she explained.

'Together they are trying to form a link between this world and the Void. In doing so, they are eroding the barriers that separate the two realms. These rifts between the worlds will become more common as the two continue to look at creating a more permanent opening, more so in places of majik, like this forest.' She gave a small shrug. 'Kurgyres are opportunistic creatures, and I was not paying enough attention.'

'Neither were they,' Lann said, glancing at the sword by his side.

'No, they were not. And thanks to you, they won't be back, to this world or any other.' Fleya took a moment to study her nephew, thinking how much older he seemed; he had changed a great deal in such a short period of time. Although Lann had asked the question, this was not the first time Fleya had pondered the circumstances surrounding the creatures' appearance in the wood. First a wyrewolf and now kurgyres had appeared in Lann's vicinity, and she now suspected they had come here to kill him, and that Gord, and now herself, had merely been unlucky victims. Not wanting to scare her nephew, however, for now at least, she decided to keep her theories to herself. 'The god Rakur also told me how we might find this young necromancer,' she said.

'He told you where Kelewulf is?'

'Oh, come now. Do you really think the trickster god would come right out and *tell* me the location? No … but he did tell me who might know.'

There was something in the way she said this that told him she was already worried about whatever lay ahead. He waited.

'King Mirvar's son, Erik, is the key. He is in prison for his father's murder, but I believe that Kelewulf is the real killer. We have to go to Stromgard and prove his innocence.' Fleya stood. She moved towards the front door and picked up the large bag she kept next to it.

'That sounds straightforward.' Lann looked over at her, noting how she was checking the contents. 'What aren't you telling me?'

'Rakur also told me we only have five days in which to save the new king. Two of these have already been wasted during my recovery. We must leave for Stromgard today.'

Stromgard

11

Erik Rivengeld looked across at the big, sleek rat sitting in the middle of the prison cell they both occupied. The creature used its front paws to comb its face, before turning its attention back to the morsel of bread that had fallen to the floor.

Why, rat, with all the other places in Stromgard you could be, would you choose to be here? Erik thought. He had no such choice. He had to either remain in this desolate prison, or else admit to something he had not done, and pay with his life.

Murder.

The word was bad enough. It had a nasty sound to it. And the particular murder he was accused of was the most heinous of all.

Patricide. Regicide.

A sob escaped him. The desperation he felt threatened

to crush him, but he could not allow that. He could not give in to despair and self-pity. Not now. Taking a deep, shuddering breath he imagined what his father would say to him right now.

Don't you cry, boy. You are a Volken prince.

No, not a prince; not any more. He was a Volken king. A harsh, humourless bark escaped him.

A king? A king in chains, with blood and dirt in his beard.

Astrid had been to see him yesterday. She believed him. The question was: did he believe in himself? Because there was a tiny part of his brain that whispered that maybe, just maybe, he was not innocent of the crime. The doubt came from the blank spots in his memory – two or three days when he could not remember where he had been and what he had done. Two or three days during which Mirvar was murdered. What if a madness had come upon him, and he'd done the deed without remembering? Or maybe it was the other way round, and murdering his father had caused his mind to erase the wicked act and the moments surrounding it? But why? Why would he kill a man he loved so much?

When his father had acceded to the throne, Erik could not help but wonder what it would be like to be king. Then, he saw only the glories of the role: the great stone chair in the longhouse, the white bearskin robe, the bejewelled sword hanging at his father's side. And at times, when he was off guard, he'd allowed himself to anticipate his father's death and how he would take Mirvar's place on that great seat. But these were merely the imaginings of an immature young mind, and in the years that followed, Erik came to see the terrible burdens of the role. The weight of responsibility for the people of Stromgard and the kingdom beyond rested so heavily on his father's shoulders that it threatened to crush the great man at times. It was an onerous load Erik was only too happy not to have to carry.

That word floated into his mind again.

Murder.

His father had deserved a hero's end. He should have died with his people, axe and sword in hand, charging into battle and cutting enemies down like wheat. Instead he had died in his bed, writhing in agony. Erik's cousin, Kelewulf, had volunteered to ride out in search of an antidote for the poison, leaving just as the witnesses started coming forward: people who'd told how they'd seen Prince Erik at some of the less reputable market stalls, buying the articles necessary to kill a man. The witnesses were many, and they spoke of how the prince went about his work with little care for who saw him. The same items had later been found hidden in his room, along with discarded clothes reeking of the vile concoction he'd prepared. And just like that, to the people of Stromgard, he'd gone from a beloved king-in-waiting to a monster.

Majik. Dark majik was at the heart of this. Groaning, Erik rested his head in his hands. What part had Kelewulf played in all this? As a youngster, his cousin had let slip his interest in majik. But without any formal training in the Art, Erik didn't see how Kelewulf could be capable of weaving a web of corruption and deceit of the kind he now found himself trapped in. And even if he was, why would he do such a thing?

Not for the first time since his arrest, he remembered the incident in the boatyard ...

A few nights prior to his father's murder, Erik, unable to sleep, had been out walking. Without knowing why, he found himself down by the harbour, where, except for a few stray dogs and the seals hunting out in the waters of the bay, he was alone. Or at least he thought he was, until he caught the sound of two people speaking. Walking towards the source of the noise, he noted the unmistakeable glow of a lamp from the building where the longships were built. The place was out of bounds for almost everyone but the shipbuilders, and none of them would be here at this time of night. The previous year, some coastal villages had suffered attacks after their own seagoing vessels had been sabotaged, so as Erik crept forward he loosened his dagger from its sheath, cursing himself for not having a weapon of more substance with him. As he paused at the open door he realised he recognised the voice he was hearing.

Without announcing his presence, he crept through the opening, coming to a halt in the shadows, from where he saw Kelewulf standing next to the hull of a wooden longship. The lamp his cousin held at his side illuminated an ornate and freshly inked tattoo he'd had done on the back of his hand. Kelewulf was talking in a strained voice, but for the life of him, Erik couldn't see to whom the words were directed.

'Why does it have to be so? Teach him a lesson, I said. Not … not this.'

Erik, thinking the other person might be hiding in the shadows, was surprised when his cousin went on, answering his own question.

'Chaos, remember? You wanted chaos.'

'Surely there is someth—'

'You went into this venture willingly. You agreed with—'

The young man stopped then, his body tense, his head cocked to one side. 'We are not alone.'

Kelewulf twisted around, scanning the shadows. A trick of the light made it seem, if only for an instant, that his eyes were completely black.

Knowing he stood little chance of creeping away without being seen, Erik stepped out just as the light was

113

swung in his direction, making him screw up his eyes and throw his hand up.

'What are you doing here?' Kelewulf asked in a sharp voice. 'Are you spying on me, cousin?'

Erik forced a smile and gave a shrug. 'I was unable to sleep and went out for a walk.' He paused, narrowing his eyes at his cousin. 'Besides, I might ask you the same thing. It is a strange time to be out wandering around the shipyard.'

'Yes. Yes, it is a strange time to be about.' Kelewulf said, attempting his own smile. 'I, too, was unable to sleep.' He reached out a hand, touching the hull of the vessel next to him. 'They are fine things, these new longships. They will allow the people of Stromgard to launch raids further afield than ever before.'

Erik nodded. 'Well, I should be getting back. To try and grab a morsel of sleep before the dawn, eh?'

He was almost out of the door when his cousin called out to him again.

'I can make you up an infusion that will help you sleep. I shall bring it to your rooms tomorrow.'

And with that, Kelewulf had turned and walked away, leaving Erik alone in the darkness.

Dreuvn Val ... and Beyond

12

The journey from Faun Forest to Stromgard was full of wonders for a boy who had never strayed from home. Despite the urgency of their trip, and the need to make good speed, Lann couldn't help but admire the views and sights afforded him during that first day's hard ride, and he bombarded Fleya with question after question about what they saw. At the end of the day, tired and saddle-sore, they stopped on the crest of a hill overlooking a wide valley below.

Having set the ponies to graze, Lann joined his aunt on a rock, where he sat chewing on an apple and looking down on the valley beneath them. It was eerily silent; no birds sang in the skies overhead, and nothing could be heard from the banks of trees that stretched out on either side.

'It's so quiet,' he whispered.

'This is Dreuvn Val,' she said, nodding down at the landscape. 'A terrible battle was fought here many years ago in which the Volken people defeated a great army from the West.' She was silent for a while, her eyes roaming the geography of the place as if seeing things that were invisible to her nephew. 'The enemy, the Hasz'een, was a fearsome warring race that had destroyed all the peoples they'd come up against in their march east across this world.

'They are a cruel and ruthless people. Unlike the Volken, there is little honour in battle for them, and no love of the land, or the creatures and plants that live on it. The Hasz'een see the mountains and rivers not as precious living things, but as inconvenient barriers preventing them from getting where they want. No, war is all they truly care about, and they use it as a means of taking what they most prize: slaves. Those poor unfortunates left alive after their conquests are taken from their lands to work on Hasz'een cities in the West – huge, ugly places that are made of stone and rock. Those too weak to make the journey are put to the sword.

'So when the Hasz'een arrived at the lands of the Six Kingdoms, the Volken King Mjor was forced to come up with new strategies to ensure his people survived. He withdrew his forces ahead of their army, running as if afraid of them. He eventually stopped his people here.'

She pointed down into the vale, and when Lann looked again he was surprised to see a mist had filled the place. Things moved about in that miasma, figures of men and women moving around, readying themselves for battle. He fancied he could make out the clank of the blacksmiths' hammers as blades and arrowheads were prepared for the battle.

'The Hasz'een invaders, having conquered all before them, thought the fight was won and that the Volken had been broken. But Mjor was a wise ruler, and his actions had been carefully planned.' She gestured towards the land behind them, but Lann was too busy studying the fascinating scene in the mists below. 'Primed for what they believed would be an easy victory, the army from Hasz made camp in the lands to our rear, on the other side of this ridge. The Has'zeen army, outnumbering the Volken by almost two to one, were overconfident, and their preparation was not as meticulous as it should have been. They drank and sang for two days and nights, shouting and beating drums that could be heard by the Volken below. When they attacked on the third day, coming over this rise and pouring down into the valley, the ground shook so badly beneath them it was like an avalanche. Great beasts led the way – huge creatures with long horns growing from the front of their faces were ridden by men who forced them crashing into the front lines of the Volken.'

Mouth open, Lann watched as the defending army in the mist below began to defend themselves against this invisible enemy.

'It was in this way that the Hasz'een usually broke their enemy. The mere sight of these formidable armoured beasts was enough to make an army turn and flee. But the Volken are no ordinary people. They held firm, hacking at the creatures' thick legs with long axes or unseating the riders with spears until they were ankle deep in a sea of blood.'

Lann saw the front line of men and women wield these fearsome weapons. Many of them fell unmoving on the ground, only to have their place taken up immediately by those behind them.

'Hasz'een archers came next, and they turned the sky black with waves of arrows that rained down on to the Volken force. But the Volken people are strong and steadfast as the mountains they live among, and the shield wall held. Despite their losses, a great shout went up from the defenders when the archers were called to halt. Now it was the Volken defenders' turn to drum. They beat their axes and swords against shields, and taunted the archers for failing to penetrate their defences. They pointed at the horned beasts lying dead at their feet and roared in defiance. The insults were deliberate and well chosen. Enraged, the Hasz'een commanders ordered their main force down into the valley. *This* was the moment the Volken king had been waiting for. The fighting in those first few moments was horrifying. Sharp iron cleaved flesh and sinew, and the earth quickly turned red.'

Lann winced as he watched countless figures fall to invisible blows.

'Fight as hard as they might, the Volken knew there was no way they could hold off the Hasz'een ...'

'But,' Lann said, shaking his head at the carnage. 'There *is* a "but" to this story, isn't there?'

'Yes, there is a "but". King Mjor had held back a large part of his army and stationed them in those woods on either side of the valley.' Fleya gestured towards the trees. 'Once the Hasz'een were fully engaged with the Volken warriors in the belly of the valley, these new forces came down from either side, trapping the enemy.'

As she said the words a new mist poured in from the attackers' flanks, covering everything with its whiteness.

'We won.'

'Nobody won that day, Lannigon, except Kria, the goddess of death. The losses to both sides were awful, but more so for the invaders. With no means of escape, only a single Hasz'een warrior was spared to leave this valley, sent back across the waters to warn the Hasz never to come back to the Six Kingdoms. King Mjor ordered the slaughter of every other surviving enemy. It was not an order he gave lightly. There was no honour in it, and it was not the Volken way. But he'd decreed it necessary if the westerners were to be convinced never to return and try again.' She paused. 'I hope I never see anything like it again.'

'You were there?'

She nodded and turned to face him. 'I was. And so was your mother. We, and others of our kind, treated the sick and dying after the battle. Those we could not save we made comfortable, and we made sure each Volken man and woman was laid on the funeral pyres with iron in their hands so they might join their fellow warriors in the great halls.'

'What of the Hasz'een dead?'

'King Mjor ordered they be left in the open for the birds and wolves and flies to feast upon. Your mother and I hated to do that, but we did as we were bid.'

He looked over at his beautiful aunt and gave a little shake of his head. 'I always forget how old you are.'

'Despite your blade giving you the ability to see me as I really am?'

'I choose not to see that.'

'Why?'

'Hmm?'

'Why do you choose to see me like this and not as I really am?'

Lann thought about this for a second. 'I guess it's because I remember you saying how you and my mother looked alike. When I'm with you, I like to imagine how she might have been.' A wind blew up the hill, tousling his hair. 'Why are they still here?' he said, nodding down at the valley. 'The ghosts of the Volken dead?'

'This was their greatest day. Our people, for all their love of the land, are warriors. The men and women who fell here that day were part of a victory that has never been rivalled. They choose to stay here and relive that time each and every day for all eternity.'

He turned to look at her. 'You wanted to stop here for a reason, didn't you?'

'Yes.' She gave a little nod. 'The Hasz'een are worshippers of Lorgukk. Their society is built on a foundation of fear and violence, and they would like nothing more than to return and take the people of these lands by force. If their god returns to this world I don't think there is anything that could stop them.'

'Then we must ensure the dark god is not given that opportunity.'

She smiled at him. 'Yes, we must. We have another half-day's ride before we reach the harbour town of Muslvik. There we will seek passage on a ship bound for Stromgard. Time is against us if we are to save Erik Rivengeld.'

'We are not going the entire way by land?'

Fleya let out a small laugh. 'Certainly not. The mountains north of us between here and Stromgard are too dangerous to cross. We will go to Muslvik and find a captain willing to take us across the Gulf of Rikkor.'

Excitement rose in Lann; he couldn't hide the delight in his voice when he spoke. 'I have always wanted to see the ocean.'

Muslvik

13

Muslvik was like nothing Lann had ever seen or experienced. The place had an unmistakeable odour to it – sharp and metallic. When he asked his aunt what it was, she smiled and told him it was 'the smell of the sea'.

Leading his mount on foot, Lann stared about in wide-eyed amazement, trying to take everything in at once. The noise of the place had a disorientating effect on him. The clamorous din of those thronging the streets – human and animal alike – was punctuated with the cries of street merchants calling out to anyone and everyone passing, imploring them to come and look at their wares. And the people! The sheer number of people jostling for space made him feel uncomfortable. Men and women, boys and girls, passed each other in a constantly moving procession that was almost too much to take in. It reminded

Lann a little of watching the salmon during spawning season, the fish cramming every inch of the river with their bodies in an effort to reach their destination.

Sensing his unease, Fleya led them off the main street, towards a livery yard where they might sell their ponies. They had almost reached their destination when a man standing in front of an empty stall, set apart from the others, urgently beckoned them over.

The trader looked like no Volken that Lann had ever seen. Broad features were set into a face that was the colour of honey and he wore a long, black drooping moustache that had been waxed into neat tips at the ends. He was a barrel-shaped man, as if he'd spent his entire life eating and drinking with no time for exercise of any kind. 'My friends,' he cried in a strange accent. 'Come over here. Come speak to Almer.' There was something about the man and his broad smile that caused Fleya and Lann to pause in a way they hadn't for any of the previous hawkers they'd passed.

'Why?' Lann called over to him. 'You have nothing to sell.'

The man spread his arms and then gestured at himself with his hands. 'On the contrary, young sir. You are looking at what I am selling. Come.'

The pair exchanged a glance, but their curiosity was piqued and they walked their mounts over to see what it was the man wanted. Standing before the trader, Lann wrinkled his nose. Almer smelt like summer flowers and spices; the aroma was unusual and he wasn't sure he liked it. At the same time it occurred to him that his own odour after days on horseback would be just as offensive to the trader.

'Thank you for stopping. You will not regret your decision to do so.' He looked at the pair, sizing them up. 'My guess is that the two of you have come a long way to get here, no? You're in need of rest. And a good bath. No offence,' he quickly added. He moved his hands a lot when he spoke, unlike the Volken, who were much less expressive. 'Perhaps I can be of assistance in recommending a tavern where you can stay? One not full of cut-throats and thieves!' He pointed at the pair with a meaty fore-finger adorned with a huge gold ring. 'I also imagine that the pair of you were off to the livery to sell your mounts? Am I right?'

'You are,' Fleya said, a half-smile on her lips.

Almer shook his head and gestured in the direction of the livery yard. 'Do not take your ponies to this man. Not only will he give you a bad price, but your animals will end up being sold as meat.'

Reaching into his breast pocket, he pulled out a small book and flicked through the pages, muttering under his breath as he peered at words written in a foreign script.

'Yes,' he said eventually, 'I have a man that will buy your beasts.' He turned to Fleya. 'Have they pulled a wagon before?'

'Yes, but—'

'Excellent. Then I will get you a good price, more than our friend over there would give you.'

'How do we know that?' Lann asked bluntly. 'How do we know anything you say is the truth?'

The trader looked affronted. He reached inside his tunic and pulled out a large silver coin hanging from a chain about his neck. 'This, my young friend, is a seal of the Guild of Merchants from my own country. It is a very precious thing to me. That is why I keep it so close to my heart. As a member of the guild I am not permitted to lie to the people I trade with. That is why I am known as Honest Almer.'

'Honest Almer? That's what you're known as?' Fleya said. She was smiling openly now.

She looked at him for a long moment, then handed the reins of the ponies over. 'We need to buy passage – direct passage across the Gulf of Rikkor on a ship to Stromgard.'

'But what providence! My cousin, Fariz, is the captain of a ship and he is sailing to Stromgard tomorrow afternoon.'

'Is it a fast ship? My nephew and I are in a hurry.'

'Yes, yes. Everyone is in a hurry nowadays. I will speak to my cousin and arrange your passage.' He gave her a grin. 'For a modest handling fee, of course.'

'Of course.' She raised an eyebrow. 'Let me guess. The price you get for the ponies, minus your handling fee, will just about cover the cost of the trip?'

'You are as astute as you are beautiful.'

'I'm also a woman you would not want to get on the wrong side of, Honest Almer.'

The big man gave her a respectful nod. 'Lady, we have people like you in my country, who learn the Art. They are always to be respected for their skills and powers. Believe me, I know this well.' Quick as a flash, his face split into a huge grin. 'Now, for that inn with the bath and comfortable beds. It just so happens it is run by a friend of mine. Come.'

14

The inn was everything Almer had said it would be: safe and comfortable. It was busy enough that even the sight of the mysterious beauty accompanied by a boy wearing a sword at his hip only drew a few cursory glances.

They ordered food and ate it sitting next to a large fire. The exhaustion of their journey here had caught up with them, and they exchanged no more than a dozen words with each other as they spooned the rich lamb stew into their mouths.

Shortly after, bellies full, they went up to their rooms to sleep.

Lann awoke in the early hours. The candle beside his bed had sputtered out and the air was still filled with the cloying smell of waxy smoke. The room was in total darkness, but it was not this that made him anxious; he'd spent long enough in the dark not to fear it. What was worrying him was the black blade and its insistent voice inside his head. Reaching out to the bedside table he took up the weapon.

That ancient voice whispered a single word over and over.

Nir-akuu. Monsters.

Lann concentrated, allowing his thoughts to merge with the blade, as he had when he'd set off into the woods after Fleya. Something *was* out there in Muslvik, but it was not nearby and he sensed that it wasn't after them. That, however, was of no consequence to the blade. It had been fashioned by the ancient gods for one purpose and one purpose only, and he felt its primal urge to search the thing out and destroy it.

Nir-akuu.

'No,' Lann said, speaking out into the darkness. 'I will not seek out danger. Not now.' A conflict raged inside his head, and it took all his effort to push the words out as the sword and he fought for dominance. 'There will be enough of that in the days and weeks ahead without our going to look for it.'

Nir-akuu!

'No!'

Lann reached for the scabbard beside the bed. Picking it up, he plunged the blade into it until the hilt met the locket, holding it there with trembling hands as if he thought it might leap free of its own will. When he heard the handle to his door turn he spun around, only to see his aunt standing there, a candle in her hand.

The witch looked at the boy clutching the sheathed weapon and sighed. Stepping inside, she came over to his night light and relit it from her own before sitting on the edge of the bed.

'It sensed something out there. Monsters.' He took a deep breath. 'I don't think they are anywhere near … but it longs to attack them.'

She nodded. 'I heard you talking. I thought you might be having a dream –' she looked at the sword again – 'or a nightmare. Put the sword down, Lannigon.' He did so, and she smiled reassuringly at him. When she spoke again it was in the becalming voice she'd used when he'd first arrived at her house, blind and terrified. It was the voice she used when she spoke to the sick and those in need of comfort. It was like a small stream, bubbling over stones in a river that would itself eventually flow out into the sea. 'You are new to majik. It is a dangerous thing and asking anything of it can lead to the asker being consumed. It is why it takes us so long to even begin to master the Art. Some people are unable to control it properly. Those who cannot, die, or lose their minds. The stronger the power, the stronger the wielder of it must be.

130

The Dreadblade demands much of its bearer because it is itself so powerful.'

'It wants me to go out there.' He nodded towards the window.

'But you have refused it.' It wasn't a question, more a statement of fact.

'Yes. But it is not easy.'

'No. It is not.' She patted his hand and rose to her feet again. 'You are wise to resist the blade's demands. To do so now would divert us from our course, and it is vital that we reach the imprisoned king. Try to sleep now, Lann. We have a long day ahead of us tomorrow. Your first day at sea. It will not be an easy voyage.' With that, she closed the door again and left him.

Turning on to his side, he pulled the covers up against him and closed his eyes. As he felt himself slowly slide towards sleep, he heard that insistent whisper begin again.

Nir-akuu ...

15

Almer was waiting with his cousin at the dockside when Fleya and Lann came down the wooden walkway. The overweight merchant bowed low when he saw Fleya, who, to Lann's surprise, held out her hand for the man to press to his lips.

'Didn't I tell you she was a beauty?' Almer said to his cousin as he straightened, receiving only a grunt in response. The merchant's expression changed to one of seriousness. 'Fariz has bad news. He is reluctant to sail directly to Stromgard – a number of incidents have befallen vessels on that same journey in the last few weeks.'

'What sort of incidents?' Lann asked.

'Pirates,' Fariz said, looking at his aunt and speaking for the first time. He was slimmer than Almer, with a muscular build and hard eyes, but the familial connection was clear.

Almer continued. 'Rather than go directly across the Gulf of Rikkor, he will be skirting the coast—'

'No. That was not the deal we made,' Fleya responded, her voice steely.

'I know, I know. Believe me when I say I am as unhappy about this as you. It hurts Honest Almer to go back on a deal that has been struck, and I would—'

'Enough,' Fleya interrupted. Her voice was commanding. 'My requirements are simple. I need urgent passage to my destination and my nephew and I are not in a position to take a longer trip around the coast.' She turned to the seaman. 'Captain Fariz, I understand how, as a good captain, you do not wish to endanger the lives of your crew unnecessarily. But your ship needs repairs, and you need supplies. So here is what I propose. You, Captain Fariz, will get me and my nephew to Stromgard by the fastest route across the gulf. In return I will give you this.' She held out a small drawstring purse. Opening it, she shook out eight large gold coins. The startled look on the sailor's face told Lann it was far more than he had anticipated. 'I'm sure it will adequately compensate both you and your crew for your efforts.' Placing the coins back into the purse, she made a small movement of her hand and it disappeared. 'What do you say, Captain? Is the reward worth the risk?'

Fariz bit his lip. 'It is difficult to spend gold when you are dead.'

'It is. It is equally hard for me to pay you if I find myself in that same state. I am willing to put my own life in the hands of you and your crew, Captain, and I would like nothing more than to pass that purse and its contents to you when we get to Stromgard.'

Fariz gave a humourless laugh. 'Why do I feel I am making a deal with the devil?' he asked, reaching down and taking hold of the witch's travel sack. Hoisting it over his shoulder, he moved off in the direction of the gangplank leading up to the deck of his ship, calling back over his shoulder as he started to ascend. 'We leave in thirty minutes.'

Almer was staring at Fleya with a look of admiration. 'You would have made a great merchant,' he said.

The witch reached out, a small silver coin appearing between her thumb and forefinger. She dropped the money into the man's hand.

'Thank you for your trouble. That should make up the shortfall in the money you hoped to make selling the ponies,' she said gently.

'How did you know I ... ?'

But the witch was already moving away. With a gesture to her nephew, the pair moved off up the wooden walkway to board the ship.

Lann's excitement at finally being aboard a ship quickly dissipated when he spent the first few hours of the crossing draped over the bulwarks being horribly sick. He did his best to ignore the taunts and gibes of the sailors, who seemed to find this hilarious. Some of them shouted out insults in foreign tongues, laughing among each other and making their own loud retching sounds to mimic his own. But as the day went on, little by little, the boy got his sea legs until eventually he was able to smile ruefully back at his tormentors.

The vessel was nothing like he'd expected it to be. It groaned and creaked as it made its way through the ocean's dips and swells as if it were a living thing. And it wasn't just the wooden body of the ship that sang along to the tune of the sea. The great sails hummed or boomed in the wind as they strained against the rigging, which screeched and sighed in response. As he was taking all this in, Lann spotted Fariz standing beside the mainmast.

'You are feeling better?' the man asked as he drew near.

'Yes.' He nodded his thanks. 'Have you seen my aunt?'

'The witch?' Fariz shook his head and gestured towards a door that led down to the cabins at the rear of the ship. 'She went below decks almost as soon as we set sail and has stayed there.' He saw the concern on the boy's face. 'She is well. My guess is she is sleeping.' He looked up at the sails and then at the waves, then shouted something to one of the crew, who scurried off to do as he was bid.

'Have you always been a sailor, Captain Fariz?'

'When I was young I fell in love with the sea. So much so that all I wanted to do was be on it. But my parents would not hear of such a thing. They wanted me to be a merchant like my cousin Almer back in Muslvik.' He gave a little shake of his head. 'So I ran away from home and joined a ship as a cabin boy.'

'Your parents must have been worried.'

'Yes, they were. But after a few years at sea I returned. My father and mother were overjoyed to have me back. But they realised there was seawater, not blood, running through my veins and so they used their savings to buy me a share in this vessel. Eventually, after making many voyages, I managed to buy the rest of the ship and became her sole owner.'

'What's it called, your ship?'

'*She* is called *Ra'magulsha*.' He smiled when the boy repeated the name, struggling a little to wrap his lips around the strange vowel sounds. The captain patted the mast as if he were petting some giant beast. 'The name comes from the story of a princess who once lived in the lands I am originally from.'

'What happened to her?' Lann asked.

'When she was a maiden she fell in love with a merman. But their love was doomed. The young merman, Langorel, could not leave the ocean, and Ra'magulsha could not leave the land. One day, while out in her father's sailboat, the vessel ran into a huge storm. The princess fell into the sea and sank down into its inky depths where she drowned. Langorel found her. He breathed life back into her, and they were finally together beneath the waves.'

'Then it strikes me as a strange name to give to a sailing vessel,' Lann said after a few moments of silence.

'Why so?'

'She sank and died ...'

'No, little man. She gave herself up to the ocean and finally got the one thing she had always wanted. A sailor is the same. He gives himself to the sea and hopes it will give back.'

'And does it?'

'Sometimes. But more often than not, it takes.'

Lann was about to say something else when a great shout went up above him from the crew member placed high in the rigging as a lookout. 'Ship ahoy!' the man shouted. The two words had a disturbing effect on the crew and their captain. Men shouted out to each other, moving around the deck and in the rigging with renewed speed as they went about their work. Lann could sense the tension, a shiver of nervous excitement and fear running through him.

'Where away?' Fariz called up to the man. The lookout pointed to his left.

Captain Fariz mumbled something under his breath about gold and women and bad luck as he pushed past Lann, heading towards the port side so he might see the vessel for himself.

Just then, Lann saw Fleya emerge from below decks. 'Fariz is worried,' he said, hurrying over to her.

'He has every reason to be. The other ship is a pirate vessel.'

As a young boy, Lann had held romanticised notions of pirates, picturing daring and audacious men and women who roamed the seas looking for adventure. But as he grew older and heard tales of pirate attacks, he realised the truth behind his fanciful imaginings. Pirates terrorised merchant ships like the *Ra'magulsha*, taking what they wanted and killing everyone aboard. It was said that King Mirvar had driven them all away to ply their bloody trade in other waters. If that was so, it had not taken long after the king's death for them to return.

The other vessel was at least twice the size of the *Ra'magulsha* and moving towards them at a terrific speed. Even from this distance Lann could make out figures on board the other ship. Many had ventured towards the front of the deck and were holding grappling hooks and ropes in their hands. Others had drawn their weapons.

Fleya reached out and grabbed his arm, her fingers digging into his flesh as she turned him round so he was looking directly at her. 'Look after this body while I'm gone,' she said. Her eyes went from the advancing ship to the body of water separating the two vessels and back again.

'What do you mean? Where are you going?'

'Just do it.' She offered him a brief smile. 'I've become rather attached to it over the years.'

Lann was about to say something else, but the words stuck in his throat at the sight of his aunt's eyes rolling back into her head. At the same time, her legs, arms and everything else simply gave out, and her body folded up beneath her as she collapsed towards the hard wooden deck. He caught her as she fell.

Fleya was in the darkness. She reached out with her mind and sank further and further into the freezing waters, searching for the thing she knew was there. The spirits of the deep were everywhere, and they were unhappy that this interloper had dared to enter their domain uninvited. There would be a price to pay for this intrusion. But that was not her main concern now.

Deeper and deeper she went, into the dark.

Captain Fariz was at the helm, his eyes glued on the pirate ship. It was almost upon them, so close that the merchant seamen could hear the threats being hurled at them. Fariz waited until the last moment to throw his full weight into the helm wheel, giving everything he had to turn the bow of his own ship towards the pirate vessel. This audacious manoeuvre meant the *Ra'magulsha* avoided the full impact of the ugly-looking ram at the front of the brigands' vessel and instead glanced off it. Even so, the damage sustained was devastating. Heavy timbers were smashed, sending lethal, jagged splinters flying through the air in every direction. The crew of the *Ra'magulsha* were thrown around like dolls, and three men up in the rigging lost their grip. Two were swallowed up by the sea; the other's screams came to a terrible and abrupt stop as he plummeted down on to the wooden deck.

The two ships, side-on now, shrieked like living things as their bulwarks ground against each other. The pirates sprang into action, readying ropes and grappling irons to board the other ship. Seeing this, Fariz leaned into the helm wheel again, this time in the opposite direction, desperate to move the ships apart.

Lann looked down at the body of his aunt in his arms. It was like an empty husk, and he knew the thing the kurgyres had tried to take from her in the forest that night – her essence – was gone. *Where was she?*

A loud *thunk* next to him made Lann look up to see a grappling hook being dragged back across the deck and coming to a stop when it bit into the wooden gunwale. Up and down the port side of the ship more hooks and ropes appeared, pirates straining against them in an effort to bring the two ships together. Standing, Lann pulled his sword free and moved to cut the rope. As he did so the strangest thing happened. In a motion that had little to do with him, the black blade quickly swung up and around in front of him, deflecting an arrow that had been fired directly at his heart.

Looking across at the other ship, he spotted the archer, the man already nocking another arrow from the quiver at his waist. The sword had saved his life.

Other members of the crew were not so lucky. Hearing a scream, Lann spun about to see a man struck in the chest with an arrow, the force of the impact knocking him back off his feet. Lann's first thought was to protect Fleya. He dragged her as best he could towards the bulwark, hoping it would offer some protection from the lethal missiles. Glancing over the edge, he saw how close the ships now were. Pirates readied themselves to swarm across the narrowing gap.

Captain Fariz had seen the same thing. Abandoning the wheelhouse he called his men to him and set up a tight fighting square in the middle of the deck. Knives and cutlasses drawn, the crew formed a shield-wall against the arrows but the look in their eyes was enough to tell Lann they thought all hope was gone.

Suddenly a loud shout went up from one of the defenders; he was pointing at something beyond the pirate vessel. There was a moment of silence as everybody, attacker and defender alike, stared in that direction. Then chaos broke loose.

The creature was ancient. A primeval thing from a time when the old gods ruled this world and everything in it. It was this mythical beast Fleya had come into this watery world to find, but even so, she paused before stretching out to make contact with its mind. She'd never attempted something like this before, not with a thing like the giant she was now faced with. She'd have liked more time before attempting such complicated majik, but right now, time was the one thing she had precious little of. Forcing her doubts and caution aside, she merged her own consciousness with the sea monster.

It had been a long time since the creature had moved from its place on the ocean floor, and it couldn't quite understand the impetus to do so now. It had thought it would rot away in the darkness and cold it had chosen as its final resting place. For it was an ancient thing and there was little left for it to do in this world but die. But it did not feel old now. No; it felt brave, excited, in a way it had not for hundreds of years. And this alien feeling, rather than being resisted, was welcomed by the monster. It unfolded itself, stretching out with colossal limbs and feeling the seabed around it. It was to go up through the murk and cold. Up, up to the surface. Jetting water through its body, it propelled itself out of the darkness towards a light that was already hurting its eyes. All it knew was the need to hurry. It passed the body of a man sinking slowly through its watery world. The man was dead, the corpse already attracting the attention of those who would feast on it. The light was brighter than ever, and as the creature burst free of the water it let out a terrible screech against the searing pain that exploded in its head. Noises, shouts, screams and harsh, sharp sounds filled this world. The cacophony was coming from the two wooden vessels filled with men. The foreign stimulus that had stirred it from the ocean depths now urged it to concentrate on the larger of these vessels. The creature had been brought here for a purpose, and now it set about its reckoning.

The sea surged upwards, rocking both ships in its wake as the kraken emerged from the depths. An eye – a perfect circle of black set in silvery-grey – stared out from the creature's huge bulbous head, the obsidian disc regarding both vessels for a moment before sinking back beneath the waves again. A tentacle, a vast snake-like thing, rose up out of the water before slamming down against the stern of the pirate ship and wrapping itself about it.

Lann, consumed with fear and dread, had frozen at that first glimpse of the vast sea creature. Pulling his aunt's body closer to him, he muttered a prayer into her ears, hoping that his instincts were correct and that Fleya was using her majik to control the kraken. Because if that was not the case, both ships and their crews were surely doomed.

The pirate vessel was large, perhaps the largest seagoing ship in all of the seas around these parts, but it might as well have been a child's toy to the sea creature attacking it. That first tentacle pulled sharply down against the stern of the boat, sending the prow surging out of the water so that everyone aboard was thrown off their feet. The second appeared quickly after. Shooting high out of the foaming waters below, it wavered in the air for a moment before snaking out to grab hold of the mizzenmast, snapping the thing like a wishbone before sending it crashing down into and through the deck. The skewered vessel quickly took on water and was already listing dangerously to one side.

The monster was beneath the ship now. A third, and then a fourth tentacle, one from each side of the ship, wound their way across the vessel. The cracking and splintering sound of the hull being torn apart finally stirred the pirate crew from the shock that had paralysed them thus far. Forgetting all else, the brigands set about hacking and cutting at the limbs, trying to free their vessel from the gigantic beast beneath it. Below decks, men were screaming as water poured in, trapping and drowning them. All efforts were in vain. With one last terrible, ear-splitting crack the pirate ship was torn in two.

There were no cheers from the merchant ship. The crew of the *Ra'magulsha* stood, slack jawed and agog as the pirate ship and all aboard her were dragged down into the boiling waters with that terrible thing. After a few moments, Captain Fariz and some of the sailors warily made their way over to the bulwarks and looked down on to the waters. Wreckage quickly floated up to the surface, but not a single pirate body returned from the depths.

Lann stared about him at the *Ra'magulsha's* crew. Some wandered about the decks, blank eyed and shaking their heads. Others sat and hugged themselves, swearing they would never take to the seas again. Seafarers often told stories of sea monsters from the deep, but few in truth believed these creatures really existed. Now, the stuff of every mariner's nightmares had dismantled a ship before their very eyes, and they could not understand how their own vessel had been spared.

Fariz was the first of them to regain a semblance of control and composure. The captain began to bark orders at crew members, urging them to work in an effort to take their minds off the ordeal they had been through. He ordered an extra-large rum ration be given to every deck-hand, and personally went among his crew to offer them reassurance and help.

It was as this was going on that Lann finally felt his aunt stir in his arms. Relief poured through him when he looked down into her face just as her eyelids fluttered open. She looked terrible. She was barely breathing, and was so weak it was as much as she could do to raise her own eyes to meet his.

'I didn't think you were coming back,' he whispered.

She gave a small cough, a hint of a smile touching her corners of her mouth. 'Neither did I. It was not easy to do so.'

'That creature ... How did ... ?' He stopped, and turned his head at the sound of heavy footsteps approaching them. Captain Fariz's face was a mask of conflicting emotions. Relief was there, but so too were anger and fear. He stood before them, staring down at the woman before slowly sinking to his haunches.

'Was that your doing?' the captain eventually asked her, gesturing with his head to where the pirate ship had been.

She parted white lips. Her voice was barely a whisper. 'I raised the kraken, yes.'

The man nodded and got slowly to his feet again. He gathered himself before he spoke. 'I suppose I should thank you for saving the lives of my crew … but I cannot bring myself to do so. I wish I had never seen the things I did today. I will take you to Stromgard as agreed, then I will use your gold to repair my ship and pay my crew. I hope I never encounter you again, Fleya Gudbrandr.'

With that, he turned his back on the pair and walked away without another backward glance.

Stromgard

16

As the *Ra'magulsha* and her crew limped into harbour at Stromgard, Lann peered out at the place through the small porthole set in the cabin wall. He was struck by the sheer number of ships approaching and leaving the port, unloading or loading their holds with goods before setting off to sea again. And behind the bustling port rose the city of Stromgard itself: a vast, sprawling place that had expanded and grown over the years to become what it was today. He mused how he'd thought the port of Muslvik to be large. In comparison to the capital, it was little more than a village.

Lann was glad to get off the ship. The crew treated the pair with an equal measure of fear and distrust, and while the remainder of the journey had been uneventful, it was clear they were keen to get the witch and her nephew off the vessel as soon as possible.

The pair's travel sacks were unceremoniously thrown out over the bulwarks on to the wooden planks of the quayside before the ship itself had been fully brought to a halt and secured. Having paid Fariz, Fleya and Lann walked along the gangway and off the ship, feeling the eyes of each and every sailor at their backs.

The pair were soon in the heart of the city, walking up streets lined on each side with dwellings built close enough that they almost touched. They were squarer than any dwellings Lann had come across before, not like the oval or ship-shaped Volken houses he was used to.

Although the day was cool, Lann noticed the thin sheen of sweat on his aunt's forehead. Despite his ministrations on board the ship, it was evident Fleya was still weak.

'Do you need to rest?' he asked her when she paused at the base of a set of steps. 'We could find an inn and—'

'No. There is no time for that, Lannigon. Terrible things are already afoot in this place, and I fear we might be too late to stop them.'

Coming to the top of the steps, the pair found themselves looking at a small tree-lined square where a few traders were selling food to passers-by. The smell of the fish cooking on grills made Lann's mouth water and he realised they had not eaten in some time. The place was busy. People gathered to talk or sit at the small tables outside, some of them playing a game that involved moving stone pieces around on a square wooden board. At the centre of the space was a small fountain, and Lann, as thirsty as he was hungry, hurried towards it. Putting his head into the flowing water, he drank greedily from it. It was the sweetest water he had ever tasted. His thirst slaked, he turned and saw his aunt standing beside him, her expression thoughtful.

'What is it?' he asked.

'There is something wrong. These people are so angry. Angry and sad.' Fleya walked away in the direction of a woman who was standing a short distance from them.

'Good day, mistress,' Fleya said. 'Could I ask—'

'And how, pray, could today ever be considered *good*?' the woman responded, shooting her a look.

'I don't understand,' Fleya said. 'My nephew and I have just arrived by ship and—'

'My apologies. I did not realise you were new here.' The woman's smile disappeared from her face almost as quickly as it had appeared. 'But I'm afraid you will find Stromgard a poor place to visit right now. King Mirvar's son has been found guilty of his father's murder and is to be executed this afternoon.'

Lann saw Fleya's face whiten. 'The young queen has decreed this?' Fleya asked.

The woman nodded. 'So it seems. At first she insisted on his innocence, but then something changed. Jarl

Glaeverssun and the high council put him on trial while she was out hunting. Hunting! Can you imagine that? When her brother is in prison for patricide!'

'From what I know of the girl, I find it hard to believe the shield maiden would do such a thing. It is said her love for both her brother and father is as deep as the mountain lakes.'

The woman gave a little shake of her head. 'These are dark days. Many Stromgardians don't know what to think or believe any more.'

'Rumours abound that the boy really did kill the king,' Fleya said, watching the woman's reaction carefully. 'Surely the people of Stromgard welcome the verdict.'

'Many do, it's true. But there are others, those who know him, who think Prince Erik incapable of such a thing. They believe the true killer is still at large.' She shrugged, her honest face troubled. 'I only know my heart is sad that such a thing has happened to our beloved King Mirvar. He was a great ruler.'

They thanked the woman for her news and left the square, seeking out somewhere they could sit and talk quietly.

The inn they found was thin on customers at that time of day. They ordered food but left most of it untouched, their appetites forgotten in light of everything they'd been told.

'Astrid is still the key,' Fleya said finally. 'We have to get an audience with her if we are to stand any chance of reaching Erik.'

'But she believes her brother guilty – she went out hunting and left him to be sentenced to death.'

'No. That I do not believe. Despite what we have been told, I think something else is at work here.'

'Or *someone*.'

Fleya nodded.

Lann considered what his aunt had said. 'I'm assuming audiences with queens are not easy to come by. Especially at a time like this.'

'No. But weak as I am, I still have a few tricks up my sleeve.'

Astrid Rivengeld's removal from the throne had been swift. The jarls, under Glaeverssun, had come prepared, bringing their own armed guards. The soldiers outnumbered her shield maidens by three to one. Seeing the situation was hopeless, and not wanting her sisters to be hurt, Astrid had called for them to stand down. Many did, but some refused to let their queen be deposed in this way and they fought. Maarika, the shield maiden who was also the queen's closest friend, battled hardest. She took down six guards and valiantly defended her queen until she was rendered unconscious by a blow from behind and dragged from the place.

Faced with the jarls, Glaeverssun at their head, the young queen was informed of their ruling and the sentence that had been passed on her brother.

'You have no right to do this!' Astrid shouted back at them.

'On the contrary, my Queen,' Jarl Glaeverssun answered, daring to smile back at her. 'You gave me ... *us* –' he gestured at the other men present – 'the right to decide on matters that were not a direct threat to Stromgard and her people. We took you at your word and set up a court to decide your brother's fate. The people of Stromgard deserve justice, whether the miscreant is a prince or a beggar. You refused to administer that justice, so we did it for you. We put the evidence to the court and they decided your brother was guilty and should be put to death.'

'I am the queen! I have the right to decide who lives and who dies. I issue those decrees, not you!'

'That is normally the case, yes. But *not* when the throne is unable to make a dispassionate ruling. In those circumstances, the ruler can set up a council to do that for him or her. You created a privy council. You gave *us* those rights.'

Astrid stared back at him in disbelief. These men had gone behind her back and colluded to have her brother killed. She had been arrogant and believed herself

153

invulnerable. She had been foolish to underestimate Glaeverssun – thought him little more than a money counter. But he'd proven himself much more than that. 'I won't let you do this,' she said in a low voice.

'You have no choice, my Queen. The sentence has been passed.' He turned and addressed the room. 'Leave us, please.'

Glaeverssun waited until the great hall was empty except for a handful of his personal men.

Then he approached the throne so he could speak to her without being heard. 'Did you really think I would stand by and allow this kingdom to be run by a foolish girl like you? The people of Stromgard deserve a ruler that will continue the great work your father did.'

She choked back a bitter laugh. 'And are you that great ruler?'

'Perhaps. But I am not so foolish as to think that it would be an easy thing for me to take the throne without a revolt. King Mirvar was a great man, and the people would see a Rivengeld sat on that throne. That is why *you* will continue to occupy that space. You will issue the decrees agreed to by the council. You will sign the edicts we see fit and make the rulings we decide you will make.'

'A puppet queen?' Astrid spat the words. At the same time she slowly moved her hand towards the concealed knife she had strapped to the inside of her arm.

'An unfortunate term. But … yes.'

'Working for the very same people who conspired to have my brother killed?'

'Yes.'

'Are you mad? Why would I agree to such a thing?' She had her fingers on the hilt of the knife now. It was a well-balanced weapon and she knew it would fly straight and true when she threw it to kill the traitor Glaeverssun.

'Because your brother is not the only thing you hold dear, is he?' That smile again. 'We have your shield sisters in chains now. The one we had to drag out? Maarika, isn't it? I understand the two of you have been almost insepar-able throughout your sixteen years in this world. It would be such a shame if anything happened to her.' He paused, letting his words sink in. 'Your brother has been judged and sentenced. You cannot save him. But as queen you hold the lives of Maarika and the other shield maidens in your hands.' He allowed his eyes to drift from her face to the sleeve of her gown, under which lay the concealed knife. 'The weight of power is burdensome, is it not?'

Astrid let go of the knife and balled her hands into fists, her fingers curled so tightly that her nails bit into the flesh of her palms. Fighting against the rage that threatened to overcome her, she did her utmost to keep from saying or doing anything that might further endanger her sisters. She would make this man pay for his treachery. She had no idea how, but she vowed to do so if it was the last thing she ever did.

Satisfied, Glaeverssun turned to the armed men nearest him. 'Please be so kind as to escort our queen to her rooms. And do not let her out of your sight. She is not to leave this place. Is that understood? Try to get some rest, Queen Astrid. Your next official duty will be at the execution of your brother and I need you to be strong enough to face that unpleasant ordeal.'

17

Astrid sat looking at her reflection in the mirror. Red-rimmed eyes stared accusingly back at her. How could she have been so stupid, so naive? She had handed power to people whose only interest was themselves. They hadn't served her father because they loved him; they had done so because they feared him. But they had no fear of her. Now her foolish naivety had condemned her brother to death.

She looked across at the man standing guard at her door and then back to the mirror. What she saw there almost made her cry out in surprise.

The face in the glass was no longer her own. Instead, a beautiful, older woman stared back at her. The face had a finger to its pursed lips, indicating the young queen should remain quiet.

My apologies for startling you, Queen Astrid, the woman

said. Her mouth did not move, but Astrid could hear her voice inside her head.

She glanced towards the door again.

Do not worry about your sentinel. He is not privy to my words. They are for you alone. Unfortunately, I am too weak to communicate with you in this manner for long. You must trust me and listen.

Astrid studied that face for a moment, then gave a tiny nod.

My name is Fleya. I have travelled here to Stromgard from my home east of the Maiden's Fingers with my nephew Lannigon Gudbrandr. We had hoped to speak with you and your brother, but it appears the gods have conspired against us. Know this, Astrid: your brother is not your father's murderer. That deed was committed by someone known to you, someone who is in league with a powerful sorcerer who escaped death until he could find a new physical body to inhabit. A body like Kelewulf's.

Astrid's hand flew up to her mouth as she let out a strangled cry, the sound drawing the attention of the guard, who looked round at her suspiciously. Dropping her head into her hands, she pretended to weep until she was certain he'd turned away again.

That calm voice spoke again.

Your cousin has a dark heart, Astrid, and the lich has made it darker still. Together, they want to bring this world into chaos and will use anything and anyone to achieve that aim.

Do not speak, Fleya said as the girl made to do so. *I need to find Kelewulf. With the aid of this lich, he has the power to bring about the end of this world and the freedom of the people in it. I think your brother knows where he can be found.*

The woman paused, making sure she had the girl's full attention.

Is Brant Skifrmunn still the greatest sword in Stromgard?

Astrid gave a tiny nod of her head.

And is Brant still in love with his childhood sweetheart, Princess Astrid?

The young queen's brow furrowed as the witch quickly explained her desperate plan …

18

Astrid watched helplessly as Erik was brought out to jeers and insults from the crowd. In those first few seconds the sunlight blinded him. She watched as he strained to see the faces of those who had gathered to watch. There were few there to support him, and she wondered if Glaeverssun had had a role in choosing the audience for this terrible business.

'King-killer!' an old woman shouted, lurching at the prisoner and spitting at him. His guards pushed her away, but without much conviction.

Try as she might, Astrid couldn't help but look at the apparatus that was to end her brother's life. The gallows had been hastily erected. A rope hung from a cross-beam, the other end tied to the saddle of a horse. There would be no quick death, dropping from a height mercifully high enough to snap the neck. No, her brother was to be pulled up into the air and strangled, kicking and twitching like a puppet while the crowd jeered and hollered. She had seen men and women killed like this before, seen eyes bulge in faces turning purple-black, tongues loll from mouths.

Astrid stood by Jarl Glaeverssun's side, acutely aware of the armed man stationed behind her. Pale and stony faced, her stomach tied itself in knots as her heart pounded away inside her.

Erik looked terrible, his body emaciated and his face swollen with new cuts and bruises.

Nevertheless, he walked with his head held high, looking his accusers in the eye as he passed, as kingly as if he were leading the army of Stromgard out on a raid against an enemy. He was their father's son in every way. Mounting the steps, he faltered for a moment, then turned and fixed the executioner with a stare as the man went to put the noose around his neck.

'STOP!' a voice called out, and such was the power of that voice that every head turned.

Into the mob strode a woman, her face covered by a hood.

'Who dares interrupt the business of the kingdom?' bellowed Jarl Glaeverssun, his face flushed.

'Business of the kingdom?' Fleya said, rounding on the man and walking towards him. 'A king decides the business of the kingdom. You are no king.'

'Who are you? Guards! Take this woman away. Perhaps some time in the stocks will teach her some manners.'

As the armed men moved towards her, Fleya pushed the hood back from her face. When she raised her arms, the cloak fell away and the crowd gasped. The witch was dressed in grey, the robe marked with ancient, powerful symbols that only those who had mastered the Art dared wear, and it was the sight of these majik runes that stopped the guards in their tracks. Out of the clear sky a dark cloud gathered, its colour perfectly matching Fleya's outfit.

Slowly lifting her right hand, she pointed her forefinger at the jarl – who visibly flinched. The look she gave him would have withered most men, but he somehow managed to meet her stare.

'You, Jarl Glaeverssun, presume to cast judgement on a king? I, Fleya Gudbrandr, sorceress of the Seal of Sigr, high priestess to monarchs of old, vassal to the gods, ask by what authority *you* dare do so.' The jarl stuttered for a moment, but Fleya was in no mind to let the man speak. 'This sentence is a travesty. This young man is no more guilty of killing King Mirvar than I am. I demand you free him immediately. My Queen! What do you have to say?'

Astrid stepped forward, her heart pounding. 'I say—'

'Enough!' Glaeverssun yelled, having finally recovered a little. 'This is a matter for the people of Stromgard. This is of no concern to you, witch! This man –' he pointed to Erik – 'has been found guilty in the eyes of the gods by the council of elders. You and your majik have no jurisdiction here.'

Fleya's eyes fixed on the jarl's, a hint of a smile briefly touching her lips.

'Guilty in the eyes of the gods, eh?'

'Yes!'

'But his fate was decided by *men*. Men like you,' she added with a sneer.

When she spoke again, it was to the crowd. 'The Volken people used to have a means of deciding who was and who was not guilty in the eyes of the gods.' The witch turned her eyes on the young queen now, giving her an almost indiscernible nod of the head.

Astrid spoke in a loud voice that sounded a lot braver than she really felt. 'The witch is right. My brother demands the ancient rite of trial by combat, as is his noble birthright. If he is guilty of this terrible crime against our father, let the gods truly decide his fate!'

The crowd became an animated hubbub of noise.

'There has been no such a trial in more than fifty years,' Glaeverssun spluttered.

'There has never been a public execution of a king accused of murdering his own father!' Astrid countered, her voice strong now. 'Extraordinary circumstances demand extraordinary responses, and the people of Stromgard deserve to know the truth!'

The crowd began to murmur their approval. Glaeverssun watched, his eyes darting. His guards were outnumbered by about four to one, and it was clear the situation could quickly get out of hand.

He turned to address Astrid, speaking to her in a hushed voice so only she could hear. 'You think you are clever, don't you? You think you and this witch have bested me? Well, let us see. You may yet regret this little stunt.' He turned to the crowd, holding his hands up for quiet. 'The queen speaks true. It *is* the right of Erik Rivengeld to demand this ordeal.' He looked at the expectant faces turned in his direction. 'Champions must be chosen to represent both sides.' He glanced at the accused young man standing beneath the gallows, a sneer forming on his lips. 'Unless the king intends to fight himself?'

'My brother is clearly in no state to do so,' declared Astrid. 'But we will give those who found him guilty the first choice of champion.'

There was a pause, everyone in the crowd waiting for the jarl to name his participant. 'The council chooses Frindr Oknhammer as its combatant!'

This announcement was met with a loud gasp. Glaeverssun turned his attention back to Fleya, and was clearly pleased to see she appeared to be as taken aback by this unexpected turn of events as everyone else.

Astrid swallowed. Oknhammer was a mercenary warrior, a savage man with the reputation of selling his sword to the highest bidder. It was rumoured he'd killed a hundred men, others said that the number was much greater even than that. But the man was not a Stromgardian, and his services had never been used by either her father or uncle.

Fleya met the jarl's look. 'Frindr Oknhammer is not here in Stromgard,' she said. 'What game is this?'

'A deadly one,' Glaeverssun answered, allowing himself to smile now that he had regained the upper hand. 'Oknhammer arrived here this morning at my request. I had no idea we would have to call on his help so soon.' He gave Astrid a sad look. 'You ask for trial by combat? For your brother to be judged by the gods? So be it.' Turning, he gestured for a nearby guard to fetch the mercenary.

The look that passed between Fleya and Astrid was a miserable one. They had expected Glaeverssun to pick Brant Skifrmunn, the finest sword in Stromgard and Astrid's unrequited sweetheart. Fleya had already spoken with the warrior, and he had agreed to their scheme: he would wait to be summoned and then denounce the trial and declare his fealty to Erik. They were certain that nobody would step forward to challenge Skifrmunn, and Erik could be freed without the need for any bloodshed.

The mercenary had not been part of their plan.

There was a hush as Oknhammer entered the square, the crowd parting before him like a wave. The man was a giant, towering above everybody else around him by almost a foot. Although the weather was mild, he still wore a great bear fur around his shoulders. It was said he was only eleven years of age when he killed the beast. Armed only with a knife, the young Frindr had refused to run when the bear attacked him in the hills near his village. When he was discovered, pinioned beneath the creature, covered in blood, he was thought to be dead. But it was the bear's blood that soaked the earth, and the unconscious young Frindr was merely trapped beneath the creature.

But you didn't need to know the story of Frindr Oknhammer's childhood to know what he was. One look at his cold, dead eyes was enough to tell you everything about him.

Astrid searched the crowd, seeking out Brant Skifrmunn. But when her eyes met his she saw only fear. Her admirer might be the best sword in Stromgard, but it was clear he had no wish to fight the giant.

'Well?' Glaeverssun said, one eyebrow raised first at the queen, then at the witch. 'Who is to champion the king-killer?'

Astrid implored Brant with her eyes, but he responded by lowering his head in shame before turning away. Panic coursed through her – that and a dreadful realisation that she had condemned her brother to yet further agonies.

Lann observed the exchange between Astrid and Brant, and he'd watched the beautiful young queen's heart break as Fleya's plan unravelled before her eyes. It was a terrible thing to witness: the devastation of hope. He was aware Glaeverssun was talking, the man's tone triumphant now as he addressed the crowd.

The dark blade stirred at his side.

'… Does this not tell you everything you need to know?' the jarl shouted, pointing at Fleya. 'The witch and the killer's sister invoke the right to trial by combat, and have no champion to fight for them. They have proven the gods wi—'

'I'll fight for the true ruler of Stromgard!' Lann shouted.

The jarl turned towards the speaker, his mouth opening in amazement when he saw who had voiced the words. 'Is this a joke?' he asked.

Fleya too had spun around at the sound. Her look, in contrast to Glaeverssun's, was one of horror. 'Lann!' she hissed. 'Don't do this. You can't!'

He stepped forward, ignoring her and directly addressing the jarl. Clasping his hands together in an attempt to stop them shaking, he did his best to do the same with his voice.

'I would not joke over the life of my king. I will fight your mercenary.' He glanced over at Oknhammer. 'There could be no better way to prove to the people of this kingdom that Erik Rivengeld is innocent than for me, a mere boy, to defeat this mighty warrior. That could only be done if the gods will it.'

The jarl, stunned, was lost for words. Eventually he turned to Astrid. 'Does Your Grace accept this ... champion?'

'Will nobody else step forward?' Astrid looked around at the men in the crowd, all of whom found something of interest on the ground beneath their feet. Only the boy with the black scabbard hanging at his waist stood tall and stared back at her; and the witch, whose eyes begged Astrid not to utter her next words.

But she had no choice.

'Then I accept him as my brother's champion.'

19

'What madness possessed you to offer yourself up to fight that monster?'

They were sitting in a room off the great hall waiting for the queen. Fleya was more furious than Lann had ever seen before. He stared stubbornly back at her.

'Nobody else would.'

'What kind of answer is that?'

'We came here to Stromgard to speak with Erik. We can't do that if he's dead.'

'And if you're dead too? How does that help!?'

'I don't intend to die.'

'You are not a fighter, Lann. That creature Oknhammer is a ruthless killer, a man who has lived his entire life with a sword in his hand.'

'I have a sword too.'

'But you have had no training. No combat experience.

He will cut you down like a dog.'

'The black blade won't allow that to happen.'

Lann watched Fleya throw her hands up in despair at his response. He wondered if her anger and fear were a result of her not seeing this outcome to her plan, the Art, for once, letting her down in her moment of need. His own emotions were harder for him to identify. Gone was the dread he'd felt when he had first offered to take part in the trial. In its place was a modicum of … calm? Not confidence – he was in no way confident at having to face Frindr Oknhammer, but he was no longer terrified. He leaned forward to speak.

'I never told you what happened on board the *Ra'magulsha*. You were gone, seeking out that thing from the depths. An arrow was fired at me by a pirate archer. It was a true shot. A deadly shot. But the arrow was not allowed to hurt me. I …' He paused, and placed his hand on the dark scabbard at his side 'The Dreadblade deflected it from its path. The blade is sworn to protect me, just as I am sworn to protect it.'

Fleya sat back, small lines creasing her forehead as she took this in.

'Does it talk to you now? The blade?'

'Yes.'

'And what does it say?'

'I don't understand all the words. Not yet. But … it's

looking forward to the battle. Oknhammer has done terrible things. Horrific things. The Dreadblade was forged to defeat monsters.'

'Frindr Oknhammer is a man,' Fleya pointed out.

'Not all monsters are from the Void, Aunt. Some are men with souls so black that even Lorgukk would not be able to tell them apart from his own minions.'

They turned at the sound of the door opening, standing together as Queen Astrid entered the room. And as her eyes met Lann's, he had no difficulty reading her thoughts.

'Great,' Lann mumbled under his breath. 'Somebody else who thinks I'm mincemeat.'

20

In keeping with tradition, the accused's champion was first to arrive. A cart had been sent to collect Lann from the rooms he'd stayed in overnight, and he was grateful; his legs were shaking so hard he could barely stand. The ride was slow, the driver plodding the old horse up the dirt streets so that everyone could get a look at the 'champion'. Lann, his heart heavy with dread, knew it was his funeral procession.

The blade had abandoned him.

He had woken up this morning to silence – the sword deathly quiet for the first time since he had accepted it from Rakur. The whispers in that ancient tongue, so familiar to him now, were gone, and with them any remote chance he might have had of surviving today.

He'd spent most of the morning pondering this. How could he have been so wrong about the blade? He and the thing were not 'one' as he had thought. No, the Dreadblade wanted nothing to do with this trial, and it would allow him to perish. In doing so, perhaps it might find a new owner, one who understood the true nature of the pact between the blade and its wielder. Perhaps it had decided it would be better served by a man like Frindr Oknhammer. Had he condemned his aunt to the same fate as Erik? And Astrid? These thoughts, and a million others, piled in on top of one another, a relentless torrent of doubt and fear so great he was no longer able to even think straight.

When the cart finally came to a halt, Lann somehow managed to get his treacherous legs to work as he climbed down into a sea of waiting faces, all wearing one expression: disbelief.

Someone shouted a command, and the crowd in front of him gave way, pulling back on either side so he might walk through. There were murmurs, but no words. No encouragement was offered him. The people of Stromgard knew they were here to see this young man die.

Twenty strides by twenty strides was the size of the square, each corner marked with a spear, buried point up in the ground. A rope had been strung up between the spears to define the space, and as he approached this, it was lifted by one of the guards to allow him inside.

To one side of the square was a priest in a long, hooded robe the deep red colour of blood. The garb marked the man as a minister of the new religion, a belief that worshipped not many, but one single god called Geshtrik. Without lifting his head to reveal his face, the priest raised an arm and pointed to the left side of the square, signalling that this was where the boy should stand.

The noise from the crowd swelled now as Lann's opponent arrived. A new wave of dread flooded him and he fought the need to be sick.

Frindr Oknhammer smiled as he walked through the throng, closely followed by Jarl Glaeverssun and other members of the council. Lann was faced by a wall of scowling people at the mercenary's back. Searching for just one friendly face, he glanced behind him to see his aunt, accompanied by Astrid and Erik Rivengeld. Fleya did her best to smile encouragingly at him.

Oknhammer looked across at Lann as if the boy were something nasty he'd found on the bottom of his shoe. He wore studded leather armour behind a huge shield with a black bear's head painted on the front. If anything, he looked even larger close up than he had the previous day.

The giant frowned across at his opponent. 'Where's your armour?' he growled at Lann. 'And your shield?'

Lann had refused both when they were offered to him, reasoning that speed and flexibility would be his only assets against this opponent. In truth, he knew that neither of these qualities, nor any other, would make any difference to the result of this fight. As his aunt had suggested, Oknhammer would simply cut him down like a dog.

'I require neither,' Lann said, his voice sounding smaller and higher pitched than he would have wanted.

'You want to fight in the old style?' Oknhammer nodded his approval. 'I like that. It'll be quicker.' He threw off his shield and unbuckled the leather armour covering his torso, forearms and lower legs, revealing a host of ugly scars on his flesh. The sight of so many battle wounds made Lann wonder how the man was still alive. The warrior, seeing the boy's expression, smiled; a cruel smile that never quite reached his eyes. 'You think you can add to them, boy? Maybe.' He tapped the sword at his side. 'Maybe when you're skewered on Widowmaker here, your eyes bulging like a frog as your lifeblood pours out, you might take some small solace in the fact that you marked me.' He looked Lann up and down, and then spat on the ground in a gesture of utter contempt. 'But we both know that will not happen, don't we? No, you will die quickly, pissing in your pants like the frightened little boy you are.'

Lann swallowed. He knew that Oknhammer's words were meant to sting and dispirit, that warriors used tactics like this to scare and distract their opponent. But the mercenary needn't have bothered. Because Lann couldn't be any more afraid if he tried. There was no warrior's

175

bravado to dent, no gallantry to undermine. There would be no songs sung of this day; of when the boy took on the mercenary and showed the people of Stromgard what it truly meant to be brave. He was just a frightened little boy, a terrified idiot who'd made a dreadful mistake and put himself in this position – one for which he would pay the ultimate price.

Shhhhk! He looked up sharply at the noise of the blade called Widowmaker being drawn from its sheath. It was a huge sword, and would have taken a normal man two hands to wield, but Oknhammer brandished it as easily as if it were the wooden toy Lann had played with as a lad on the farm, pretending to be a Volken warrior. Lann's hand shook as he reached over and placed it on the hilt of his own blade.

And, just like that, the Dreadblade awoke. The noise that filled Lann's head was a harsh, piercing cry; a war cry that demanded he draw the weapon free of its own confines. He willingly did so. The black sword was like a living thing in his hand, filling him with a new emotion, something he thought had deserted him forever. Hope.

He held the blade out before him, the doubts and fears he'd felt only moments before now disappearing. And in his head, he could hear the sword's voice as it repeated a phrase over and over: *Kurum-na murt. Kurum-na murt. Kurum-na murt …*

Something must have changed inside Frindr Oknhammer in that moment too, because his sneering arrogance momentarily faltered, as if he, too, could hear the cry of the black blade and knew what it wanted.

'That is a strange sword,' he whispered.

When Lann spoke, he was hardly aware of the words that tumbled from his lips. They were not entirely his own. They were his and the blade's both, united in the face of an enemy that would do them harm.

'It is as old as the world itself. It has tasted the blood of countless battles, and has been wielded against mighty enemies. The gods themselves fear it and named it Dreadblade. Today it will be the end of your reign of terror. For you have committed crimes of blood that have gone unpunished, Frindr Oknhammer. You have killed the innocent and the weak. You have turned your weapon on those you served, those who trusted you. You have used it on women and children. And you have done so without remorse.' He raised his voice. 'You claim to be a warrior, but you are a murderer without remorse. And today, you will be made to pay for your wrongdoings.' As Lann uttered these last words, a galvanising force, like a lightning bolt, shot through him. He felt the hairs on his neck stand on end. He had never felt stronger.

'Who told you these things?' Frindr bellowed, looking around him as if he might find the answer in the crowd.

'Who? I shall kill that man when I have done with you, boy!'

'No man.'

'A woman then. The witch!'

'No woman.'

'WHO?' Oknhammer roared.

'The sword you hold in your hand told me. The blade you call Widowmaker. It knows all your darkest secrets. You have ill-used that weapon, killer.'

The mercenary looked from the blade in his hand to the black one in his opponent's. Deep frown lines beetled his brow.

'I will cut out your tongue with this "ill-used" sword, boy.'

'We'll see.' Lann stared back at the man. '*Kurum-na murt,*' he said. The words escaped his lips unbidden, the Dreadblade and its wielder speaking in one unified voice.

'What was that you said?'

'*Kurum-na murt.*'

'And what does that mean, boy?'

Lann looked at the giant from beneath his eyebrows, a small smile playing at the edge of his mouth. 'Death is coming,' he replied.

Oknhammer, quivering with rage and roaring with fury, took off across the square, his weapon raised over his head to smite the boy with one fell blow. Lann was vaguely aware of Fleya crying out a warning from behind him, but he paid it no mind.

The giant moved quickly for a man of his size, but Lann stepped to one side, the Dreadblade coming up to meet the huge broadsword as it crashed down. The clash of metal sang to the gasp of the crowd. The Dreadblade was already sliding across the sharpened edge of Widowmaker, silver steel screeching in protest.

Lann and the black sword were one. Blade moved arm, and arm moved blade, neither controlling the other. The reverse-sweep cut through Oknhammer's left calf.

The mercenary's roar was filled with both anger and pain. He swung his great sword again, the blade horizontal, at a height designed to take Lann's head from his shoulders. But this blow too was deflected by the black metal of Widowmaker's nemesis. Thrown off balance, and unable to twist round in time because of that first wound, the giant gasped as the boy whipped the sword round to cut a blow in his hip, the blade sinking deep and bringing a hiss of anguish to the man's lips.

Oknhammer knew that the greatest warriors were able to accept the pain of a terrible blow, yet counterattack as if it had not occurred. A sword-strike into bone, like the one just inflicted upon him, would almost certainly result in the opponent's blade becoming lodged. So with no room to make a cutting attack, he quickly pointed his sword to the skies, pulled his elbows in, and struck down with the heavy pommel at the base of Widowmaker's grip, aiming to turn his enemy's head to pulp.

But the boy wasn't there. Oknhammer gasped, reeling round to see his foe take a step backwards, sword moving snake-like in the air, his lips moving silently as he repeated those strange words over and over again. The mercenary took a moment to glance down at his wounds and the bloody rivers that accompanied them.

Anger was an emotion that had always sustained Oknhammer – that and its brother, hate. He knew that others believed anger was the enemy in a battle, but he'd found it fuelled him. Giving in to his rage, drinking it in, he rushed forward again. Using a technique that had never before failed him, he feinted low, as if to strike at the boy's leading leg and so draw a defensive parry, but then whipped his hand round and up, extending the broadsword fully to skewer his opponent.

The black metal blade in his opponent's hand moved too quickly, however. It was like a shadow that easily countered his attack, deflecting the strike down and to the side, and causing Oknhammer to overbalance. He righted himself, and lunged.

He didn't feel the blade enter, but he heard the crowd's cries of amazement, as if from far away. The lad was so close to Oknhammer now that the giant could simply reach out and crush him – wrap his big arms about the miserable wretch, and squeeze the life from his puny bones. He would enjoy hearing the sound of cracking ribs accompanied by the boy's screams. But Frindr's arms would not move. His hands and legs and head refused to obey, and the blackness that had started at the edge of his vision swiftly swam in to blot out the world forever.

The giant figure of Oknhammer fell backwards, and then he lay, unmoving, on the blood-stained dirt.

Lann looked down at the body of the man he had killed.

The sword repeated its warning one last time before falling mute again. The crowd, too, was hushed now. The only sound to break the stunned silence was the sobbing tears of the victor before his knees gave out and he crumpled to the ground.

Fleya was the first to reach him. Drawing her nephew into her arms, she managed to get him back to his feet, shaking her head at the others who tried to come to his aid. She could feel his pain, feel the waves of sadness and despair leaching out of him, so that his hurt became her own. Supporting the full weight of him, she looked at the black blade at their feet, and knew there was no way she could bring herself to touch the thing. In the end, it was the red-robed priest who retrieved the weapon, carefully wiping it on the hem of his costume before replacing it in the scabbard at the boy's side.

Fleya straightened up to her full height and called for silence.

'This,' she said, nodding down at the dead figure of Oknhammer, 'is your proof of Erik Rivengeld's innocence.' Turning her head, she eyed all those present. 'Does anybody here doubt that? Does anybody here wish to speak out in defiance of the gods and what they have shown you here today?' She waited, and although she'd addressed the crowd, her eyes were now firmly fixed on Glaeverssun, as if daring him to be the one to speak. 'No? Then I suggest you arrange for King Erik and the princess to be escorted back to the great hall so he might get on with the business of ruling Stromgard and his people.'

Vissergott

21

Kelewulf stared out of the window of the tower at the waves crashing into the shoreline far below. The storm was waning now, but the sea still battered the land, throwing great white plumes into the air as it did so. He marvelled at the relentless power of the ocean.

He'd come to this place after leaving Stromgard, drawn here by its solitude and inaccessibility. It held many memories from his childhood; not all of them good.

Vissergott had been his mother's sanctuary, a headland she visited whenever she needed to escape the pressures that a queen to someone like his father felt. She had brought Kelewulf here on a number of occasions, letting him explore the shoreline down below while she watched him from this window …

* * *

It was the same window he'd watched his mother throw herself from.

The memory of that day was burned indelibly into Kelewulf's mind.

His mother had brought him here following a terrible row she'd had with his father. Before that day, Horst Rivengeld had always let the two of them go off. But this time he followed them from Stromgard. In a fit of rage, he'd confronted his wife.

'You will return to the palace with me,' he had bellowed.

'I will not,' Kelewulf's mother had replied, her voice calm in the face of her husband's wrath. 'And you cannot make me, husband.'

'I am your king! You will return and you will bring the boy. His place is in Stromgard. Where, by the gods both old and new, he will learn the Volken ways. Not here, where you fill his mind with useless books and talk of majik!'

On and on he'd raved while his wife stood, calmly staring back at him, a serene ocean before his raging storm, until he'd told her she could go to hell.

She'd smiled back at him then. 'Perhaps, my lord, I shall do just that.'

Kelewulf had watched her as she turned to the window. He'd screamed out for her to stop, but to no avail. He would have followed her out of this opening and into the night, had his father not grabbed him and wrestled him to the ground …

He shivered, now. What must it have felt like, launching herself from this height and plummeting down into those unforgiving rocks below? Had she thought of him, or had escape been the only thing inside her head that day?

Crossing the room, he lowered himself into a chair. He was exhausted. Occasionally it was necessary for the lich to return to the phylactery, due to the tremendous strain its occupation of him placed on Kelewulf. This was one of those days, and the young necromancer was glad for the brief respite.

You need to look after our body, the lich would tell him. *Do not push yourself so hard that we cannot complete our work here.*

Tired like never before, it occurred to him he was unable to remember the last time he'd slept or eaten, and this last thought made his stomach growl angrily. 'Get something to eat, then rest,' he mumbled to himself.

Getting up, he was about to go down to the kitchens when an almighty crash below – the force of which was powerful enough to make the entire edifice shake – stopped him in his tracks. He hurried to the window again and, with a mixture of horror and fascination, stared down at the creature he and the lich had summoned to do the work they were incapable of doing themselves.

The Earth Elemental, a colossal, man-shaped thing made out of rock and stone, lumbered towards the vast block it had dropped. The creature was capable of moving the huge things, each of which were taller than Kelewulf, without tiring. And yet it was clumsy to the point of being downright dangerous. Only yesterday Kelewulf had almost been crushed to death beneath one of the blocks when the creature had dropped it.

The Elemental was hauling the cube-shaped blocks into place. There were nineteen so far and they would eventually form a great arch that would dominate a large section of land out there.

These blocks – objects created from powerful majik – were strange to look at up close: formed from black, glass-like material known as shadowglas, sinister-looking things moved around inside them, things that were there one moment, gone the next. Each took almost half a day to produce and the effort of doing so had exhausted Kelewulf's reserves of majik and willpower.

He needed to create eleven more, or so the lich said. The mere thought of the energy the task would take filled him with dread.

When it was finished, the arch would become a portal between this world and the Void. But it would only be open for a matter of minutes due to the vast effort required. Any longer might kill him. And yet, in those short moments, the terrifying panoply of monstrous creatures that would enter this world would make it quake.

Without warning Kelewulf's knees buckled beneath him and he only just managed to stop himself from falling to the hard stone floor by clutching the heavy curtain hanging beside the window.

The reminder of his weakness was a timely one. He needed to restore his body's strength, and quickly, because unleashing the monsters here at Vissergott was only the start of their plan – an audition of their combined powers. Afterwards, he would have a long and difficult journey ahead of him. A journey that would enable him to achieve his ultimate goal: the return of the dark god Lorgukk to this realm.

But that was not possible without the heart. The heart was the key to everything, and it was thousands of miles away in the lands of Hasz.

With no heart, there could be no return of Lorgukk. And with no Lorgukk, Kelewulf would never realise the immeasurable power he'd always sought – because the dark god would surely grant his redeemer anything their heart desired. He could be Lorgukk's commander-in-chief, the most powerful mage the world had ever seen, and together they would create a reign of terror.

Kelewulf regretted that he would not be around to see the panic and pandemonium the portal would cause here in the Six Kingdoms, but he satisfied himself that the Volken people would eventually know it was he who was responsible. He could almost hear the lich's voice inside his head. *They underestimated you at their cost. We will make them pay. Just as we made your cousin Erik pay.*

Kelewulf frowned, remembering what they had done. Without the lich inside him, whispering its dark thoughts so that they seemed almost his own, he knew that he had never wanted his uncle dead. He had planned to merely weaken the king, and to throw suspicion on the girl, Astrid, who had always hated him. That had been before the incident in the boatyard. Following that night, the lich had argued that Erik had seen or heard too much. They must create an environment of chaos, one in which the finger of blame could not fall upon them, and then they would leave Stromgard. Through a fog that threatened to envelop his mind at the time, the lich had argued that Kelewulf's uncle should die and his cousin Erik would face execution for his murder. Among the fear and confusion Kelewulf must have agreed, although he had no recollection of doing so. And so the lich had taken over the prince's body, and made him commit the terrible deed. *The perfect crime* was how the lich had described it. *A world of chaos, remember?*

What have I done? The thought had no sooner formed than Kelewulf banished it. He could not let sentiment weaken him.

He shivered. He felt, he realised, empty without the lich, as though he were half a man. The power he'd always craved was at his fingertips when the creature was in possession of him – a wealth of knowledge acquired over many years. But he resented having the creature privy to his every thought and emotion.

He shook his head as if to clear it of the jumbled thoughts and emotions he felt. Exhaustion was making him confused. Confused and … weak.

He must not let his resolve break now. He would find a way to acquire the heart, and through it he would return Lorgukk to this realm. Then the world would quiver, hailing him, Kelewulf, for his might and power. He wouldn't need a crown or a throne. And he wouldn't need the lich. Kelewulf could command his own army of hellish creatures and strike horror into the hearts of those who had sneered at his frailties. Those who had, like his father, mocked his inability to wield a sword or a shield would bow down on the ground at his feet and beg for mercy.

With this thought in his head, he turned from the window and crossed the room to the straw pallet set up in the corner. Lowering himself down on to it, his head had no sooner hit the pillow than he was fast asleep.

* * *

The lich was pleased. Once again, the boy thought himself alone, when all along he was there, just hidden. The lich would need to be careful, however. Subtlety and cunning were needed. Now was the crucial time if he was going to wrest control of this physical shell for himself, and he couldn't rush this; the boy needed to think himself in charge, until it was too late. No, little by little, the lich would erode the boy's mind from within until there was nothing left. Then, and only then, would Yirgan, the last great mage, truly show the world what he was capable of.

Stromgard

22

'Would killing him give you a feeling of retribution? Would you feel justice has been done?' Astrid asked her brother, her eyes unblinking and fixed on his.

It was a slanting, quizzical look that reminded him of their father.

'Yes, I think it would,' Erik said, from atop the throne that had almost been denied him. 'He's a traitor.'

His sister nodded thoughtfully, her expression unreadable. The only other person in the great hall, aside from the guards, was the witch, and such was her beauty that Erik found it hard to look at her without the colour rising to his face.

It was Fleya who spoke next.

'Granted, his methods were underhand and deceitful. I myself hold little regard for the man, but I believe Jarl Glaeverssun, at least in his mind, was acting in a way he thought would benefit the kingdom.'

'By wresting power away for his own benefit? By trying to have me killed?'

'That sentence was decided by the court.'

'A court *he* set up.'

'King Erik,' Fleya continued, her voice calm and equable. 'In his place, with the same evidence, you would almost certainly have come to the same judgement. I understand that you seek vengeance, but it is time to think like a king. It is time to think like your father.'

'I shared a cell with a rat.'

'The same cell the jarl now resides in,' Astrid pointed out.

Her brother hesitated.

Fleya studied the new king as he considered their counsel. Like his father at the same age, he was handsome and well built. The Rivengelds came from good stock, and she doubted there was a more handsome family among the Volken people. The young man had the opportunity to be great.

She had seen what a great king he could be if he chose the right path in life; and how poor choices could ruin him – especially during his early years on the throne. *This* was one of those moments. For whatever reason, she knew that the destinies of Glaeverssun and Erik Rivengeld were closely entwined with a thread that was not supposed to be cut. Not yet, at least.

The fire in the long trough down the centre of the hall made a loud *pop*, an ember leaping clear of the flames but dying before it reached the packed earth of the floor. The sound shook the witch from her thoughts, and seemed to have the same effect on the king, who had clearly come to a decision.

'Your words are wise. I will spare Glaeverssun's life, but he is to be banished. He has done too much harm here to be trusted. He will leave Stromgard this evening, on foot, with what he can carry and no more. If he is seen in this kingdom again, his life will be forfeit.' Erik nodded to himself and rose from the throne, signalling the discussion was ended. He stepped down from the low dais so that he was on the same level as the two women. 'How is your nephew?' he asked Fleya, his voice gentle.

'Physically, he is unharmed. But he still will not speak. He is in shock.'

The young king sighed. 'I have seen this before. In men returning from wars. Something happens to them, something that is related to the things that they do in the heat of battle.'

Fleya nodded. 'Lann killed a man. The weight of such a deed is causing great distress to his young mind.'

'The man was a vile murderer,' murmured Astrid.

Fleya shrugged. 'It doesn't matter what sort of man Oknhammer was. Lann took another human life, a

193

terrible deed that he must somehow find a way to make peace with.'

'I am sorry that I was the cause of your nephew's pain,' the king said. 'I am in his debt.' Turning to glance at his sister, he added, 'We both are. So too are the people of Stromgard. I would like to grant him a jarldom. The very same one Glaeverssun is about to vacate. The people of those lands need a good man as their Protector.'

'That is a kind offer, but—'

'Good. Then it is decided.'

The witch nodded her thanks. 'Your Grace, we know now that the person who killed your father – and framed you for that murder – was your cousin Kelewulf. It is vital that I know where he is. The fate of this kingdom, possibly the world, might depend on it. Do you have any idea where he might be?'

Erik shook his head. 'I wish I did.'

'Is there no childhood place that was special to you both?' She watched him closely as he frowned in thought. 'It might have been little more than a cave, a forest clearing or a building in some remote spot. Somewhere that you went as children, long since forgotten. Does nowhere like that come to mind?'

'I'm sorry, Fleya,' the king said. 'It is strange – I feel like I *do* know such a place, but when I try and recall it –' he shook his head in frustration – 'my mind is a complete blank.'

My mind is a complete blank ... Fleya reached out and placed her hand firmly on the king's arm.

'King Erik,' she said, fixing his eyes with her own. 'Is ... is your mind "blank" in the same way it was when you tried to remember being in the market and acquiring the poisons that killed your father?'

The significance of her words seemed to strike the king like a physical blow. 'You mean that this memory could have been deliberately removed too?'

'I believe so, yes.'

'Then there is no hope of discovering this place you seek.'

'Not necessarily.' She moved nearer to him, her voice little more than a whisper. 'Memories of a life are not so easily stolen. They can be buried, yes, but not erased. With your permission I might be capable of restoring that which was hidden from you.' She paused, looking her king in the eye in a way that left him in little doubt he would rather not hear the words she would speak next. 'But it would bring back *all* the memories you were robbed of.'

There was silence as the weight of this sank in.

Fleya studied the young king's face. Despite being a puppet of another creature during the deed, Erik *had* killed his father – a man he loved more than any other living being. She knew he was glad to have no memory of the vile act. Even so, Fleya could also see how he desired justice, and in the end this emotion was the stronger of the two.

'How?' He looked down at his hands as he wrung them.

'Your memories have been obscured using strong majik. They can be unlocked in the same way too.'

Erik swallowed. 'If it will find my detestable cousin and the lich responsible for the wrongs done to my family, I will do it.'

The witch nodded. 'Tomorrow. I will need time to prepare myself.'

'Tomorrow it is.'

23

Sitting at the edge of the bed, lost in his thoughts, it occurred to Lann that somebody was knocking at the door to his room.

'Lann? May I come in?'

It was a woman's voice. But not his aunt's. Dimly he remembered that Fleya had knocked earlier. He had not answered and she eventually left.

How long had he been sitting here like this? He stared down at his bare feet resting on the stone floor. They were blue-tinged and numb with cold. Raising his head, he noticed the untouched plate of food on the small table a short distance away.

'Who is it?' he asked in a voice he hardly recognised as his own.

'Astrid.'

Astrid? The princess. He recalled her face: beautiful

and fierce, with large, grey eyes and a determined chin.

He wanted her to go away. Why wouldn't they *all* just go away?

He sighed and lowered his head again. A small beetle had appeared from a crack between the flagstones. Having squeezed its chitin-covered body out of the tight space, the shiny black thing proceeded to make its way through the gap made between his feet. What must that colossal, flesh-coloured valley look like to the little insect? And did it know the precarious nature of its journey – how, at any instant, those vast walls could simply lift up into the air and come down again, crushing it to death?

Another knock. 'Please?'

'Go away,' he whispered under his breath, but he heard the door creak open.

She didn't come in immediately, and Lann guessed she must be standing on the threshold, looking in at him. Then he heard the tread of her brisk steps. There was a scrape of wood on stone as she moved the small table and used it as a seat, so she could sit directly in front of him. Leaning forward, she dipped her head, making it impossible for him to avoid her face as she peered up at him.

When he sat up she mirrored the movement.

'I wanted to come earlier, but your aunt said you wanted to be alone.'

He gave a small shrug in response.

198

She paused before going on. 'I wanted to thank you. What you did—'

'What I did was kill a man.'

'I understand how you feel.'

Her response lit a hot spark of anger inside Lann.

'Do you?' He held her eyes with his own. 'Have you ever killed anybody?'

'No.'

'Then you don't know how I feel.'

'I can't ...' she started to talk, then stopped.

He looked down at the floor again, but the beetle was gone, disappeared under the bed.

'Then tell me.'

'What?'

'Tell me how you feel.' She paused. 'Tell me. Because I need to know. Please.'

He struggled to organise his thoughts, to find a way that might even begin to explain. Eventually he came up with a single word to describe himself. 'Empty,' he muttered. That was it. That was how he felt. *Empty*. As if somebody had taken a great spoon and scooped out all the good and decent parts of him, leaving this worthless husk behind.

She nodded, then took a deep breath before going on. 'I'm sorry. I really am. I can understand that you don't want my thanks. But ... you saved my brother. You saved me.' She frowned, considering her words. 'And there are others who owe you their thanks, those you will never meet. Frindr Oknhammer was a man of violence, who killed indiscriminately for anyone willing to pay his price. He had done so in the past, and he would have gone on to kill again. But you stopped him. So, I'm also thanking you for their lives too.'

'Killing is killing.'

'No.' Her voice took on a hard edge that made him look up. 'Not *all* killing is wrong, Lann. These times we live in have shown us that. My father killed thousands.' She paused, as if it were difficult for her to utter these words. 'He killed them with his armies so his own people could live and prosper. It's what a king does. Maybe those deaths left him feeling like you do now … Empty. And yet, he was not a bad man. He did what he felt had to be done to protect his people. He taught me that sometimes it is hard to do what is right. So no, killing is not just killing.'

They sat in silence for a few moments. Lann eventually broke the silence.

'Thank you. I think I needed to hear that.'

'Good.' Her voice changed and became softer again. 'I know it isn't an easy thing to live with. But you saved many lives. Remember that, Lann.'

He gave her a nod.

She stood and held out her hand. 'Now. Come with me.'

'What for?'

Her expression was impish now. 'You'll need decent clothes.'

'Clothes?'

'You don't want to meet King Erik looking like a street beggar, do you?'

He paused, but it was clear she was not going to leave. Her hand was still held out to him, her eyes fixed on his.

'It's not a request, Lann,' she said. 'This is a royal order. Now, come on.'

24

'… The lands running down to the Gulf of Rikkor are now owned by Jarl Lannigon Gudbrandr.' King Erik smiled down at Lann, giving him a small nod. 'He will safeguard and serve the people therein and be fair in all his dealings with them.'

The king, dressed in white furs and with the gold and silver circlet of his office resting on his head, was almost unrecognisable as the same young man who had been led out to the gallows so recently. Lann himself was dressed plainly in brown woollen trousers and a studded leather jerkin. He was also wearing the fur-lined grey cloak Astrid had insisted he have, held in place on his shoulders by a beautifully carved whalebone pin. The quality of the clothes and shoes was like nothing he had ever owned before.

He felt his aunt nudge him in the small of his back and

realised the king had stopped speaking and was expecting an answer. His heart was racing in his chest.

'My liege. I am just a boy from the Maiden's Fingers and in no way worthy of this tribute. You do me much honour by bestowing these gifts upon me.'

Erik shook his head. 'You are no longer the boy from the Maiden's Fingers, Lannigon Gudbrandr. You are Jarl Gudbrandr now. You are a man, and you will govern these lands wisely. And in doing so, you will expunge the memory of the previous incumbent, the traitor Glaeverssun.'

When the king stood, Lann knew it was his cue to step forward. The Volken ruler embraced his new jarl, the act a signal that the festivities should commence.

25

The longhouse was full of music and celebrations that night. Food of every kind was brought to the tables in quantities that made Lann stare. Ale was poured into horn cups by serving girls and boys, musicians played and sang while guests laughed and shouted and argued. In a rope circle at one end of the longhouse, huge oiled men wrestled each other in competitions of strength and agility. Lann and his aunt sat at the king's table where they wanted for nothing.

It was shortly after the festivities began that a well-built, older man approached the table and Lann. His long hair was braided on one side of his head and his beard, grey in places, reached almost down to his chest. Astrid made the introductions.

'May I present Jarl Mardl, former Master-at-Arms at Stromgard.' Although she spoke pleasantly enough, there was something in her tone that suggested she was not a great fan of Mardl.

'It is a pleasure to meet you,' Lann said, taking in the man's imposing figure and the leather patch over his right eye.

Mardl gestured at the puckered white scar that extended above and below the patch. 'When I lost my eye I was no longer able to fulfil my role. But I still have a keen interest in fighting skills and run a small school for young Volkenfolk in weapon-lore. I was hoping to talk to you about—'

'I thought I had been quite clear earlier, Jarl Mardl,' Astrid said coolly. 'Jarl Gudbrandr has no interest in discussing the fight. I hope you are not getting forgetful in your old age.'

An amused smile played about the older man's lips. 'I must admit, Your Grace, the temptation to ask just a few questions was too great ... I have never seen so remarkable a combat.'

'But I told you—'

'It's all right,' Lann said, nodding at Astrid. 'I guess I will have to talk about it at some time or another.' He turned to Mardl. 'And please, my name is Lannigon. I doubt I will ever get used to being addressed by my new title. What did you want to know?'

'Where to begin! Such extraordinary prowess. You must have learned from a true master to have dared employ such an audacious gambit.'

'Gambit?'

'Oh, come now. I have witnessed it before, but never have I seen it carried off quite so well. To bait your opponent into a hasty attack when you are looking so weak. By the gods, your hands were so low you practically invited the Ubrfullen attack!'

'The what?'

The look the Master-at-Arms gave him suggested he thought the young man was deliberately teasing him. 'And yet when your opponent rose to your exquisitely presented bait, you deflected his blows with great skill, transitioning what appeared at first to be a clumsy defence into wonderful attacks. I particularly admired the Shiluer move you made to end his first press.'

'Shiluer?'

Mardl's face hardened. 'It is rude to mock others, Jarl Gudbrandr.'

'It is. But I am not mocking you. I have no idea what you are talking about.'

'Who taught you to fight?' Mardl snapped, any hint of friendliness now gone from his words.

'Nobody. I am … self-taught.'

'You expect me to believe that? How many bouts have you fought?' He leaned in closer. 'Where did you get that black blade?'

'Which would you like me to answer first?' Lann said, his

own annoyance coming to the fore. He ticked his answers off on his fingers. 'I was never taught sword-play – you can believe me or not.' He moved on to the next finger. 'I've never fought before, so that was my first. And my blade? I am afraid that it is none of your business.' The sword stirred at Lann's side as if it appreciated this final response.

Mardl flushed with anger. He went to say something, but stopped. Turning on his heels, he stomped away, muttering loudly about young upstarts and lack of respect for elders.

'That went well,' Astrid said, grinning. 'Don't worry, he'll get over you teasing him like that.'

Lann shrugged. 'I wasn't teasing him. Everything I just said was the truth.'

'Now you're teasing me.' Astrid's smile faded at Lann's expression. 'Y-you mean to say that was all true? You've never been trained in sword-play?'

'No. I grew up on a cattle farm. The nearest I came to a sword-play was swinging the yard broom about.'

She stared back at him. 'Then you are a fool, Lannigon Gudbrandr,' she said, shaking her head. 'I thought you were … I … I thought you had … You could have been killed!'

She turned away and stormed off, her cheeks flushed. Lann caught Fleya smirking. 'What is she so annoyed about?' he asked.

Fleya shrugged. 'Princess Astrid is clearly concerned for your safety,' she said, but her face suggested Lann was clearly missing something. Turning away, she laid a hand on King Erik's forearm and stood.

'My apologies, King Erik,' she said with a bow. 'But I too must leave the celebrations early. I have much preparation to do before our meeting tomorrow.'

Left alone, Lann picked at the sweet hilfenberries that had appeared on a plate in front of him while watching the revellers. Amidst the jollity he felt that he and Erik alone were sombre. It wasn't immediately obvious – Erik raised his cup to Volken nobility and warrior alike, smiling and nodding at their jokes and even making a few of his own – but Lann saw how serious the king looked when he thought no one was watching. Lann could guess why. Tomorrow Fleya would attempt to restore the king's memories, and Erik clearly dreaded what he might discover.

Turning his attention away from the king, Lann spotted one other grim face in the crowd: the red-robed priest who had presided over the trial by combat. The man's eyes were fixed on him. After a moment, Lann rose and walked the length of the hall to speak to him.

'Congratulations on your jarldom,' the man said as the youngster drew near.

'Thank you,' Lann answered, after a brief hesitation.

'The honour is strange to me still. It feels too … grand, somehow.'

The priest nodded, the ghost of a smile crossing his lips. 'How refreshing. Most men would kill to receive such an honour.'

'I *did* kill for it,' Lann answered with a shake of his head. The image of Frindr Oknhammer's bloodied corpse flashed into his mind's eye and he struggled to fight back the gorge that rose up inside him.

The priest nodded his head. 'The king merely wishes to show his gratitude.'

'I know it *is* an honour,' Lann answered quickly, thinking he might have offended the man. 'And I am not ungrateful to King Erik for bestowing it on me.'

'But …'

'But it's not what I am.' The priest raised his eyebrows and Lann continued. 'Many of the men in this room were raised to take on the position of leaders and rulers. It is what they were *meant* to do. Prince Erik –' he stopped, correcting himself – '*King* Erik himself was tutored and trained specifically to take the throne.'

'And you, Lannigon Gudbrandr? What were you meant to do?'

'I was raised to work on a livestock farm.' He frowned at his answer and gave a small shake of his head, knowing that that was no longer the case. 'But now? Now I don't know.'

'A great warrior, perhaps?' the priest said.

'I hope not. I have no taste for killing,' murmured Lann.

'The weapon hanging at your side would suggest otherwise,' said the priest. 'As would the words you spoke when you fought Oknhammer. *Kurum-na murt*? Death is coming.'

Lann stared. 'You know that language?'

'It has not been spoken for hundreds of years. But yes, I know some of it. It is the language of the gods. The old gods.' He fixed the boy with a look. 'The *true* gods.'

Lann gestured at the priest's red robes. 'You are a minister of the new religion. I thought only country oafs like me or witches like my aunt believed in the old gods now. What do you know about them?' Lann asked.

The priest looked down and frowned, as if seeing the garb for the first time. 'I wear the robes of one who believes in this new god, Geshtrik. But I am no more a priest for this false deity than you are.' He ran a hand over the fabric. 'They hide me. Just as *you* wear your own disguise, Lannigon Gudbrandr-who-was-Fetlanger.'

Lann shook his head. 'I wear no disguise.'

The man frowned. 'Not knowingly.'

'The way you speak in riddles – it is like one of the old gods.'

'Oh? Which?'

'Rakur.'

'You speak as if you have met the immortal one.' That quizzical look again, but this time Lann met it only with a stare of his own. 'Rakur is indeed a riddler. But questions lead us to truths. Not all riddles are childish puzzles.' The man paused. 'The sword,' he said, effortlessly switching the subject in a way that caught Lann off guard. 'It is dangerous. *You* must be the one to control it, and not the other way round. Like the trickster god, it is adept at bending others to its will and making them its slave. If that should happen, it may not just be your enemies it would seek to kill. Other owners of the blade have lost those they loved to that baleful weapon.' The man went quiet, lost in thought or memories.

'You have not told me *your* name.'

'No, I haven't, have I?' He smiled again. 'Would you like to see something?'

'What?'

'It is not far from here.' Lann tried to read the man's enigmatic expression. 'I mean you no harm, Lannigon Gudbrandr.'

Lann considered the man's words and eventually nodded. 'All right.'

At this, the red-robed stranger turned and left the building, not once bothering to look back and check if the boy followed.

* * *

Sconces holding burning torches lined the walls of the temple, the flames casting shifting shadows on every surface. The walls of the place were painted in a deep red that quickly turned to black in the shadows.

'I thought you said you were not a celebrant of Geshtrik.'

The priest, a short distance ahead, directed his answer over his shoulder. 'I told you no lies this evening, Lannigon Gudbrandr. Nor shall I. I have no love for this new god.'

'Then what are we doing here?'

'This temple is built on the site of a much older one. Much of the latter still exists, even if it is not immediately obvious.' He stopped before a huge altar. Behind it loomed the figure of Geshtrik. The god, like the altar, was carved from a dark, almost black, wood. Naked, except for a small loincloth, the god held a kid goat under one arm, a flaming torch in the other.

'Help me to move this to one side,' the priest said, ignoring the statue and nodding at the opposite end of the altar. Heaving aside the thing between them revealed a metal-reinforced wooden hatch set into the floor. There was a recess, into which the priest placed a flat, thin object of the same colour and material, rotating it until the two pieces slotted together. There was a muted *click*. Lifting the hatch up on its hinges, he exposed a dark cavity from which no light came.

'What is it?' Lann asked.

'An entrance.'

Fetching one of the burning torches, the priest illuminated the first few steps of an extremely steep and narrow stairway. Beyond this, lower down, was utter blackness. Without saying a word, the robed man set off down the steps, leaving Lann little choice but to follow.

The descent into that dark fissure was claustrophobic and Lann had the strong sense that the walls were pressing in on him. Even when he put his hands out, brushing his fingers against the rough stone, he was hardly able to banish the notion. As the unease he felt increased, the temperature all about him dropped, until he reached the bottom. The priest stood waiting for him and it was cold enough for his breath to hang in the air before his face.

'This way,' the priest said, turning to walk off down a passageway carved into the stone to their right.

Lann paused for a moment. The place had an earthy smell to it. *Like a grave*, he thought.

Lann felt the change in the air as he emerged into a wider space. The red-robed man stood in the centre of the room, before a large metal bowl set into the floor. As Lann watched, the priest touched the flaming brand to it, igniting a substance inside and filling the place with a dancing, shifting light.

The room was circular, with a floor of a highly polished grey stone that was cold underfoot, and walls adorned with hand-painted images. Lann took a step closer and peered at the first image. The background was black, but in the centre was an egg with a crack running down the outside.

'The First Egg was all that existed in the darkness before time began. From the Egg came the giant spider, Shi'ith,' the priest said, narrating the story for Lann as he moved on to the next panel, this one of a spider with all manner of people and things atop it. 'She was assigned the role of carrying our world on her back, but she had no love for the task. In particular, she despised the humans she was made to carry. So she tried to throw off her burden and destroy it forever. But the great god Og stopped her from doing so. He killed Shi'ith and tore the legs from her body. And from each of the legs came a new god, each one charged with caring for the world and its inhabitants.' Lann moved on again. 'But Og did not kill Shi'ith fast enough, and she was able to lay an egg of her own before her demise – an egg full of the hatred she felt. That egg, and all the darkness it carried, hatched to create a powerful and malevolent creature.'

'Lorgukk,' Lann said in a low voice. Absorbed in the story and the images, he had not realised he was already a third of the way around the room.

'Yes. The dark one's hatred of the other gods was a powerful force and he used it to create more creatures like

214

him to fight at his side. And so began a war that might have destroyed the world of men. But the spider's spawn and his foul army were stopped. The black blade was entrusted to the god Trogir to cut down that monstrous army, and it did its job well.'

Lann studied the painted panel before him. The previous three or four had depicted terrifying battle scenes, Trogir scything through hordes of creatures in his attempt to reach the hulking, horned thing looming at the rear of those forces. This next panel, however, stopped Lann in his tracks. There were no figures in this panel. Instead it was of an ornate stone archway at the centre of which was a perfect blackness. Around the edges of this arch were signs and symbols he recognised as being the same ones he'd seen on the staff he'd once held in a dream.

'The Nemesis Arch,' the priest said, studying his face. 'While Trogir waged his war, the other seven gods had not been idle. They built this structure using all their might and wisdom, a thing capable of transporting the dark god from this world and trapping him forever in the Void. When Trogir finally fought Lorgukk, he drove him towards this arch with the aim of forcing him through it.'

It was a story Lann was familiar with. Indeed, he had seen similar friezes, albeit in a much poorer state, in an old temple not too far from the Maiden's Fingers. There, the image of Trogir bundling Lorgukk through the archway

215

was the final panel. In the circular room he now stood in, there were more to come.

In the next picture, Lorgukk teetered on the threshold of the dark oblivion described by the arch. The dark god's left hand appeared to be reaching into his own chest.

The priest continued: 'The dark god knew he must leave a part of himself behind if he were to ever return, so he tore free his own heart and managed to throw it, unseen, behind him into the human world.'

'What happened to it?'

'It was lost. Some say the old gods destroyed it. Others say it was rescued by the people of the West, a terrible people who were later to become the Hasz'een. We must pray they never cross the seas to these lands again.'

'They were defeated when they last came. At Dreuvn Val.'

The priest nodded. 'Your aunt has taught you well. But that defeat has never been forgiven in the land of Hasz. One day, they will seek revenge.' He paused. 'One way or another.'

'The heart? It is the dark god's only hope of ever returning to this realm?'

'That is what is said, yes. But there is still some of our legend to tell.' He nodded for the boy to move on to the next panel.

'Trogir and the Dreadblade had vanquished their enemy

216

and driven the monsters out of this world. But the victory came at a high price. The power of the Dreadblade sent Trogir mad. He believed the world would be better under the dominion of just one deity: its saviour. So he set about trying to destroy the other gods. But his efforts with the dark god had left him weak, and he was no match for the Seven. They wrestled the black blade from his possession, and Morinar, the sea god, called up a great storm that swept Trogir up to drown him in the Sea of Tears.'

'Were they successful? Did he drown?' Lann asked, staring at the last panel beside the doorway. It depicted an ocean in the midst of a terrible tempest. There was a vast circular void among the waves, a swirling vortex into which the mad god, carried on the winds, was pitched.

'Some say so.' The priest paused. 'Others say he escaped the storm, only to wander the earth for hundreds of years, unaware of who and what he was.'

'And the Dreadblade?'

'Lost. To this world, at least.' He glanced at the scabbard hanging at the boy's side. 'Until now.'

Lann considered everything the robed man had told him. 'Why did you bring me here?'

'To show you the dangers of what you seek to do. And to show you that defeating the dark god alone may not be enough. The greater battle for you, Lann, might be the one you must fight with yourself.'

'Do you really think I can stop Lorgukk if he is returned?'

'That will depend on many things, Jarl Gudbrandr. But it *has* been done before.'

'By a god,' Lann said with a shake of his head.

'Yes, that is true. By a god.'

Lann turned slowly on the spot, taking in the images one last time. It was not a complete surprise to find the man in the red robes had disappeared when he finished. Even so, he had no wish to stay in this place on his own a moment longer than was necessary. Grabbing the torch, he hurried back along the corridor to the stairs and the exit.

26

Fleya had requested that they be alone for the ritual to restore Erik's memory and, despite the protests of his guards and advisors, the king agreed.

They both sat on the floor in his private chambers. At any other time, the young king might have relished the idea of being in such intimate company with this beautiful woman. But this was no ordinary situation. Large wooden shutters at the windows banished the daylight, and the only illumination was from tallow-and-beeswax candles that sputtered and spat in their holders, filling the room with an unpleasant, slightly meaty odour. Around the pair, describing a circle on the floor, was a length of hemp rope, tightly knotted where the two ends met. In the centre, between Erik and Fleya, were three items: a dead songbird, a loaf of bread and an empty drinking horn.

A number of minutes had passed since the two had

taken up their positions, and neither had said a word to each other during that time. Indeed, the witch hadn't moved a muscle since she'd lowered herself to the floor, where she sat with her legs crossed beneath her. Eyes closed, chin tilted slightly up, Erik watched as her breathing became increasingly shallow until it seemed she was not breathing at all. The only evidence that she was even alive was the tremendous heat coming off her, as if she were in the grip of some terrible fever. He had never seen anyone perform majik like this, and it made him uneasy. She had told him nothing about what to expect, and this only fuelled his apprehension.

Trying to take his mind off things, he took the time to study the woman across from him. Her most striking feature – her eyes – were hidden from him, but even so, he doubted there was a more handsome woman in Stromgard. She could not know it, but the young king felt drawn to her in a way he had not been to any other female before. It was foolishness on his part; he was well aware of the vow that witches had to make if they were to engage in the Art.

Still, he told himself, there was no harm in looking at her.

Fleya had not eaten or allowed a drop of liquid to pass her lips at the feast the previous evening or indeed during the entire day. Her physical body protested at this abstinence,

220

but she ignored the thick tongue in her dry mouth and the angry rumblings of her stomach. There would be time for eating and drinking after she'd completed what she needed to with the king. It was complicated majik. Undoing another's work always was, and this was no backstreet dabbler's labours she was trying to counter.

Kelewulf and the lich were a formidable force, wielding considerable talent and power. But it helped that King Erik was such a willing participant. Had he not been, she might have had no option but to force him into remembering, and that was fraught with danger. The complexities of a human mind, and the damage that could be done if the majik were botched, made things extremely complicated.

She reached out with her mind towards the swirling mass of energy that was at the heart of the Art. Having made the link with that mysterious force, she retreated back into her human body and allowed her physical and psychic forms to recombine. She slowly raised her arms, holding them out towards the king, waiting for him to take them in his own. When she felt his large hands clasp hers, she silently began to recite the sacred words.

Erik wasn't sure what he had expected to happen when he placed his hands in the witch's – a sudden wave of energy, or a bolt of light, perhaps? – but the silence and calm that followed felt anticlimactic. He started to wonder if the spell was working at all when something extraordinary happened.

The drinking horn had been empty when Fleya had placed it on the ground. Now, as Erik watched, it slowly filled up from the bottom with what appeared to be ale. The liquid increased and decreased in volume, sometimes draining down to nothing again before refilling.

More incredible still was the loaf of bread. As he watched, Erik witnessed the round loaf become increasingly pale until it was almost grey in colour. The uncooked dough then shrank in size, changing in appearance and texture until it eventually transformed into the flour it had originally been made from.

As astonishing as these sights were, filling him with wonder and setting his heart racing, it was the bird's transformation that was truly miraculous. When he'd first sat before it, he'd wrinkled his nose at the creature. It cannot have been long dead, but its body was already brittle and hardened by exposure to the elements. Its eyes had gone, taken by insects or some other feathered creatures, and the bluish-black plumage on its body had lost the shine of vitality. But as he watched, Erik saw both eyes and feathers restored. Blood, too, appeared to fill the creature's body once more, plumping it out as he stared in disbelief. When it first moved, the king gasped; then the creature pushed itself up with its wings to awkwardly regain its feet.

It was then that he noticed how charged the air was, like the atmosphere before an electrical storm. The hair on the witch's head had started to lift, sticking out on all sides, and he felt his own hair do the same. The heat and oppressive air became too much for him, and he was suddenly unable to fill his lungs. He gasped silently for air, like a fish removed from its watery world. Forgetting all about the miracles he had just witnessed, he felt himself quickly slide into a state of panic. His heart raced, hammering a frantic rhythm that demanded oxygen he was unable to feed it. Bright spots of light danced in front of his eyes, and he felt the world slide away from him as unconsciousness threatened. He managed to wrench one hand free, feeling the grip on the other intensify in response. He wanted to get to his feet, but knew it was useless. A terrible rasping croak, like the sound a crow might make, escaped him.

Eyes still closed, Fleya groped beside her for the knot in the rope. Expertly, only using one hand, she shook the knot free and opened the circle.

Air rushed in and the pair sucked it in greedily, the world returning with each subsequent breath. The sudden dissipation of the heat sent a cold shiver running through Erik and he looked down at the trio of objects again.

The loaf, the drinking horn and the dead bird were exactly as they'd been at the start, and he wondered what sort of trickery had made him imagine he'd seen them otherwise.

Fleya finally opened her eyes and looked across at him. 'I'm sorry,' she said, her eyes full of compassion.

Erik let out a sob.

He remembered everything.

The loud knock on his door roused Prince Erik from his sleep. Pulling on a robe against the cold, he crossed the room and opened it.

'Cousin,' Kelewulf said, standing in the threshold. 'As promised.' He held out a small phial. 'To help you sleep.'

'Thank you.' Erik took the little bottle and hesitated. 'Would you like to come in, cousin?'

Kelewulf nodded and entered, crossing the room to a chair by the window. In the light, Erik noticed how his cousin's forehead was damp with perspiration.

'You look tired, Kel,' said Erik gently. 'Are you unwell?'

'No, I'm fine … fine …' murmured Kelewulf. 'But yes, I – I am tired.' He dropped his head into his hands. 'So very tired.'

Erik watched in alarm as Kelewulf slumped forward in a faint. He hurried over, getting to his knees before his cousin and lifting his head so he might feel at his neck for a pulse. As he did so he noticed the dark smoky tendrils beginning to escape from between Kelewulf's lips. And, as he opened his own mouth to cry out, the smoky stuff came out in a great rush and entered him, filling first his lungs, then every part of him with its darkness.

The memories from that point on were terrible and painful ones. He walked with his own legs, looked out of his own eyes and spoke with his own lips, but it was not he who was in control of these actions. The thing – whatever it was – controlled him entirely, using his thoughts and memories to seem normal to those around him while carrying out the terrible acts Erik would later be accused of.

He remembered walking into the marketplace and shopping for the ingredients to create a deadly poison. Worse still was how Erik was made aware of the thing's ultimate intention, and how the creature seemed to revel in the whole affair, keen that Erik should know what he would be making and why.

He had manufactured the hideous brew in his sleeping quarters, tears blurring his vision. The tears were his own, but the manic laughter that accompanied them was not.

He remembered too how he'd gone to the kitchen and doused his father's meal with the stuff. Then he'd taken up his seat by Mirvar's side and sat watching him spoon the food into his mouth, knowing dimly that each mouthful spelled the end for the man he loved. Except he hadn't loved him in those moments, had he? His feelings for his father, like those for *everyone and everything else, were not his. They were the spite-filled thoughts of another.*

His mind wiped, he had known nothing more, except the grief and horror of finding his father dead. And then the shock of being accused. His cousin and the lich had quickly departed Stromgard and left Erik to take the blame, knowing he would be found guilty of the murder. But he knew where Kelewulf was now. He remembered: a place where they had played together as children, exploring the dark rocks along the shore while his mother watched from above.

The king looked up at Fleya. The witch was on her feet now, looking compassionately at him. He struggled to identify how he felt about what she'd done. Anger was his foremost emotion; anger and resentment. But there was something else – a kind of relief. At least, awful as it was, he knew the truth.

He rose and stood before the witch, trying to show strength and bravery as his father would have. But he knew that she could see through this pretence.

'It wasn't your doing, Erik.' Fleya reached out and pushed back a hair that had fallen across his face. 'You were no more a part of those terrible deeds than I was.' Taking a small step backwards she looked him up and down, and nodded. 'You will be a fine ruler for your people, my King. Mirvar will be proud of the man he left to protect the kingdom.'

'I appreciate your words,' he said. 'And I will endeavour to see that they are borne out.' Pulling himself up to his full height, the ruler strode over to the window on trembling legs and threw open the shutters, allowing the daylight into the room before turning to face her again. This time his expression was grim. 'But before I can begin my reign, I must avenge my father's murder. I know where Kelewulf is.'

27

'I'm going with them,' Astrid said, fixing her brother with a look that probably worked on every other person in the kingdom.

'You most certainly are not.'

'You can't stop me.'

Erik gave his sister a stony look. 'I think you'll find I can do exactly that.'

'They need me,' she said, nodding at Fleya and Lann.

'You are a princess of this kingdom. You are not—'

'I think we've already established I am not really princess material.' She grinned fiercely when he flushed at her words. 'I have made my peace with that, brother. I *am* a shield maiden, though. I am trained in combat and am the best archer in all of Stromgard.' She paused and shot Lann a look. 'I'm the best fighter in this long-house right now.'

'You might be the best archer, sister, but—'

'Best *fighter*,' she repeated. 'With whatever weapon you choose to name.'

Erik snorted. 'I find it astonishing you can say such a thing when you witnessed what Jarl Gudbrandr did to the mercenary Oknhammer!'

'Really? Well, let's see, shall we?' Reaching into a sack by her side, Astrid pulled out two heavy wooden training swords. Lann just about caught the one she threw in his direction. 'Well?' she said to the young jarl. 'Shall we show our king what kind of fighter you are?' She nodded at the sword in his hand. 'Prepare to defend yourself, Jarl Gudbrandr.'

'Astrid, I want you to stop this—'

The king didn't get to finish because his sister launched herself towards her opponent. Lann managed to get his sword up in time to clumsily parry her attack. With little more than a twist of her wrist, Astrid jabbed him in the chest with the blunted end of her weapon hard enough to knock the wind out of him. Taking two strides back, she turned to her confused-looking brother.

'That – that doesn't prove anything,' he said. 'Jarl Gudbrandr simply allowed you win.'

'Allowed me to?' Astrid's eyes narrowed. '*Nobody* allowed me to win, brother.' That wild look was directed towards Lann again. 'Another bout, "champion"?' she asked.

'No,' he spluttered. 'I mean, look, can't we just talk—'

Astrid didn't wait to hear any more; she moved in to attack again.

Lann, his chest aching, gripped the sword and prepared to defend himself. He saw her attack coming easily enough: a big swing from the outside towards his shoulder. He brought his own weapon round to block it, but her stroke was just a ruse designed to provoke such a move on his part. Astrid stepped a little to her right, rotating her hand and whipping her sword down in a chopping blow on to his wrist. At the same time she kicked out with her left foot, catching him a painful blow in an area that he definitely did not want to be kicked in. All the air rushed out of his lungs and he folded forward, clutching himself in pain. Astrid, grabbing his injured sword hand, twisted it viciously enough for the wooden weapon to fall to the floor with a clatter. The new pain made him straighten up again, only to find Astrid's sword at his throat.

The girl smiled sweetly over her shoulder in Erik's direction. 'Want to see some more? Maybe he let me win again. Or was I lucky?'

Erik sat back on his throne, mystified. 'I don't understand,' he admitted.

Lann was relieved when the shield maiden removed the wooden blade from beneath his chin and stepped away. His chest, wrist and another particularly delicate region all hurt like hell, and it struck him that he would have died twice over in the last few moments had they been using real weapons. Worse yet was that he knew Astrid had not even been trying particularly hard. Fleya's amused expression was equally annoying. 'Oh, I'm sure you find this highly entertaining,' he muttered to her.

Another thing occurred to him: the blade at his side had remained completely inert throughout the exchange. There had been no strange whispers or words in his head, no urge for it to be unleashed so it might come to his aid. It seemed everyone and everything in the longhouse were conspiring to make him look like a fool.

'Explain this to me,' Erik demanded of Fleya. 'Was it your majik that allowed Lann to beat Oknhammer the other day?'

'No, Your Grace. There is no such majik that I know of.'

The king waited. Eventually Fleya broke the silence.

'Lann is no traditional warrior, my liege. And the sword he carries is no ordinary weapon. Neither can it be wielded by just anyone. It is an ancient blade that was put into this world for a special purpose, and I still have no idea why my nephew was chosen to carry it. But together they won you back your life and your crown. That is as much as I know. I can tell you no more.'

Erik considered her response and the words she had used. He turned to his young jarl. 'Is this true?'

Lann nodded. 'It is. I am sorry, King Erik. I am new to this, and it is as strange to me as it must seem to you.' He frowned, trying to find the right words. 'The sword … speaks to me. It is an ancient and long-dead language. But at times I can understand it.' He rested his hand on the pommel of the weapon. 'The blade scares me, I'm not ashamed to admit that. But it has saved lives. Mine – twice – my aunt's and yours. It gave me back my sight when I was blind. But Astrid is right, I am no warrior. I hardly know how to hold a sword. As you have just seen, I have no training.'

'If you had drawn the black blade against my sister, would it have killed her?'

The question caught Lann by surprise, but he didn't hesitate in his response. 'No. It would not have harmed Astrid.'

'Another one of these things you simply "know"?'

'It is.'

'Still, such a weapon is a dangerous thing. Especially in the hands of one so young.'

'Some might say the same of a crown on the head of a young ruler, King Erik.'

The king regarded Lann for a moment, then surprised them all by bursting into laughter. Nodding his head, he looked at the younger boy again, as if appraising him anew.

'Perhaps I have been too hasty. My sister *would* be an

232

asset on your journey. She could teach you combat skills in case you and your black blade ever get separated. A Rivengeld should be part of bringing my father's murderer to justice, and as I must stay here and rule ...' He turned to Astrid. 'You have my blessing, sister. Just make sure you come back to me when you have dealt with our odious cousin.'

'I will, brother.'

'Good.' He nodded at Astrid and Lann. 'The two of you should prepare for your journey. All of Stromgard is at your disposal. And you, witch,' he said, turning to Fleya, 'I would welcome your counsel now.'

'Of course.'

The king waited until the two younger people had left before he slumped into his great chair in exhaustion.

'Are you unwell, Your Grace?' Fleya asked.

'I did want to rule, you know,' he said quietly. 'But I never thought it would be like this.'

She nodded sympathetically. 'The ritual to restore your memory will have diminished your strength. I will make you up some restoratives.'

'Are you satisfied with the decision to allow my sister to join you and Lann? I should have consulted you first.'

The witch glanced towards the door. 'She is a resourceful young woman and a great fighter. I have no doubt Lann can learn much from her.' She hesitated.

233

'But?'

'But she has no knowledge of the Art. There will be dark majik ahead, and I fear for her.'

He nodded thoughtfully. 'The lich – the thing that inhabited my mind and body – it could do the same to her, couldn't it?'

'It could.' She paused. 'I am having a small pendant made by your royal blacksmith. Marked on it will be powerful symbols that should help to protect her.'

'This pendant is already being made?'

'It is.'

He frowned. 'It seems that you had foreknowledge Astrid would be joining you.'

'I thought there was every chance a Rivengeld would be coming along. I just didn't know which one.'

He stared broodingly into the distance. 'I wish that it were me.'

'You have much work to do here. It would be reckless for you to leave your kingdom after everything that has happened so recently. Kings are cursed with always having to do the things they must and not the things they want.'

'Can you see the fate of my sister on this quest?'

'No. But you know that Lann and I will do everything in our power to keep her from harm.'

He nodded his thanks, suddenly looking extremely weary again.

'You are not sleeping,' she said. It was more of a statement than a question.

'No.'

'You are having nightmares since the restoration of your memories.'

'I have had some strange dreams, yes.'

The witch offered the king a sad smile. 'They will not last forever. Your mind has been wounded by terrible traumas, and dreams are its way of coming to terms with those things. It is beginning to mend itself.'

He nodded his appreciation. 'I find that I can be honest with you. When this enterprise is at an end, will you grant me the pleasure of your company again? Return here with Astrid and Jarl Gudbrandr, even if for a short while?'

She hesitated and was about to say something when she stopped herself. Instead she smiled and bowed her head. 'I would like that very much, Your Grace.'

'Please,' he held up a hand. 'When we are alone, I would like you to call me Erik.'

'I think I would find that hard, my King, but I will try.'

28

'**P**ut your weight on your left foot and hold the point of the sword down and to your right. No, point it at the ground just ahead of your right foot.' Lann and Astrid were standing in an open space in front of the shield maidens' longhouse. It was used exclusively by the female warriors for all their training and she seemed more at home here than he'd seen her at any other place in Stromgard. Astrid leaned forward and adjusted the angle of the wooden weapon. 'That's better.'

'It feels strange.'

'Stop moaning. This is the Iron Door Guard. You lean forward a little and offer the head as bait to the attack.'

'Offer my head?' He stared at her, trying to ascertain if she were joking. The look he got in return was a hard one.

'To draw an attack, yes. I'm not suggesting you just stand there and let your opponent cut it off. Once your adversary makes his move, you quickly straighten up, removing the head as a target.'

'Oh, that's comforting.'

She ignored him. 'Alternatively you can step in, block, and counterattack with the Wrath Cut we worked on earlier.'

They'd been practising for hours. Astrid's knowledge of the martial arts was inexhaustible, and she was equally comfortable with the sword as she was with the axe and spear. He knew this from bitter experience, and his body bore the cuts and bruises to prove it.

'How good are you with that?' he said, nodding at the horn bow.

'Better than you.'

'That would not be difficult.'

'It's my favourite weapon.'

'How about a demonstration?'

'Are you just trying to get out of any more training?' she said.

'Yep.'

She shook her head, but gave him an unexpected smile. Walking over to the bow and quiver, she slipped the latter over her shoulder and removed an arrow, nocking it on the string in a smooth, practised motion.

'Pick a target,' she said, looking across at Lann.

He looked out over the training area. About halfway

across, maybe forty strides away, was an old wooden bucket. He pointed to it. 'That.'

'Really? *That's* what you want me to hit?'

'Too far away?'

The look she gave him suggested otherwise. Lann watched as she took aim, pulled the bowstring taut, then turned her head to look back at him. 'I'd have liked more of a challenge.' She had hardly let the last word out when, her head still turned away from the target, she released the arrow.

Lann watched it *thunk* into the centre of the pail, knocking it back across the ground until it rattled to a stop. He applauded the shot, his admiration tinged with jealousy. He was nothing without his sword; she handled weapons as though she had been born to it.

'How about you set me a real challenge?' she said. 'Something up the far end of the training square.'

He turned and looked, wondering what might be considered a good target. 'That shield in the far corner. How close can you get to the centre?'

'Ah. Now that *is* a good test.' She narrowed her eyes, murmuring to herself. 'I'll have to allow for the wind coming from the left once the arrow flies beyond the shelter afforded by the longhouse ...'

'Too hard? I can pick something else.'

But she wasn't listening to him. She gave a little nod

to herself, then swiftly nocked another arrow on the bowstring. She was a lesson in concentration as she aimed, her breathing steady and controlled. It seemed to him that she had to miss, aiming as far away from the target as she was. He watched in fascination as she loosed the arrow into the air. It flew true for a while, then gravity and the wind acted on it and swung it down and round towards its target. It hit the edge of the shield, where it shivered for a second before becoming still.

Lann went to clap his hands, but Astrid swore, then swiftly pulled another arrow from her back, nocked it and took aim.

The second arrow hit the shield almost dead centre, and Astrid turned and grinned at him. 'I allowed too much for the wind on the first shot,' she said. 'Bit of a stupid error, really.'

'You hit it,' he pointed out.

'Yes – but it wasn't the shot I'd pictured in my head.'

'Is that how you do it? Picture it in your head?'

She frowned, as if trying to figure out how she *did* do it. 'Yes. I imagine the arrow drop and the effect of the wind and the distance to the target, and I *see* it happening before I release. That, and hundreds of hours of practice, of course.'

'It's very impressive.'

'I'll teach you.'

Lann shook his head and nodded down at the wooden sword in his hand. 'I'm having enough problems with this. Let's just try and get that right, shall we? But not today,' he added hastily. 'I'm a walking bruise right now, and I don't think I could handle any more pain being inflicted. If it's all the same with you …' He thought she might insist, but instead she gave a nod.

'Hungry?' she asked.

'Starving.'

Lunch consisted of a stew, dried meats, great hunks of fresh bread, and cheeses that tasted a whole lot better than they smelt. They sat together at a small table in the kitchens behind the longhouse. The place was run by a surly old man who'd lost an arm and an eye in battle ten years earlier.

'*You* lost your sight, didn't you? What was it like?' she asked between mouthfuls of stew.

The question took him by surprise. She had a habit of doing that to him: saying and doing things when he was least ready for them. He pointed this out to her. 'You don't mince your words, do you?' he said.

'I know,' she said, lowering her eyes. 'I'm sorry. It's probably something to do with never having to apologise for my actions. "Spoilt" – that's what my father would have called it. That, or just plain "rude".'

'It's all right,' he said, waving the apology away. He

swallowed the mouthful he was eating and went on. 'It was frightening, at first. I hadn't always been blind, and I guess, like everyone else, I simply took my ability to see for granted. So when it was taken away from me, I had no idea how I might cope.' He paused, remembering. 'Almost a year I spent in the dark. A year of being scared and … alone.'

'You had Fleya.'

'I did. And I wouldn't have been able to get through those times without her. But I missed the visual world so much it hurt. When I was given the chance to see again, I grabbed it. Perhaps a little too hastily.' He tore a piece of bread from the loaf and spread butter across it. 'But I don't regret my decision. And I don't take the things I see for granted any more. Take this meal, for instance. I look at the things on this plate in a way I never would have before. And that's just food.' He grinned and nodded in the direction of the open window. 'Don't even start me on the sky.' A thought occurred to him. 'I'd never seen the sea until we came here. If I'd not had my sight restored … well, I never would have. Imagine never having the chance to see that fantastic chaos of water – the power and beauty of it.' He looked across into her eyes and took in her face. For some reason he flushed. 'I'm sorry, I'm going on a bit.'

'No. No, you're not.'

He frowned. 'It came with a price, getting my sight back. I see and hear strange things now. Things I'd rather not.'

'Monsters? Like the one that made my brother do those terrible things?'

He nodded.

The sword's voice, having been silent for some time, caught him by surprise when it gave a long, whispering sigh.

'What was that?' Astrid said, looking about her.

'What?'

'Nothing. I ... I thought I heard something.'

Lann stared at her before eventually standing up and brushing the crumbs from his clothes on to the floor.

'Come on,' he said. 'I think it's time we found my aunt and checked on the supplies. We have a long ride ahead of us tomorrow.'

'Aye, a ride through lands that may not welcome Stromgardians like myself, let alone strangers like you and your aunt.'

'What do you mean?'

'Our neighbours have not been too friendly of late. It would be better for us all if we can cross those lands unnoticed.'

Vorneland

29

Lann, Astrid and Fleya set off early on horseback, Astrid on her beloved chestnut mare, the others on mounts personally chosen by the king from his own stables.

Compared to his hill pony, Lann's new mount, a grey called Mistglar, seemed huge when he'd first taken to the saddle. However, he quickly got used to the change, and it was not long before both rider and horse formed an easy understanding.

The trio were not alone on the first leg of their journey. Despite their protestations that they would be less noticeable on their own, Erik had insisted a number of his household guard escort them to the border with the neighbouring kingdom, Vorneland. From that point they would be on their own.

'The Vornelanders are wary of outsiders,' the king had

explained before they'd left. 'And there have long been concerns about the newly appointed queen.'

'In what way?' Fleya had asked.

'Some say she has slaughtered her way to the throne, killing her husband, his brother and others. All of the children sired by the two men, including her own young son, have disappeared.'

'Disappeared?'

Erik had nodded his head gravely. 'Before his death, my father sent trusted emissaries in his service to find out what was happening. Although I do not know all of the details, I do know my father believed the queen to be ruthless and dangerous even before she ascended to the throne. My advice would be to avoid contact if you can.'

Despite everything they'd been through recently, not to mention the enormity of the task that lay ahead of them, the three companions found themselves in high spirits. Their time in Stromgard had been a difficult one, and even Astrid was glad for the opportunity to be away from the place. It was only when she was far from the coastal city's boundaries that it occurred to her that she might never again see her homeland. She halted her mount. Turning in the saddle, she looked back on the capital and the surrounding landscape, trying to see it as Lann now saw the world – with appreciation and gratitude for its beauty. Strong emotions filled her, and she took a few moments to compose herself again. If the others noticed her farewell to the place of her birth, they were kind enough not to say anything when she spurred her horse forward to rejoin them.

By the afternoon they reached the foothills that marked the start of the range known as Grunwelfe. The mild weather of late had caused the pastures to erupt in a sea of colour as wild flowers bloomed among the grass, bringing with them a host of bees and small butterflies.

'It reminds me of the hills near the farm where I grew up,' Lann said to Astrid when she saw him smiling at the view. 'When my mother died, I'd ride out on my own for hours on end. I spent a lot of my time in wild pastures like this.'

'I'd like to see the Maiden's Fingers one day.'

'Maybe when all this is over, I'll take you there. Compared to the place you grew up in, it would seem dull and uninteresting, but it was home to me.'

Reaching up, she touched the small medallion hanging around her neck. Fleya had given it to her before they'd set off with instructions not to take it off unless she wanted to invite dangerous majik. It was another reminder of how strange and perilous the enterprise they were under-taking was.

As they were crossing a river at a natural ford, she took a moment to study the boy riding alongside her.

He was handsome in a way that was not obvious. Steely grey eyes stared out from a strong face, and the first wisps of his beard were beginning to show on his jawline. More endearing still was the way he seemed completely oblivious to his good looks. She blushed a little when he turned to catch her regarding him. 'You look good on that horse,' she said, nodding at both rider and mount.

'It's a fine animal.'

She gave a little laugh. 'And so it should be. It was my father's own horse.'

Lann stared across at her to see if she might be joking with him. He looked down at the animal in astonishment. 'Why would Erik give me such a thing?'

'My brother holds you in high esteem, Lannigon Gudbrandr. Mistglar is a fitting gift for Stromgard's newest and youngest jarl. I hope she proves as good a companion to you as she did for my father over the years.'

It was late in the day when Fleya called out for them to halt. They'd reached the pass in the hills that would be the safest and easiest route into Vorneland.

'We will stop here and make camp. We are close to the border and I would like to send our escort back before the night is completely upon us.' The witch waved away the guards' protests, pointing out they were anyway no more than a couple of miles from the frontier.

They watched the Stromgardians ride off, then set about putting up a shelter for the night.

Astrid's bow skills provided two fat rabbits, which they roasted with the herbs Fleya gathered. Bellies full, the three sat beside the fire, staring into the flames as they contemplated what might still lie ahead.

'What is your cousin like?' Lann asked Astrid, after a while.

'Kelewulf?' She started saying something, but stopped herself. Instead she thought for a moment before responding. 'Erik always felt sorry for him. My cousin lost his mother when he was young – they were very close, and Erik put any strangeness down to that. I don't really know why, but I've never liked him. He's clever, but … false.' She gave a little shake of her head. 'I don't think he likes people very much.'

Lann nodded thoughtfully, then turned to Fleya. 'This lich,' he said. 'Who was it before?'

'A powerful sorcerer with a similar dislike of this world to Astrid's cousin. He seems to have found the perfect partner with whom to reignite his hatred.' The firelight danced across her features and Lann could see the consternation on her face. 'His name was … is … Yirgan.'

The name was familiar to Lann, and he remembered how Fleya had told him how the sorcerer had risen to power. A servant of the dark god Lorgukk, his majik had become so great, it threatened the very existence of the world until the gods themselves were forced to intervene and stop him. If the gods couldn't destroy the man, what hope did they have?

She sighed. 'We should rest now. We have a long journey ahead.'

The trio pulled their blankets up around themselves and closed their eyes to the world. But all of them found sleep hard to come by that night.

Lann woke to the sound of a voice calling his name. When he opened his eyes, he was standing in a pasture not unlike the one they'd travelled through earlier that day. It was neither night nor day, but the world was bathed in a weird pink light. The sword was gone from his side.

It occurred to him that he was dreaming.

He looked about him and spotted a strange circle of stones to his left. Each of the nine megaliths that formed the ring was square in shape, and twice the height of a man. They were old, those stones; that much was obvious even from this distance. Covered in lichen and moss, they looked like great hairy giants who had hunkered down close to the ground to shelter themselves from the weather. Stranger still was the pulsating glow that surrounded them, marking this place as one of power and majik.

The sound of feathered wings close to his head caused

him to look up and then duck as the crow flashed past. Despite the creature's speed, he caught the flash of green in its eye. Lann watched as the bird banked in an arc around the stones once, and let out a loud caw before dropping down into the circle and out of Lann's eyeline.

Intrigued, he walked in the direction the bird had taken, his feet moving soundlessly over the ground. Indeed, with the exception of the crow's calls, there was no sound of any kind in this place.

He rounded the nearest stone and stood at the edge of the giant circle. He was only half surprised to discover that the black-feathered bird was no longer there and that a woman had taken its place.

When she smiled at him his heart clenched. She looked very much like his aunt, but her eyes were wider, her lips fuller. Long hair the colour of polished copper hung down to her shoulders, where it came to rest on the black, heavy woollen cloak she wore, fastened on one side by a silver brooch in the shape of the bird that had preceded her. And he knew – knew in his very bones – that this woman was Lette, his birth mother.

Lann went to call out to her, but no sounds would form, and when he tried to enter the circle and go to her, he found that his way was blocked by some invisible force. He instinctively knew there was no point struggling, and the sad look she gave him confirmed he was not permitted to enter this place at this time.

She put her hand up to her lips and kissed the tips of her fingers, silently blowing it towards him. That smile again on her face, she reached for something on her arm and—

'Wake up, Lann,' Fleya said, shaking him gently out of that world and back into his own.

Opening his eyes, he stared into a face that was almost identical to the one he'd just been dragged away from. 'I had a dream,' he said, his voice little more than a whisper. 'About my mother.'

'Lae Fetlanger?'

He shook his head. 'No, my real mother. Lette.' He recalled the kiss she'd blown him from her fingertips, tears of happiness and sadness welling up in his eyes as he did so.

The look Fleya gave him mirrored his emotions. 'I wish I had shared your dream.' She sniffed and turned her head towards the morning sun. 'We must be going, I fear we have another long day in the saddle ahead of us.'

After a short ride of no more than an hour, Lann spotted the circle of stones from his dream. Reining his horse to a stop, he stared across at it, his pulse racing at the sight.

'The Ring of Brodgor,' his aunt said, drawing her horse beside him. 'An ancient place. A site of worship.'

'For which god?' he asked.

'One of the old gods. Storren.'

Storren, god of the earth and all things that grow from it, breathe life into these seeds that they may awaken and flourish. His aunt had invoked the god's name on many an occasion when they had been planting in their small garden back at the cabin, and the habit of doing so had rubbed off on him when he took it over.

'The god has always been popular among farming communities,' his aunt went on, 'but this holy site has been left unused for some time.' She gave a little shake of her head. 'It is a shame when the old ways are forgotten.'

'Storren is also popular with witches, is he not?'

'He is. Most of the medicines and treatments we make are produced from plant matter. Those of us who study the Art offer up thanks to the god responsible for those things.'

Making a sudden decision, Lann urged his horse forward towards the circle. Exchanging a glance, Fleya and Astrid followed.

'Lann?' Astrid said. 'Is something the matter?'

He didn't answer her, but dismounted and approached the circle. He hesitated on the border – where his progress had been barred in his dream – and then took a step inside.

'What is he doing?' Astrid asked the witch, her eyes fixed on Lann as he approached the centre of the circle and stopped. He stood there, staring down at something on the ground before slowly reaching down and picking it up.

'What have you found?' his aunt asked.

He held the small bauble up so that both of them might see it. Whatever it was, it appeared to be the same colour and finish as the metal of the Dreadblade.

'More gifts from the gods?' Fleya said, the strain in her voice clear to hear.

'Not from the gods this time,' he answered with a little shake of his head as he walked back towards them. 'And this was not left here for me.'

'Then for whom?'

'Astrid.' He lifted the trinket up, offering it to her.

Fleya gasped as she saw the armlet up close, the thing causing a great surge of emotion to rise up inside her. She knew the item well. The last time she'd seen it was on her sister's arm. She had been wearing it the night she died, shortly after giving birth to Lann.

Astrid stared at the black metal band, but made no move to reach out and take it. Without being able to explain why, she felt afraid to do so. There were intricate markings on its surface, but they were strangely difficult to fix with the eye. The more she tried to do so, the more they appeared to shift and blur. She looked to Fleya, as though seeking advice.

'It was my sister's,' the witch said in response. 'She received it as a gift, but I never found out who from. It was very special to her. Now she means you to have it.'

'A majikal item,' Astrid said. It was more of a statement than a question. Before meeting Lann and Fleya, the world she inhabited had not involved majik or the Art. And though she had seen the great good it could do, she still harboured deep-seated anxieties about this new supernatural landscape and the things that came from it.

'It is, yes.'

Astrid frowned. 'My father always told me to be careful when accepting gifts, and that those given most freely were often those that carried the most risk. You yourself told me you wished Lann hadn't taken the sword when it was offered him, and that it was as much a curse as it was a blessing. How do I know *this* gift won't prove to be the same for me?'

Fleya shook her head. 'Items of majik always demand something from their bearer.'

'Lann?' Astrid said. 'Why should I take this thing?'

'I don't know,' he said gently. 'There may be a price, as with the Dreadblade. All I know is that, last night, I saw my mother in this place, and she left this here so I might give it to you.'

'Lette was here?' Fleya gasped, staring out to the spot where Lann had crouched down to pick the item up. When she finally managed to tear her eyes away she turned them on Astrid. 'My sister was the best and kindest human I have known. If the armlet could cause harm she would not have left it for you.'

Astrid gingerly reached out and took the bangle. Still not sure she was doing the right thing, she slipped it over her wrist and up on to her arm; as she did so, it was as if a filter were removed from her vision.

The first thing that struck her was the glow that surrounded each of the nine stones. The auras were like nothing she'd ever seen before: blue and green shifting patterns danced off their outer surface. There was nothing sinister about that other-worldly radiance; quite the opposite: she felt it was a place of safety, of … sanctuary. She turned to comment on this to Fleya but the words were strangled in her mouth by what faced her. Gone was the beautiful woman she had first seen in the mirror on the fateful night before Lann declared himself her brother's champion. Instead, a wizened and shrunken version stood before her. The sudden transformation caused her to gasp in surprise.

'I told you I was older than I looked,' the witch said with a smile. As she did so, the young Fleya seemed to shine through again, and the older version faded into the background. 'Now you can see the world as Lann and I do, Princess Astrid.' Her gaze went past the girl towards the stone circle. 'I would spend a moment here. With my sister.'

Understanding that his aunt needed to be alone, Lann gestured for Astrid to join him on the other side of the perimeter.

Alone, Fleya approached the spot where the armlet had been left. Taking a shuddering breath, she spoke to her sister.

'I need you to forgive me, Lette,' she said, fighting back the emotion that threatened to take over. 'I'm sorry for the way I behaved. I had no right to say the things I did when you told me you were with child. I was scared. I was scared for you …' She paused and took another deep breath. 'But if I'm honest, I was more scared for myself. I didn't want to be left on my own.'

She pictured her beautiful sister. Her favourite memory of Lette. Of them playing together in the snow, laughing and screaming as they threw snowballs at one another. They must have been about eight years old at the time, not long before they were sent away by their mother to learn the Art. Lette had got chilblains that day, and Fleya had held her hand as their mother rubbed the blood back into her feet, chiding them both for being silly and staying out too long in the freezing temperatures. Despite the pain their mother's ministrations caused her, Lette had smiled back at her sister throughout.

She wiped at the tear that slid down her face. 'I was wrong. You knew the truth I refused to see. That you were not leaving me alone. You left Lannigon behind in the world with me. And I have tried to do as I promised the day he came into this world. I have tried to keep him safe.' She shook her head. 'But now, after all this time, I seem to be doing the opposite – I find myself leading him *towards* danger. I can't keep him hidden any longer. The gods themselves have interfered with the path his life is taking, and try as I might, I can do little to stop them. He is like you and I: a leaf blown hither and thither on the breath of the gods.' She let out a little sigh. 'I miss you, sister. I miss you every day.'

As she turned to leave, something made her pause. Looking up, she smiled and then laughed as a black feather fell through the air in a graceful spiral towards her. She reached out her hand and allowed it to land on her palm, the feather brushing her skin with the softest of kisses.

'I love you too.'

She took care putting the feather into a pocket inside her cloak. Then, gathering the garment about her, she left the Ring of Brogdor and rejoined her travelling companions.

30

'What was it like?' Lann asked Astrid once they were on their way again.

'What was what like?'

'Living with a father like Mirvar Rivengeld?'

She took a few moments to consider her answer. 'Exhausting. He was so good, so … *loved*, that we were terrified to let him down in any way. Erik and I couldn't really be ourselves unless we were alone, and we hardly ever got to be. That's why I wanted to become a shield maiden. The maidens were not interested in who I was. The only thing they cared about was whether I could fight.'

It wasn't the answer Lann had expected. He'd always thought it would be the greatest thing to be born into a family like the Rivengelds, to have everyone look up to you and admire you.

'The woman who left me this …' She gestured at the armlet. 'Your mother. What was she like?'

'I never knew her. She died giving birth to me. All I know is she was a witch, like Fleya. Last night, in my dream, was the first time I'd ever laid eyes on her.'

'And the woman who brought you up? Who was she?'

'Lae Fetlanger.' A memory of her came to him. She was standing outside the farmhouse, laughing at his attempts to catch a chicken that had escaped the coop. The sun was on her face and she looked beautiful. 'I couldn't have asked for a better mother.' As the words escaped him, he realised just how true they were. Lae *had* loved him like her own son.

'I sense a "but".'

'She was married to a man called Gord – the man I thought was my father. He never liked me, and I could never understand why. That is, until I found out the truth.'

'It is not in some people to give their love freely.'

'No.'

'You were lucky to have Lae. Just as I was lucky to have Mirvar. We were loved by good people.'

They rode in silence for a short while, taking in the landscape of this new kingdom.

'Do you think the rumours about the new Queen of Vorneland are true?' Lann asked. 'That she killed to take power?'

Fleya, having caught up with the pair, answered. 'It

would not be the first time a blood-drenched monarch has sat upon a throne of the Six Kingdoms. Favner Lurvald is a woman obsessed with power.'

'You know her?' Astrid asked.

'I met her once, although she was young at the time. Her ambition was evident but I sensed something more dangerous lurking inside her. Marrying a king was not enough for her – she wanted to rule. It seems she has achieved her goal now.'

'It's unusual to have a queen on the throne, isn't it?' Lann said. 'Why do our people think a man should reign? Women should be given the chance to show they can rule every bit as well as their male counterparts.'

'Unlike me, you mean?' Astrid said in a loud voice.

'No.' The word came too fast and too loud, and his face flushed crimson again. 'That's not what I meant. You did the best you could. You were just, er … What I mean is …'

He stopped when he saw both women laughing. Cursing himself, he mumbled under his breath how he should, in future, keep his mouth shut on matters he had no real grasp of. His reaction, however, only resulted in more hilarity.

'It's all right, Lann,' Astrid said, waving away his embarrassment. 'But you're right when you say it is unfair. As queen regent, Favner would be forced to hand the throne to the next heir apparent once he became of age. In this case, her young son.'

'The one who has disappeared?' As he said these words, the sword, silent until now, let out a strange noise, and a small frown clouded Astrid's face, as if she too had heard it.

'I think your brother's advice to steer well clear of any contact with the new queen is well given,' Fleya said. 'Vorneland is not the kingdom it once was.'

The remainder of the day went by peacefully as they rode through a largely agricultural landscape. The only sign that people lived here was the occasional column of smoke drifting up from the chimney of the odd farmhouse they passed.

They built no fire that night – 'Just in case,' Fleya said. 'Try to get some sleep now,' she went on, hunkering down among the furs that made up her bedding. 'If we make the same time tomorrow, we should make it all the way through Vorneland by noon. After that, the tower where Kelewulf and the lich have absconded to is a relatively short ride.'

Something at the edge of his consciousness made Lann open his eyes from the deep sleep he'd been in. He stared up at the deadly spear tip inches from his face, and the group of men surrounding him. His breath caught in his throat. Very slowly he felt down by his side and was shocked to discover the black blade was not there. Frowning, he tried to make sense of what was happening.

If one of these men had taken the Dreadblade, why hadn't the sword warned him?

Careful not to make any sudden movements, he slowly glanced to his left, his heart sinking when he saw that Astrid and Fleya also had spears pointed at them.

Their captors ignored the trio's furious questions and protestations as they were dragged to their feet. Then, with their hands bound behind them, they were bundled up into their saddles.

It was only when the trio were trussed up on their horses like this that the leader of the group stepped forward. Dressed in leather and fur, with a long braided beard of the style that was common in these parts, he looked up at them and addressed them for the first time. His voice was calm and pleasant, which seemed at odds with his rough appearance and the manner in which he and his men had just captured them.

'You are trespassing in Vorneland territory without permission of Queen Favner. If you do as you are told, you will be brought before Her Grace unharmed. However, I will quite happily present you to the queen in a less than pristine condition if you choose to give us any trouble. Is that understood?'

'And you are?' Fleya asked.

'Captain Rinkor of the Queen's Guards.'

'Since when is it a crime to cross these lands?' Astrid

asked, fixing the man with a haughty stare. 'The Volken people have always been permitted movement across any of the Six Kingdoms in times of peace.'

Her outburst was answered with a shrug.

'Do you know who I am?' she asked hotly. 'I'm—'

'An innocent young woman scared out of her wits at being captured like this,' Fleya said, cutting her off and shooting the girl a look. 'And so she should be. If the warriors of Vorneland are stopping travellers and threatening them like this, who knows what else they are willing to do.'

Captain Rinkor turned to face Fleya, his own expression grave. 'I am a father as well as a warrior, and you have my word that no man in my charge would ever harm a woman. The men of Vorneland are not barbarians like the Northmen, or mindless thugs like the Hasz'een.'

'Even the Northmen do not make prisoners of those entering their lands.'

'No, they just cut their hearts out and feed them to their ice-wolves.' The man shook his head and went on. 'There have been thefts of livestock of late. That alone gives us the right to take you captive. The queen will judge you fairly, I am sure.' There was something about the way he lingered a little too long over these final words that struck Fleya as odd; as if there were much more he would have liked to say. Instead, he turned his back on them and mounted his own horse. 'Now, perhaps you'd all do me the service of remaining quiet for a while. If you feel you cannot do so, I'm sure we can arrange to have you all gagged for the remainder of the journey.' He raised an eyebrow at them and nudged his horse forward in the direction of Queen Favner's court.

The settlement was small compared to Stromgard, but busy with people trading goods and services. Carts full of agricultural produce made their way up and down mud tracks with simple wooden buildings on either side. The great longhouse at the heart of the community was impressive, however, and it was to this place the captives were brought.

With their hands still bound, they were ushered towards the entrance. Against the brightness of the morning light, the interior appeared dark and foreboding.

As they entered the place Fleya cast a glance in her nephew's direction. Lann hadn't uttered a word since their rude awakening at the hands of their Vorneland captors.

The captain called them to a halt before a dais that was made out of a giant millstone.

The Vorneland throne was carved from one huge piece of wood, fashioned to depict heads of wheat and corn as well as vegetables and other plants and foodstuffs; the legs had been shaped to represent livestock of every kind.

A woman sat on the throne. Dressed in a long blue dress

which perfectly matched the polished stones set into her crown, Queen Favner stared out through eyes the colour of storm clouds. Below the silver circlet on her head, long grey hair hung down almost to her hips. A great hound, its own coat shot with white and grey, slept at her feet. The only other people in the place were the queen's personal guards, and a small retinue of courtiers who were arranged in the area immediately behind the throne.

'Well, well, what have we here?' asked the woman atop the throne in a voice that portrayed little emotion.

'Your Grace,' Fleya said, speaking for the others and giving the ruler a small bow. 'We have no idea why we have been brought before you like this. We are merely travellers passing through Vorneland and have committed no crime.'

'No crime? How would you know? Only a king, or indeed a queen, has the right to decide what constitutes a crime in their own kingdom.' She gazed over their heads into the middle distance. 'The right of travel in Vorneland is no longer free to all. Your very presence on its lands is, in itself, a crime.'

'Since when?' Astrid asked.

There was no answer. The queen, a blank look in her eyes, stared out at something unseen beyond the long-house. When the silence continued, some of the courtiers began to shuffle their feet.

Eventually Favner gave a tiny shake of her head and fixed Astrid with a cold look. 'Did you say something, child?'

'I asked you when Vorneland had taken the decision to stop free travel rights.'

'How pretty you are, child. And young. But youth can make one foolish.' The smile she gave the younger woman was anything but friendly. 'You would do well to hold your tongue in my presence, little one. That is, if you still wish to have one in your head. Or, indeed, a head at all.'

Fleya shot Astrid a look that told her to do as she was bid. 'If I might address the queen?' she asked, pleasantly. 'May I ask why we have been brought here?'

'Not so foolish, this one,' the queen said absently. 'I could list several reasons.' She ticked them off on her fingers. 'You were trespassing on lands that I rule. You came armed. You may be responsible for the recent disappearances of livestock. But really, you are here ... because I will it.' Her expression turned absent again and she subsided into silence.

'Your Grace,' Fleya said gently, her unease growing by the second. The queen half turned her head in the witch's direction. 'I should like to pay my respects to the prince. Your son. Where is he?'

'Gone,' Favner said dreamily.

'Gone where?'

'I sent him away. For his own safety. To a holy order of priests, so they might teach him the ways of his people. Away, away, away. Gone.' She started to hum.

'She's lost her mind,' Astrid said under her breath.

A man standing a short distance away from the queen gave a loud and deliberate cough that had the desired effect of bringing the monarch's attention back into the room. When she looked up this time, Favner shot them a disconcertingly brilliant smile.

'You have arrived in time for my wedding! I insist you join me in the celebrations.' She looked at Astrid, her eyes narrowing at the girl. 'I know you. Mirvar Rivengeld's daughter. Did he send you?'

Astrid looked across at Fleya for help, but the witch was too busy studying the queen.

'M-my father is dead,' she said. 'You … you sent a representative to attend the funeral, Queen Favner.'

'Did I?' she sighed and shook her head. 'There have been too many funerals of late. My husband, the old king, is dead, you know.' She paused. 'Did I tell you I am to be married?'

Fleya had seen madness of this sort before: a sickness of the soul brought on after committing foul and dreadful acts. She had seen how the pursuit of power could destroy a person, leaving them mentally scarred. The healer in her wanted to help the deeply troubled individual sitting on the throne before her, but there was no majik she knew of that

266

could save the soul of somebody who had committed the wicked deeds Favner had in order to gain her throne.

'Exciting, isn't it?' the queen went on. 'A wedding. Tomorrow morning.' The queen pointed a ringed finger at Astrid, treating the girl to a conspiratorial wink. 'And your father played no small part in the whole affair.' She gave a little clap of her hands. The gesture was almost childlike.

'My father?'

'My husband-to-be was first sent to these lands by Mirvar Rivengeld many moons ago. Since then he has been back and forth, back and forth between our kingdoms. But now he has returned for good!'

'May I ask his name?' Fleya said, her voice laced with dread.

No sooner had the question left her lips than a man stepped forth from the deepest shadows at the rear of the great hall, making his way through the courtiers until he stood beside Vorneland's ruler.

Mounting the dais to the wooden throne, the exiled jarl, Glaeverssun, took up Favner's hand and planted a kiss on it before looking back to the trio.

'Princess Astrid, my dear. Isn't it wonderful news? And imagine my surprise when I heard the three of you were in these lands!' His hideous smile broadened. 'Your arrival here is like an early wedding present – isn't that so, my dear?' He nodded at the queen before returning his attention to his prisoners. 'I myself have been crossing over the border to Vorneland for well over a year now. Your father had heard reports that Queen Favner might be experiencing some personal issues. He was concerned the rumours about her could spell trouble for the region, so he sent me here regularly to check things out. During my visits the queen and I became rather … fond of each other. So, when I was so rudely expelled from my own lands and kingdom –' he shot the trio a less than friendly look – 'I came here to ask for succour.'

'And for the queen's hand in marriage,' Astrid said, unable to keep the sarcasm from her voice.

He gave a coy little smile. 'In fact, Queen Favner did *me* the honour, and I accepted with all gratitude.'

Fleya let out a little hiss of disgust.

'How did you know we were in Vorneland?' she asked. She directed her question to the queen, but it was Glaeverssun who answered.

'I still have friends in Stromgard. They told me of a covert mission – two women and a boy leaving the palace on the king's finest horses, and how the lad carried a black blade at his side …'

At the mention of the Dreadblade, Lann lifted his head and glared at the disgraced jarl through red-rimmed eyes.

Glaeverssun motioned to the guards hovering behind the trio. 'Take our guests to their living quarters, please.'

He grinned at them. 'You will not find them particularly appealing, I'm afraid. But they're no worse than the ones I found myself in after I displeased you, Princess.'

'I should have let my brother kill you!' Astrid cried over her shoulder as the guards led them away.

The man pursed his lips at this, as if weighing her words. 'Yes, Princess. I really do think you should have. Still, we all make mistakes, don't we?'

'Come to bed,' Queen Favner said, patting the pillows beside her. She was sitting up, surrounded by countless cushions. Her hair hung down over the front of her shoulders and the white, high-necked gown she was wearing. She smiled and beckoned to him from across the room.

A shiver ran through Glaeverssun. The thought of marrying this woman repulsed him. The queen was deranged, he had no doubt about that. He'd watched her slow decline as her wits deserted her over the last year or so and she was getting worse.

He had managed to turn the situation to his advantage, of course. King Mirvar, uneasy at rumours coming out of this region, had sent him here as an emissary. He had no doubt that Favner had committed wicked and terrible deeds on her way to the throne, and these acts had corrupted her soul and left her grip on reality broken.

Instead of reporting this to his king, however, he'd kept the information to himself and had used his visits to wheedle his way into her affections. She trusted him more than many of those in her own court.

When he had come to her following his exile from Stromgard, Queen Favner had listened to his story of betrayal and treachery, and quickly come to his defence. The marriage proposal had come from her – but the seed had been planted by him long ago.

'Bed?' she suggested again.

'Not now.' He turned his attention to the black blade. The sword sat on the table, still sheathed. He'd not plucked up the courage to pick it up yet, but he knew it was a weapon of great power. What had the boy called it? Dreadblade. It was a weapon that, wielded by someone like him, could make his dreams of controlling all six Volken kingdoms come true.

'You haven't looked at me since my men brought you that dreadful sword,' Favner said. 'I think –' a small smile curved her lips – 'yes, I think I will have it taken away and thrown into a lake somewhere.'

Her eyes widened when he spun round to face her, a furious expression on his face. 'You will do no such thing!' he said. 'This weapon will be the start of Vorneland's rise to power. It will bring my – *our* – enemies to their knees. It will elevate us to new heights, and—'

He stopped, staring at her as she began to laugh. 'Look at you,' she said. 'You funny little man. Making a lot of fuss over a stupid sword. The secret to Vorneland's continued power, my lord, relies on its queen and her long reign of unopposed strength. On her health. On her happiness.' She narrowed her eyes at him. 'And right now, I am not very happy.'

Glaeverssun recognised the danger. He knew exactly what this woman had done, the people she had made disappear. How she had plotted and schemed for years before her husband's *untimely* death, and he knew that he would have to walk a delicate line to avoid the same fate.

For now, at least, he told himself again.

Forcing a smile on to his lips, he made his way over to the bed.

The three captives sat in cramped wooden cells with their hands and feet bound. There was no chance of them escaping their confines, and even if they could, the prison's only entrance was guarded by a huge, heavily armed man.

Lann occupied the centre pen with Fleya on one side and Astrid on the other. He still had not uttered a word since their capture.

'Lann? Are you all right?' Fleya asked. She sighed. 'I warned you. I told you the sword could betray you. And it has done so. Betrayed all of us and allowed us to be taken captive.'

'It *knew* we would be captured,' he said slowly. 'It wanted this to happen.'

'What?' said Astrid. 'Why on earth—'

'It knew Glaeverssun was here. It also knows how much the man desires to own it and use it for evil. It knows what terrible crimes the queen has committed – she murdered her own son for the throne.'

'You're certain?'

Lann nodded. 'Glaeverssun knows it too. The Dreadblade told me.'

'Such terrible deeds come at a high cost,' Fleya said in a small voice. 'Her fixation on power, even if she had to pursue a path of death and destruction to achieve it, has brought madness on her. No person, not even a queen, can commit such vile acts and remain unchanged. And Glaeverssun is using her frailties to fulfil his own ambitions.'

'If all that is true,' Astrid said, 'why would the black blade allow us to be captured like this? Why would it put us in the hands of these evil people?'

'It must do what it was created for,' Lann answered. 'It cannot shy away from that.'

It was Fleya who finally seemed to realise what her nephew was trying to tell them. 'The Dreadblade ... It is compelled to eradicate evil.'

Lann nodded. 'I am the wielder of the sword, and it is sworn to protect me. But it is also sworn to eliminate evil wherever it finds it. It knows I am not capable of carrying out what it judges necessary here, so it will do it without me.'

'And what is it that will be done here, Lann?'

'Dark deeds,' he whispered.

It was hot under the furs. Waking with a dry mouth, Glaeverssun opened his eyes on the dimly lit room, momentarily confused as to where he was. However, it was not just thirst that had woken him. He could have sworn he'd heard somebody whispering.

He lay perfectly still, senses tuned in to his surroundings. He could call the guards – *should* call them – but he didn't want to appear foolish to them. So he lay unmoving for a few moments more.

Nothing.

Eventually, convincing himself his nocturnal imaginings were a result of the wine and the goat's cheese he'd eaten at dinner, he turned over and settled back down into his pillow again. It was as he closed his eyes that he heard the small, barely audible whisper again.

He turned to the queen, wondering if she had spoken in her sleep, but her face was calm and peaceful. How the woman slept so soundly he would never understand.

'Who's there?' he called out in a hushed voice. Then, throwing back the furs, he climbed down from the bed, the cold of the floor sending an icy chill through him.

And just then, that whisper again. Glaeverssun stood rock-still, straining his ears to try and work out where the sound was coming from, because it seemed as if it were from everywhere at once. A whisper that was more in his head than—

Kurum-na murt.

Glaeverssun gave a little shout and spun around wildly. Childhood stories of phantoms and ghouls were reawakened in him as his highly charged imagination began to run away from him. His heart beat wildly in his chest as he hurried across the room towards a lighted candle on a small stand not far away. But as his hand reached towards it, the flame sputtered and died, as though extinguished by an invisible figure.

'Wh-who's there?' Glaeverssun stammered, hating the scared sound of his voice. 'You don't frighten me, whoever you are.'

Another whisper, this time to his left.

He moved in the direction of the sound, and bumped into the table in the middle of the room. *The sword*. With shaking hands he grabbed its hilt and pulled the Dreadblade free. Despite his panic he was struck by how light the weapon felt in his hand. A shiver of excitement ran through him. He was invincible with this weapon. Invincible! Standing taller, he dared whatever malevolent being was here to show itself.

Karum-na murt.

Behind him!

Glaeverssun spun about, thrusting forward. The black blade penetrated the chest of Queen Favner as if she were a thing of air and not one of flesh and bone. Her terrible scream filled the chamber, and despite the gloom, he could make out her face: the look of disbelief, eyes widening in horror as she stared first at the weapon she was impaled upon, and then at the ugly darkness that was quickly spreading outwards across her white cotton nightgown, like some night flower opening its inky petals.

'Cold,' was all she managed to say as she reached out for him, pulling him into a terrible embrace, as if she were set on stealing his warmth to make it her own.

It was this bloody scene that greeted the guards, alerted by the dreadful scream, when they burst in through the door of the royal chamber.

'The queen!' the first man roared, hurrying across to the pair and drawing his own sword. 'He has murdered the queen!'

'No! It was the sword. It made me think—'

Glaeverssun spun around, the bloodied weapon held out before him.

275

Faced with a blood-soaked murderer brandishing a blade, the captain reacted in the way any soldier would. Metal met metal, and the murderer's explanation died on his lips as the captain buried his own weapon in his queen's killer.

Glaeverssun sank to his knees. The guards paid him no attention now, intent as they were on saving their queen. He could hear their cries for help as if from a long distance away, his hearing deserting him. His vision too was fading. A dark fog moved in, slowly obscuring everything.

As his life ebbed away, he remembered where he'd heard those whispered words before. The Gudbrandr boy had spoken them in the square, moments before he had bested the mercenary.

Kurum-na murt.

That's what the boy had told Oknhammer.

'Death is coming.'

Astrid nudged Lann awake as a soldier came into the jail, heading for their cells.

The man looked weary, with dark shadows beneath his eyes, but it was the knife he drew from his belt as he approached them that held their full attention.

'What? No wedding for us?' Astrid angrily asked him. 'I thought we were to be the queen's guests?'

'There is to be no wedding today.'

'No? What then?' she spat. 'Our execution?'

The man frowned, and looked down at the knife. 'I have been sent here to free you, not harm you,' he said, beginning to unlock the cages. 'This is to cut your bonds.'

'Who ordered this?' asked Astrid, still eyeing the man with distrust. 'I can't believe Glaeverssun would willingly let us—'

'Glaeverssun is dead,' Lann said, raising himself to his feet and wincing as the blood flowed back into his legs. He offered his hands, allowing the man to sever his ties. 'Isn't he?'

The soldier gave him an odd look, but nodded his answer.

'And your queen?' Astrid's voice was little more than a whisper as she remembered Lann's explanation of the sword's judgement of both individuals.

'Queen Favner is dead too,' the soldier said. 'At the hands of her husband-to-be. King Rinkor rules Vorneland now,' he said, pulling himself together and handing Lann the knife. 'He requests an urgent audience with the three of you.'

'Rinkor?' Fleya said. 'The captain who captured us?'

'No longer a captain. He finds himself the ruler of these lands now.'

'That is quite a promotion.'

'Indeed. I'm sure he will tell you all about it during your audience.'

'Where is my sword, the Dreadblade?' Lann asked.

The man's lip curled up in distaste at the mention of the weapon. He shook his head and tried the name out. '"Dreadblade". Aye, that's an apt name for the thing, all right. It was found in Queen Favner's chambers, her blood still on its edge. My men will not touch it, and I don't blame them. Those who approach it are filled with a terrible feeling of fear that is so great they are convinced majik is at work.' The man eyed the boy warily. 'The thing is cursed, isn't it?'

Lann's refusal to answer was met by a humourless snort. 'I thought as much.'

'A blade – even one of majik – is still only a tool,' Fleya said. 'It was the wielder of the weapon who is responsible for your kingdom's loss. You would do well to remember that.'

'Be that as it may, it is a malevolent thing that has no place inside these walls,' the soldier replied, turning back to Lann. 'King Rinkor, however, has said you may have it back. He was the only one with courage enough to handle it. He will return it to you during your audience with him.'

The news that he and the Dreadblade were to be reunited created a host of conflicting thoughts and emotions inside Lann. The separation had been genuinely painful – almost physically so – for him. And yet the sword's motives in allowing itself to be taken could be seen as reprehensible.

It had decided Favner and Glaeverssun should be punished for their crimes, and it had set about seeing that justice be done. It had killed them. It would have killed them if it thought Lann was willing to wield it in the act of doing so, but it knew he was not. Did that mean it didn't really need him? Did what happened here mean it would leave him and plunge him back into the darkness?

As these last thoughts occurred to him, an all too familiar whisper filled his head.

Nir-akuu.

Monsters.

And then a new word that he also understood somehow.

Ishmet.

Together.

Pulling himself up to his full height Lann looked the man in the eye. 'Take me to my sword,' he said.

They were given time to wash and change before they were brought before the new king.

Rinkor seemed ill at ease on his throne.

Seeing the puzzled look on their faces, he gave a small smile. 'I have the dubious honour of being the last king's bastard child.' A small shrug. 'Only a handful of people knew about my birth and I owe the reason that I am still breathing to the fact that Queen Favner was not one of them.'

Lann nodded towards the dais and the huge wooden chair the man sat upon. 'You appear to have taken her place quickly enough.'

'Believe me, young man, when I tell you I have no wish to be seated here.' His words were accompanied by a sad shake of his head. 'But Favner's murder left Vorneland without a ruler. The last time that happened, over seventy years ago, a civil war lasting eight long and bloody winters was the result.' He shrugged. 'I love my people. Even reluctant monarchs must do what is right for those they rule.' He tapped the arm of the great wooden seat with the ring on his finger and sat up taller. 'The queen did many things that demand reparation during her reign, and the first of these can be dealt with here and now. Please accept my apologies for the way in which you were treated in these lands, and for the part I played in your capture and imprisonment. You must understand that I swore a blood oath to obey all orders given me by my ruler, whether I agreed with them or not. That is a burden every soldier must carry.'

'I understand,' said Fleya quietly.

'Now,' he went on. 'Perhaps you three would be so kind as to provide answers to some questions I have.' He turned to Lann. 'Jarl Gudbrandr, answer me honestly. Did you have any hand in the killing of the queen?'

A sad smile played on Lann's mouth. 'I doubt you would

allow me to stand here before you like this if you thought I had.'

'Nevertheless, I need to hear the words from your own lips.'

Lann placed his hand across his heart. 'Then my answer is no. I played no part in Favner's death.'

'But your weapon did,' the king said. Reaching down to one side, he lifted an item up from the floor and placed it on his lap. Although it had been wrapped in thick cloth, there was little doubting what it was. 'The dark blade. It is no ordinary sword, is it?'

Lann studied the man for a moment before answering. 'It is a weapon of the old gods, sworn to eradicate evil wherever it might find it. And it found evil here.'

The king frowned. When he spoke again his voice was low.

'I, like many others, had heard the rumours. That she killed my young half-brother, lying to her subjects that she'd sent him away to be schooled by holy men. That she was also responsible for the death of the king. And others. Her evil deeds sent her mad. And her madness made her all the more dangerous. Still, I should have acted against her.'

'Why didn't you?' Fleya asked, though there was no note of accusation in her voice.

'I didn't want to believe it. That, and the fact that those who opposed the queen in any way over the last year or so are no longer with us. Glaeverssun played his part in her reign of terror. He would have her remove anyone he thought posed a danger. I didn't act against him either. Does that make me a coward, I wonder?'

'No. As you said, you were a soldier, sworn to obey, not question.' Fleya tilted her head. 'The gods kept you alive for a purpose. Perhaps you are the man to make your kingdom whole again.'

'We are sorry for what happened here, King Rinkor,' Lann said. 'Please know that my friends and I want nothing more than to leave your borders as quickly as possible.'

'But your work here, and that of the dark blade, is not yet done.' They all turned in surprise at the sound of the new voice.

The man stepped forth from the shadows. He was dressed in the uniform worn by the royal guards, but Lann recognised him immediately as the red-robed priest who had taken him to the hidden temple in Stromgard.

Rinkor and Astrid, their reactions triggered by years of combat training, drew their swords almost in unison. The man put his hands up to show he was unarmed. He seemed unfazed by this threat of violence. Indeed, the smile on his lips merely broadened.

'He means us no harm,' Lann said.

'Who is he?' Astrid asked, her sword still trained on the newcomer.

The man addressed her, but his words were for them all. 'Someone who is interested in the Dreadblade and the safety of its wielder. Please, lower your weapons, my friends.'

Astrid glanced across at Rinkor, who gave her a small nod. The pair held the swords to their sides, although neither was willing to fully sheathe their blade.

'This man and I met at the feast in Stromgard,' Lann said.

'He is no man,' Fleya said, her voice as calm as the stranger's. 'He is the god Storren.'

Rinkor let out a gasp and dropped to his hands and knees, pressing his head to the cold stone of the dais. 'You honour us, Storren. I know in the old times the gods walked among us,' the newly crowned king said, his voice hoarse. 'But I never thought I would come face-to-face with one.'

The god seemed amused by the king's reaction. 'The people of Vorneland have always been my most ardent worshippers. Even now, when belief in the old gods wanes, many here still pray my name. Please – stand, Rinkor. We have much to discuss, and I would prefer to do so with the king on his feet.' He nodded at the man. 'It may have reached your ears from some local farmers that livestock has gone missing recently?'

Rinkor nodded. 'My people think it is the work of

wolves.' He shrugged. 'Those are the creatures usually responsible for taking livestock.'

'No wolf is to blame for these attacks' The god paused and took in the faces of those around him. 'No, something far more sinister is responsible.'

'What?'

'A local farmer came to the palace this morning with the carcass of a calf in his cart. At first he refused to leave unless you agreed to see it with your own eyes. He is a desperate man.' The god paused and gave a small shake of his head. 'He has good reason to be.'

The king frowned. 'Where is this farmer?'

'Your men persuaded him to leave the animal in the ice house and sent him away. You need to see this creature, what has happened to it, and understand what it means.'

'And that is?' said Rinkor, his eyebrows raised.

The god gave him a grave look. 'All in good time.' He gestured towards the large doors at the front of the long-house. 'Shall we?'

The ice house was in a small building next to the kitchens. Throwing back the bolt that held the door in place, Rinkor stepped into the place and beckoned for the others to follow.

The calf lay on the floor in the centre of the building, its dead eyes staring up at the ceiling above it. Having grown up on a cattle farm, Lann was not unused to encountering dead livestock and he took a step forward to get a better look at the animal. The beast seemed unhurt at first glance; there were no slashes or puncture marks on its hindquarters or flanks, as Lann would have expected if it had been pursued by wolves. It was only as he moved to the front of the animal that he saw the cause of its death.

Below the neck, where the animal's chest broadened out, was a great cavernous hole. As though a giant arm had reached in and …

He turned to look at the god Storren.

'Something took its heart,' Lann whispered.

'Indeed.' The god shook his head. 'The farmer, the man your guards sent away … His daughter went missing at about the same time he discovered this unfortunate creature. You can imagine what he fears.'

Lann closed his eyes, but the image of what had been done to the young animal was seared into his brain. Feeling his gorge rising, he pushed past the others to get out of the ice house, gulping in the fresh air outside. The others quickly joined him.

'What monstrosity is responsible for this?' Fleya asked.

'The creatures of the Void are many and varied,' Storren replied. 'But I would suggest this is the doing of an asghoul.' The god turned to Astrid. 'Your cousin, the young necromancer, is meddling in things he does not fully understand.

The dark majik he is trying to perform is allowing monsters that have long waited for a chance to cross over into this world to do so. Whatever killed that calf and took the young girl must be stopped.'

'Is she still alive?' Lann asked.

'She is. For now.'

Fleya spoke. 'We have no time. We must reach Kelewulf, and fast, or this will only be the first of many terrible incidents.'

'A girl is missing!' Astrid cried. 'We can't just leave her to her fate.'

Fleya bit her lip in frustration. 'Then we have no option but to separate. The pair of you will go looking for the asghoul and the child it has abducted. I will go on alone to face Kelewulf and the lich before they can do much more harm. Join me when you are able.'

'You will need me,' Lann protested. 'The blade, at least ...'

'The majik that the lich Yirgan possessed will be Kelewulf's to wield now. But I have a few tricks up my sleeve yet.' She leaned closer to him, her next words for him alone. 'You must do this, Lannigon. You must save the child. I knew this moment was coming. I had a vision that the two of us would be separated before the end of this journey.'

'And did your vision also show you your own fate?'

She looked deep into his eyes before replying. 'It did.'

'What did you see?'

'I can't tell you that, nephew.'

Lann turned to ask Storren a question, but the god was no longer there. Turning back round, he was not entirely surprised to find his aunt, too, had disappeared.

It was at this moment that the voice of the sword started up inside Lann's head again, the word all too familiar by now.

Nir-akuu.

Monsters.

Vissergott

31

Two more blocks were all that stood between Kelewulf and the completion of the vast, arched portal to the Void.

How long it had been since they'd started? He had no idea any more. But it had taken a terrible toll. He was painfully thin now, with dark haunted eyes set in a drawn face that had changed to such a degree that he'd been shocked when he'd caught sight of himself in a mirror the previous day.

Rain had been falling solidly for some time, and his sodden clothes stuck to his skin, offering no protection from the cold wind that blew in from the sea. But the weather and its effects hardly registered with the young necromancer.

Kelewulf talked to the lich quite openly now. After all, there was no one to hear, and no one to see his strange behaviour. 'I need to rest,' he said in a small voice. 'This majik … it's exhausting me.'

The lich stirred within him. *But we are so close. There will be time to rest soon enough, after we've achieved our goal.*

'We will not achieve our goal if I collapse—'

There was a moan behind him, a terrible, guttural sound, and Kelewulf spun around towards its source. A creature had appeared out of nowhere, a hideous thing that might once have been human but was now decayed and rotten. What little flesh still clung to it in places was greyish-purple, but most of it had fallen away, revealing muscle and sinew at some points, hints of bone or cartilage in others. The smell of rot and decay that accompanied it was like nothing he'd ever experienced, and it was as much as Kelewulf could do not to gag. The thing turned its head to look at him through rheumy grey eyes, the whites of which were a foul, sulphurous yellow colour.

'Did you summon this creature?' he asked, staring at it with a mixture of fascination and revulsion.

No, the lich replied, and Kelewulf heard the exultation in his voice. *The portal we are creating is ripping holes in the curtain that separates this world from the Void.*

The undead thing lifted its chin and sniffed the air. Then it turned and shuffled off in the direction of whatever it had detected.

'Where is it going?' he asked.

To feed, the lich responded, drawing the last word out and chuckling.

There was a pause while Kelewulf took this in. He didn't dare ask what it was the creature sought out.

Still tired? the lich whispered inside his head.

He realised that he wasn't. The appearance of the revenant had filled him with a new-found vigour, and he knew he wanted nothing more than to get on with their work and complete those last two blocks.

He smiled as he closed his eyes and summoned the majik within him.

He couldn't wait to see what other horrors they might summon forth.

Northern Vorneland

32

The farmer opened the door to his farmhouse just wide enough to peer out at the visitors, a young boy and girl, their travel cloaks wrapped tightly around them to stave off the cold. The night had become even more foggy in the last hour or so, and the grey air swirled slowly behind the pair.

'Yes? Who are you?' the man asked.

'We were sent by King Rinkor,' the boy answered.

The man's eyes widened upon hearing this. 'They … they wouldn't permit me to speak to him. I begged them, but they refused me an audience. I needed to tell him—'

'That is why we have come,' the girl said, interrupting him. 'To find the creature responsible for those terrible things. And to try and rescue your daughter.'

'I … I fear she is already dead,' the man said, tears filling his eyes. 'Whatever killed the calf has her now and—'

'Do not give up hope,' said the boy gently. 'Please. May we come in?'

The farmer drew the door wider. 'I am afraid it is a humble home. We are only simple farmers—'

'My family are … were cattle farmers,' the boy said. The man stared from him to the girl, taking in the quality of their clothes.

'You're farmers?'

'Not her,' the boy said, gesturing in the girl's direction. 'She's a princess.'

The look the girl gave the boy made the farmer glad that *he* wasn't on the receiving end of it. 'And he,' she said, flashing the boy a fierce smile, 'is an idiot.' Giving the farmer a nod, Astrid stepped into the farmhouse.

They sat before the fire, warming the cold that had set into their bones during the journey and sipping warm mead from cups that the farmer's wife had brought them. The man's name was Bortib, and both he and his wife seemed stunned into silence at hearing the circumstances of Queen Favner's death.

'The new king sent you?' Bortib asked eventually. 'Just the two of you? No soldiers?'

Lann shook his head. 'We are here with the king's blessing – but we were sent here by a god.'

'A god? What is this? Who are you?'

292

'The thing that killed your animals is not of this world,' Lann said. 'It has come from another place, a place where it and others like it have waited patiently for their chance to cross over.'

The sound of a baby waking up somewhere else in the house caused the farmer's wife to hurry out of the room.

'These creatures do not fear man,' continued Lann. 'But they fear this.' He patted the black scabbard hanging at his side. The others couldn't know it, but the action caused the sword to renew its strange lament inside his head. Ignoring the voice, he carried on. 'Astrid and I are only two, but the asghoul that has your daughter would rather face a hundred mounted soldiers than this blade.' He hadn't realised he'd got to his feet, and was completely taken aback when Farmer Bortib dropped to his knees before him, grasping at the hem of his cloak and thanking him. Embarrassed, Lann helped the man to his feet and fixed him with a kind smile.

'I think we had better go to sleep. We will need your help in the morning to find the place where you discovered the dead calf. My hope is that the Dreadblade can lead us to the asghoul from there. We will leave here at first light.'

They woke to find the world covered in a wet, grey blanket of fog, its cold creeping up around their feet and legs as the horses picked their way across the ground, whickering nervously.

'It has been like this for days,' Bortib said, sitting astride his pony.

Astrid shivered. There was something about the fog that made her deeply uneasy. It swirled and eddied, rocks and bushes looming out of it and disappearing again.

They rode in silence until eventually Bortib pulled his mount to a halt. Peering through the miasma, he pointed up ahead. 'I found the calf near the foot of those hills.'

'And your daughter was taken from the yard behind your farmhouse?' Astrid asked.

'Aye. Saffren was feeding the hens. My wife went to fetch her in for her tea, but she was nowhere to be found. We searched everywhere for her. That's how I discovered the dead animal out here.'

'You can go back now,' Lann said to the man in a quiet voice. 'This is the place. I can feel it.'

'I'd rather stay. I can fight. I can—'

'No. This is no place for you.'

Bortib opened his mouth to argue but Astrid stopped him. Reaching across, she placed her hand on his.

'Please,' she said gently when he turned to face her. 'Go back to your wife and baby. We do not doubt your bravery, but Lann and I stand more chance of rescuing your daughter if we do not have the worry of keeping you safe. We will do everything we can to bring Saffren back to you, I promise.'

There was a pause, and then the farmer gave a sad nod of his head before turning his mount around and moving off dejectedly.

'The sword speaks to you, doesn't it?' Astrid said once the man was gone. 'That's why you've been so quiet all the way here.'

'It does. It tells me that the creature is close by.' He paused, then added, 'It knows we are coming for it.'

'How? How can it know?'

'The sword told it.' He nudged his horse forward into the foothills. 'It told the asghoul to be ready.'

'So much for the element of surprise,' Astrid muttered under her breath.

After a short ride they spotted a land-hollow up ahead, a small but dense wood of evergreen trees growing up from it. Fog flowed down into that depression in the land, pooling and thickening as it did. With the bottom of the trees hidden, the visible portion of the plants appeared like a wooded island in a bleak, grey lake.

'There,' Lann said, nodding ahead. 'We should leave the horses here and proceed on foot.'

'Do you have any idea what an asghoul looks like?' Astrid said in a low voice as they walked down to the edge of the woods.

'No, but I think we are soon to find out.' He nodded at the bow in her hand. 'You should stay back a little and use that. Just try not to shoot me in the back by mistake, eh?'

'You've seen how good I am with this, Lannigon Gudbrandr. If I shoot you in the back, it will not be by mistake.' The serious expression on her face gave way to a broad grin, and the pair shared a smile at this gallows humour. As he turned away she considered her feelings for him – how he stirred up conflicting emotions and feelings in her. Sometimes he was infuriatingly innocent, at others wise beyond his years. She shook her head, telling herself to concentrate on the matter at hand.

Trees, their trunks wet with moisture, loomed out at them as they reached the bottom of the slope and made their way into the wood itself. The sound was all wrong, distorted and muffled with strange echoes that tricked the mind as to the direction of noises. The temperature was different, too: it was a good deal lower than it had been in the foothills.

Astrid unslung her bow and drew an arrow from her quiver as Lann passed her, walking fearlessly ahead towards an unknown danger. He was hardly recognisable as the boy she'd bested at sword skills. Was it purely the black sword's influence? Or was it something else? Something that had been there all along, but hidden somehow?

Just then, the forest suddenly went quiet; unnaturally

so, as if everything in it were holding its breath and waiting to see what would happen next. She'd almost forgotten the black bangle she wore around her upper arm, but it seemed to tingle and tighten a fraction in that moment.

The asghoul appeared out of nowhere. One second it wasn't there, the next it was, materialising out of the mist behind Lann. The thing was hideous. Horned antlers protruded from a misshapen head that looked as if it had been made from melted wax. Its eyes were deep set and blank, and like its head, the creature's body and limbs seemed too long, as if grotesquely stretched. The thing's elongated hands ended in black and wicked-looking claws, and she watched as the creature pulled back its arm, ready to thrust those deadly daggers through the flesh and muscle of the boy before it.

'Lann!' she managed to call out. But he was already moving, swivelling on his heel, the sword moving round in a deadly arc that should have scythed the creature's body in two.

But the blade cut only mist. The asghoul had disappeared as quickly as it had appeared.

'It came out of nowhere,' Astrid whispered.

If Lann was shaken by the experience, he didn't show it. When he spoke, his voice was calm and assured. 'Thanks for the warning,' he said. 'But we were lucky it materialised behind me and not you.'

'We should proceed together,' she told him. 'That way we can keep an eye on each other's backs.'

He nodded his agreement, then paused, frowning, and she guessed the blade was speaking to him again.

'The girl,' he said, nodding off to his left. 'She's this way.'

They set off again, cautiously moving through trees that seemed even more sinister now, their branches recalling the asghoul's antlers.

Astrid was aware something was watching them. The armlet tingled against the skin of her arm, alerting her to the monster's presence. Sometimes she thought the thing was to her left, sometimes to her right or behind her, as if it were shifting around, waiting for its moment.

Out of the corner of her eye she saw Lann come to a stop, his body tense. The bangle prickled a warning at the very moment the snap of a twig behind her told her she was the one in danger this time. Dropping her shoulder, she threw herself into a forward roll and was able to avoid the asghoul's deadly claws as they raked the air where she'd just been. Pulling the string of her bow and unleashing the arrow before she was even back to her feet, she was rewarded when the projectile found a home in the creature's shoulder, the hit accompanied by a terrifying screech that echoed through the trees. The second arrow was nocked and almost loosed when the creature winked out of existence again.

Lann was quickly at her side, the concern on his face clear to see as he took in the sight of blood leaking from her left boot. The monster had caught her foot as she rolled away. Astrid felt sickeningly dizzy for a moment as the pain of the wound swept through her.

'It'll be fine,' she said, doing her best to give him a reassuring smile. 'And I'm not the only one bleeding now. The monster has one of my arrows in it.'

'At least we know it can be hit. And it'll be warier now.'

They carried on, picking their way through the mist. Astrid's heart was hammering in her ears. Despite her trust in the armlet to give her a moment's forewarning, her wounded foot meant she might not react quickly enough when the monster next appeared. In all her time out with the huntsmen in the forests near her home, she'd never felt as if she were both the hunter and the hunted at the same time. And never had she stalked so deadly a prey.

As they came upon a small clearing they saw a girl bundled up against the roots of a huge tree, her eyes widening in a mixture of surprise and hope as she saw them. That she was Bortib's daughter there was no doubt: the fiery red hair atop her head was the same colour as her father's. A great wave of relief filled Astrid at the sight of the child, and she wanted nothing more than to free the farmer's daughter and be gone from these woods as quickly as possible. When they drew closer they saw that she was bound by thick vines, lashing her firmly in place.

Lann hurried forward and began to slice through the girl's bonds with the Dreadblade while Astrid kept watch. When the bangle around her arm tingled, Astrid had no time to call out. The asghoul was ahead of her, its hand raised, deadly claws extended to slash into Lann's back. Astrid raised her bow and loosed the arrow in a single fluid movement, sending the missile, not into the exposed back of the asghoul, but straight through the rear of that clawed hand, the power of the shot twisting the creature about and pinning the hand to the trunk of the tree the girl was secured to. Lann reacted in the same moment the arrow was loosed from Astrid's bow. He rose quickly to his feet, instinctively swinging the sword up and round, so that its deadly edge carved clean through the monster's forearm, which now hung from the tree like some terrible effigy.

The scream the creature let out sent icy shivers running through each of them. The asghoul looked from Lann to Astrid, then backed away, snarling and hissing as it clutched what remained of its ruined limb. It snapped its teeth in their direction, but it was clear to both that the monster was fearful in a way that it had not been before.

'It can't dematerialise now.'

Lann and Astrid spun around at the sound of a familiar voice. The god Storren stared across at the asghoul with open disgust. 'It needs to be whole to do that. Separating the arm has trapped it here.'

Astrid was the first to react, confidence filling her for the first time since they'd set foot in the woods.

She pulled her bowstring back and took aim, letting the arrow go and watching as it found a home in the asghoul's chest, sinking the creature to its knees. It screeched angrily at them, slapping at the arrow shaft and snapping it before swiping out with its remaining arm in an effort to wound the onrushing boy. But the black blade easily deflected the monster's feeble attack, and when the dark weapon swung through the air one last time it was to separate the creature's head from its body.

Astrid was already at his side, and the pair stared down at the creature for a moment. Then, without a word, they turned and held each other, as if to reassure themselves that they were unbroken and alive.

'You did well,' the god said, nodding at them both. 'An asghoul is a formidable opponent. Perhaps there is hope for this world yet.' He gestured at the decapitated head. 'Take some of the monster's antler.'

'We didn't come here to collect hunting trophies,' Astrid said.

'No, you did not. But such an object is capable of closing a portal into the Void. You must be quick. A dead shadow creature like an asghoul cannot stay in this realm for long.'

Astrid watched as Lann, the Dreadblade already raised over his head, brought it down to hack off a sizeable section of the antler. He picked it up just as the body and the severed arm of the asghoul disappeared.

'How—?' Lann turned to talk to the god, but there was nothing but mist where he had stood moments before.

Kneeling next to the girl, Lann wrapped his cloak around her shoulders. 'We'll get you home to your parents soon. But first we need to tend to my friend's wounds, all right?' She nodded back at him, and he noticed how blue her lips were. 'And while we're at it, I think you could do with warming up.'

They built a fire large enough to take the chill out of the air, and Astrid held the shaking child while Lann foraged nearby for plant stuffs he knew could help to stop infections. Having returned with what he needed, he set about putting stitches into the flesh of her calf before bandaging the leaves he'd gathered directly on to the wound. The gash was deep, and his needlework wasn't anywhere near as accomplished as his aunt's. Despite this, Astrid never complained once; in fact, he caught her looking with interest at his work, her grey eyes wide and serious.

Despite their exhaustion, none of them wished to stay in that place a moment longer than necessary. Having extinguished the fire, Lann carried the youngster back through the woods; slowly, so that Astrid would not have to struggle too much on her wounded leg.

Both of them noticed how the mist had already begun to thin.

'You are sure you will not stay?' Bortib asked, repeating the offer he had made moments earlier. He and his wife were beside themselves with relief at the return of their daughter, who was now safely tucked up in bed inside the farmhouse. 'Not even for one night?' The four of them were outside, Lann and Astrid making last-minute checks of their horses and equipment.

'We cannot,' Astrid answered. 'Another of our party is heading towards danger, and we need to reach her before she meets it.'

'There will be more monsters, won't there?' Bortib asked, his wife by his side now.

It was Lann who answered. 'I fear there will be, yes. That is, unless we succeed in what we must do next.'

'Then we wish you all the luck the gods can send your way. Here.' The man held out a tiny leather pouch.

Thinking it was money they were trying to offer, Lann shook his head, but the farmer reached out and pressed it into his hand. It was fantastically light.

'Seeds,' Bortib said, nodding his head. 'There is something about you, Jarl Gudbrandr ... something that tells

303

me you've grown from the land before. Take these, and I hope they will remind you of us when you finally get a chance to sow them.'

A memory came to Lann then: of tending Fleya's garden, the sun on his back and the smell of soil and the feel of the rich earth beneath his fingers. He swallowed at the lump that rose in his throat. Putting the little bag safely inside a pocket, he nodded his thanks and climbed up into the saddle of his horse.

The pair didn't look back as they rode away, but they knew they were being watched and prayed for. They knew, too, that these small acts of goodwill would have to sustain them through the horrors that lay ahead.

Vissergott

33

Fleya was almost there now. The horse, like her, was weary as it plodded up the hill that rose steadily ahead of them, its head hanging low to the ground. Urging the beast on, she reached the top of the ridge and looked down on the broad headland that was known simply as Vissergott. What she saw filled her with dread.

'By all the gods, Kelewulf, what have you done?' she murmured under her breath.

Below her, massive, glassy black blocks of shadowglas had been placed on top of each other to form a distorted and misshapen arch. The thing was huge, a vast and terrible portal. She eyed the shadowglas blocks and suppressed a cold shiver of fear. It was the same material that the gods had used to fashion the Nemesis Arch when they'd banished Lorgukk and his evil minions from this world, and now it was being used again to try and return them.

She had never seen so much of the stuff, and a part of her marvelled at the sheer force of will and majik that must have been needed to create it. Cursing under her breath, she turned her attention to the creature working below her. Kelewulf and the lich had summoned an Earth Elemental to help them carry out the task, and the huge, hulking golem was down there now, moving what appeared to be the last of the vast black blocks across the landscape to complete the final part of the edifice.

The structure was not even complete, and yet it was already beginning to wreak horror and chaos on their world. More and more fissures in the fabric that separated the two realms were opening up, letting creatures like the asghoul through. If Kelewulf successfully managed to activate a huge opening like the one she saw below, who knew what chaos and destruction would follow?

A cold wind blew in off the sea up ahead of her, tousling a strand of hair across her face.

She stared at the portal again, deep in thought. Fleya doubted such a thing could be held open for any length of time. The effort to do so would be immense, beyond anything even the undead lich was capable of. They could not bring Lorgukk back – not without the heart. So why bother to create it?

It was an act of evil, perpetrated by a maniac hell-bent on causing death and destruction. She wondered to what depths young Kelewulf had sunk even to consider such a thing, and how much dominion the lich held over the human body it inhabited. Her heart sank, both in sorrow and fear for the boy's soul.

She had to stop them. But how? There was no way she could simply confront the giant Elemental down there. It had been summoned not just for its colossal strength, but to act as a guardian for this place. A place that was …

She stood perfectly still, then, looking out over the landscape and the sea beyond. Vissergott was a headland. The tower had been built here because it was easy to defend against any attack made on it from the *land*.

But there were other elements.

She made her way along the ridge towards a small, stone structure that must once have been used by a shepherd in these parts. Sure enough, when she ducked inside, the little beehive-shaped place still had the unmistakeable whiff of livestock inside its crumbling walls. It was an ideal place for her needs; the opening looked out and down on to the headland. For centuries, she thought, the men and women who had worked these lands would have sheltered here.

Fleya took up her own position in the doorway, lowering herself on to the floor and pulling her cloak around her against the chill sea air.

She emptied her mind, and transported herself into the

place where she could tap into the Art. Her eyes were open, but she was looking at two realms now: the one before her, and the swirling vortex of power that she aimed to draw her majik from. She knew she would have to drink deep from that well, and that she would leave herself vulnerable by doing so.

The majik stirred inside her, and an icy shiver of fear ran down her spine. Turning her hands so the palms were facing up towards her, she intoned the words of the summoning, concentrating on the land and sea below her, and on the steely grey waters beyond the headland in particular. She felt powerful and filled with energy, but also became conscious that her presence here was no longer a secret. The lich was aware that something was attempting sorcery.

The waters beyond the headland began to move in an unusual way, swirling and churning the surface as if something just beneath were trying to break free. A noise, like water poured from a great height, filled Fleya's head. Doing her best to keep focused, she repeated the spell, the words merging with the now tumultuous noise that seemed to come from everywhere all at once.

Suddenly, without warning, a huge, winged dragon made entirely of water erupted from the sea and took to the air. Its enormous shadow hung over the land below, and great showers of seawater fell from it, soaking the earth. The creature's wings beat the air over the headland as it scanned the landscape below for something. Its mistress.

Already exhausted by her efforts, Fleya stumbled to her feet and out of the stone building. Looking up through the torrents of salty rain, her heart soared as the creature turned towards her. That great wet din still filled her head, and through it she could hear the creature, demanding to know why she had brought it here. Staggering slightly, the witch made it to the edge of the ridge.

When she looked down on the Earth Elemental a gasp escaped her lips. Perhaps spurred on by her presence, the creature had increased its efforts – the last block was about to be put in place. Pointing a shaking finger at the creature of rock and stone, she screeched her command to the skies, demanding the Water Elemental do what she had summoned it for.

Even before the words were fully out of her mouth, the Water Elemental had folded its wings and was diving downwards, falling from the heavens at great speed to try and intercept the stone golem before it could lower that final glassy block.

Fleya screamed in frustration as she realised she was too late.

The air changed, and a crackling discharge, like that released in a lightning storm, was emitted as the block was lowered into place. At the same time, the Earth Elemental turned its face towards its attacker, looking up and swinging an arm clumsily in an attempt to hit the thing streaking down towards it. Making no attempt to dodge the blow, the dragon opened its mouth and spewed forth a great column of seawater that struck the thing of rock and stone at full force in the chest, knocking it back off its feet. Mud and clay, boulders and stones as big as a man, fell from the Earth Elemental as it struggled upwards again. But the winged thing was no longer there. In one motion it climbed vertically, then turned over in the air so it was directly over its opponent.

Folding its wings again, the Water Elemental dropped out of the sky a second time. Head down, its long neck stretched out, it emitted a blood-curdling screech as it plummeted straight down, twisting at the last possible second to slam its vast tail into its foe. The Earth Elemental shattered like a china doll, bits of it flying in every direction until there was nothing left of the creature but scattered debris.

A small whimper escaped Fleya as the last of her strength threatened to leave her. With what remained, she begged the dragon to dive one last time; to smash those black glass towers in the same way it had smashed the golem.

But the Water Elemental was equally spent. Weakened

to the point that she could hardly stand, Fleya looked on in horror as the great flying creature fell to the ground as a sheer mass of water that quickly turned it to a sodden, boggy mess.

The witch clenched her fists. This was not over. She had to get down there to stop the portal being activated by the lich. She had to—

Fleya heard the footsteps behind her, but it was too late. Pain exploded behind her eyes, and then darkness consumed her.

Lann and Astrid rode through the night, ignoring their fatigue and fears as they hurried towards Vissergott, pushing their horses to the limit in the hope of getting to Fleya before she was forced to take on Kelewulf and the lich alone. Bent over the necks of their beasts, they hardly spoke a word throughout the long ride.

Their encounter with the farmer and his family had stirred up something inside Astrid that she had not expected: she was homesick. She found herself longing for news of her brother. She'd left without telling him how proud she was of him or how much she loved him, and, with the realisation that she might never see him again, those missed words hung heavily on her.

Her musings were abruptly cut short when the black bangle on her arm suddenly sent a painful shock through the limb, the sensation greater than anything she'd experienced when it had warned her about the asghoul. At the same time, Lann reined his horse to a halt, turning in the saddle to look across at her, the look of fear on his face perfectly matching her own.

'Something's happened,' he said, his head cocked to one side as if he were listening to something she couldn't hear. 'It's Fleya.' He gave her one last look before kicking his heels into the horse's flanks and urging it on at a full gallop.

Fleya slowly emerged from the blackness. Her head throbbed and she did her best to ignore the terrible pain behind her eyes. Her hands were tied behind her, the leather cords pulled wickedly tight so they bit into the flesh of her wrists. Flexing her fingers to try and get some blood flowing into them caused her to gasp in pain. Her feet were tied in a similar fashion.

She was still outside, but she was no longer up on the ridge. The wetness of the ground, coupled with the briny smell of seawater, suggested she must be down on the headland. The cold had soaked into her clothing and she let out an involuntary shiver.

'Good, you're awake,' she heard somebody behind her say.

More pain flared as she turned her head in the direction of the voice.

Kelewulf Rivengeld was hardly recognisable as the young man she'd met in Stromgard a few years earlier. During that first encounter she'd been struck by how different he was from his father or uncle, both of whom were thick-set Volken men. But at least he'd appeared healthy enough. Now he looked ... withered – like a once healthy plant that had endured a long drought and was hollowed out from within.

He was standing in a circle that had been gouged into the earth and filled with small stones and pebbles. She herself had used similar circles on many occasions.

'The Water Elemental was rather impressive. I should like to know how you managed it. Sadly for you, it was also a complete waste of time and effort.' He smiled down at her. 'It has left you exhausted. What a shame.'

'Who's talking to me right now?' she asked softly. 'Is it the young man I met once, full of potential and promise? Or the dark thing that is forcing him to do its bidding?' She waited for a response, continuing when none came, 'For that is what has happened here – you know that, Kelewulf, don't you? Regardless of what agreement you thought you had with Yirgan, he is slowly but surely possessing you. You are his dupe. A victim. Have you seen yourself lately? The way you look? Do you think the lich cares about you?'

Her questions drew nothing but mocking laughter.

'The lich and I are one now. We share common goals and desires that can only be realised by staying together.'

'Kelewulf, listen to me. Concentrate on my voice, and not the one inside your head. You can break this covenant. You can free yourself of the creature that occupies you. You can—'

'Silence!'

The boy threw an arm out, and the remaining words were shut off as Fleya felt an invisible hand squeezing her throat. She couldn't breathe, the pressure was too much, and as she gasped for air a wicked smile spread across Kelewulf's face. He was enjoying watching her eyes bulge in a face that was rapidly turning from red to purple. A black curtain began to obscure Fleya's vision and she was about to pass out again when she witnessed the smile falter. In its place was an odd expression: one of confusion and doubt.

'Enough. Please. Do not kill her.' The pressure released, and Fleya guessed that the boy had wrestled control back from the lich, even if only momentarily. She greedily sucked air into her lungs, warily watching the young man.

That there was a conflict going on inside him was clear. His face twisted into a terrible grimace one moment, an angry mask the next. Not only did his face contort, his whole body jerked and writhed as if he were struggling to control it.

'She is dangerous to us. I should end her now.'

'She is more useful to us alive. The boy is coming. And he brings with him the Dreadblade. He cares about the witch. We can bargain with her life.'

'You meddle too much, lich. Remember who is the master and who is the servant here.'

A small gasp escaped Fleya. Her situation was even more perilous than she'd imagined. *It was the boy, not the lich, who had the upper hand!* The realisation made her skin crawl. *How could she have misjudged the boy's power so badly?*

As if sensing this, the young man looked down at her with a sneer.

'Do you still think I am its puppet, witch? Hmm? You're right about one thing: the lich did indeed try to take over. It went against the agreement we made when I first summoned it. But I was prepared. I did not enter into the covenant lightly. I had planned for Yirgan's betrayal. Because I knew it would eventually come. I'd equipped myself with spells and protective wards, all kept hidden from the lich, of course, to ensure that such a thing could not happen. And now the lich's powers are mine, and it is little more than my slave. I will dispense with it soon. Its usefulness is wearing thin. But who knows? There might be a thing or two it could still teach me, I suppose.'

'You're a monster,' Fleya croaked.

'A monster, you say?' He laughed. 'In a few short moments I shall open a portal to another dimension. Then you will see what monsters truly are.'

'This is your world, Kelewulf. This is the land of your people. You cannot unleash the horrors of the Void on them. People will die.'

'Oh, I do hope so.'

Fleya gave a small shake of her head. 'Whatever you do, you can't bring her back. You know that, don't you?' She stared into his sunken eyes, willing him to hear her. 'Your mother is gone. I know how you've carried the anger of her loss with you all these years, and that burden has warped you, Kelewulf. But it is not too late. The portal is not yet open. You can still change.'

'Change? I *have* changed!' He gave her a cruel smile. 'Oh, you mean change for the better. Into something like you. And why would I want to do that, hmm? You talk as if I should care what happens to this world and its people. But this world has done nothing for me. My people don't give a damn for anybody unable to swing a sword or axe. This world gave me a father who treated me like dirt. And it allowed him to take away the one person who cared for me. The people who you are so concerned about made me feel small and weak and useless. And now they shall suffer as I did.'

'Your mother was not well. Your father treated her

badly. But hear me, Kelewulf,' Fleya pleaded. 'She would never have wanted this.'

'She wanted me to be strong ...'

'Not like this. This is not strength. Strength is living in the world and changing it for the better. You will change this world into an even more terrible place.'

'Gods and monsters roamed this realm once. Who's to say that was not a better time than this?'

'Because this is the time of man. Those days are gone.'

'We shall see.'

'Kelewulf! Please, I beg you! STOP!'

But the boy wasn't listening any more. His head was tilted back, and she saw his eyes roll back as the words of an ancient language spilt from his lips.

Fleya felt the power that was being called upon: a wrenching sensation that caused her to let out a small cry of fear. She bucked her body, twisting it in an effort to roll towards the safety of the small circle that he'd created around him, but it was hopeless. She could feel the coldness of the Void seep into her bones, she could hear the anger of the creatures within it: howls, screeches, moans and screams of excitement filled the air around her as the light inside it waned.

Then they came.

Not in ones or twos, but in a horrifying flood of teeth and claws, scales and feathers, wings and tentacles. Some were large, others small, but all were terrifying. Things which belonged in the darkest recesses of the imagination or in stories designed to scare children. Ghostly wraiths, demonic chimeras and ghastly undead things appeared out of nowhere, filling the air with their cacophony of sound until her ears hurt.

She sought to summon a spell of protection, already knowing that the majik would not come. Kelewulf was right; she was spent, and could do nothing but accept her fate.

She turned to look back at the young necromancer again, noting how he, too, appeared to be on the point of collapse, his entire body trembling with the immense effort he was having to expend to keep the portal open. She understood the willpower and energy such a feat required, and a tiny part of her couldn't help but marvel that one so young and untrained was capable of carrying it out. What little colour there had been to his skin had now disappeared completely, leaving him the colour of bleached bone. He'd badly bitten his tongue during the spell, and blood ran from the side of his mouth on to his neck and clothing. A great convulsion went through him, and she watched as his knees buckled. He almost collapsed in that moment, but somehow he found yet more strength to continue. She doubted she'd ever met anyone with such raw power. And she knew there would only be one outcome if Lann, even with the Dreadblade, tried to stand against it.

The terrible cold that had signalled the merging of the two realms disappeared, and she knew the portal was no longer open.

Fleya did not know how much darkness and terror had leached from that realm to this. But she knew that the world would never be the same again.

She felt the thing behind her before she heard it. A dark, horned thing that came at her with its claws raised, its lips peeled back to reveal row upon row of jagged teeth.

Fleya had seen the monster before; seen this exact moment. She had seen her own death in a vision on the night before she and Lann had set out from her home, and she knew that right now, at this very moment, he and Astrid were running towards her from the hills above, trying to save her from her fate.

She knew all these things.

Just as she knew they would be too late.

34

Lann and Astrid approached the hilltop overlooking Vissergott at a full gallop, and both were nearly thrown from their mounts when the creatures skidded to an abrupt stop and reared up, rolling their eyes in fright. Despite their urgings, neither animal would go on.

Lann could not blame them. He had felt it too: an omen of evil that affected both human and horse at the most basic of levels.

'We have to hurry,' Astrid said, climbing down from her saddle and moving towards the bluff. 'Lann?'

He hardly heard her words due to the clamour of noise that filled his head. The black blade's usual mutterings had risen to a screeching jumble of warnings and urgings and demands. He staggered as he climbed down from his horse. When he looked at his right hand he saw that the sword was already firmly in his grasp, even though he had no recollection of having drawn the blade from its scabbard.

Nir-akuu. Nir-Akuu. Nir-Akuu! NIR-AKUU! NIR-AKUU!!

'Lann?' Astrid took a step in his direction, but halted when he held a hand out. There was a dangerous look in his eye, something she had not seen before.

'I am your keeper and will do your work,' Lann said through gritted teeth. He was looking out at a point in the distance beyond her, and Astrid knew he was speaking to the blade. 'But I cannot do those things if you fill my mind with this noise. Relent, and we will do what must be done ... together.'

The sword did as it was bid, and Lann was able to relax ever so slightly as the tumult in his head subsided. The incessant voice of the sword was still there, but Lann could hear his own thoughts now. Shaking his head as if to clear it, he focused on Astrid and gave her a small reassuring smile.

The pair hurried up to the edge of the hill overlooking the headland, but were stopped in their tracks by what they saw below.

'Kelewulf,' Astrid said in a small voice, and Lann followed the direction of her gaze.

A thin boy was standing inside a small ring marked out in the ground. A short distance in front of him, bound by her hands and feet, was Fleya. One side of her pale face was covered in blood from a head injury, and she appeared to be talking to the young necromancer, even though it was clear she was struggling to do so.

Whatever she said was ignored by Kelewulf. Lann and Astrid watched as he tilted his head back and started to intone words in a strange language, the sounds drifting up to them on the wind. Even from where he stood, Lann could make out the fear and desperation on his aunt's face, and he fancied he heard her cry out, begging the young man to stop.

Lann began moving in the direction of his aunt when the sword sang its harsh battle cry again in his head. At the same moment, a horde of vile and terrible creatures appeared from within the huge arch-shaped construction, those at the front pushed out by the mass of others behind them as they surged forward. Things no human eyes should see spilt out into this world, causing him to shrivel inside with terror. As he watched, one of the monsters raised its head in Fleya's direction and started moving towards her.

He heard Astrid shout out, and it was this sound, not the screaming cries of the Dreadblade, that spurred him into action. He wasn't aware that he had set off down the hill, his legs only just staying beneath him and finding the next footing as he hurtled down the steep slope.

He too was screaming now, a great war cry that echoed

the words of the blade, the two in unison once more as they sought to prevent the shadowy thing from reaching Fleya. There was a harsh, fizzing sound above him, and he caught the flash of the arrow in flight as it cut through the air not far over his head. Astrid's aim was true, and he saw the arrowhead find a home in the foul creature's chest, knocking it back for a moment. But it was only for a moment. The monster swiped at the arrow in annoyance, snapping the wooden shaft with a swat of its claws, even as a second found a home in its shoulder.

Time seemed to slow – a cruel trick of the mind that made Lann realise that no matter what he and Astrid tried, Fleya's fate was sealed. The monster was almost on her, reaching out with long, curved talons to tear her apart. Without faltering, Lann raised the black sword, lifting his arm up over his shoulder before launching it forward again with all his might to hurl the blade.

End over end the dark blade tumbled through the space between the youth and the monster. He could hear it as it flew, and he knew the monster heard it too. But the dark creature would not be distracted from its goal. Its eyes still fixed on the witch, lips peeled back in a ghastly grimace, it swung its arm in a wide arc, raking those awful claws through Fleya's body. Lann shuddered when he heard his aunt's terrible cry of pain – a cry that was echoed, too late, by her attacker, the creature falling back and crashing to the ground as the sword buried itself deep in its throat.

Running to where his aunt lay, Astrid close behind him, Lann heard the shield maiden cry out. Turning his head in the direction of her voice, he watched as she pulled her hand back and prepared to throw something in the direction of the portal, from which monsters continued to pour. The severed piece of the asghoul's antler flew out in a high arc, landing in the pulsing blackness of the opening. And as it did, he felt the world pinch back in on itself, snapping shut the terrible breach as if incensed that it had been so violated. No more of the vile creatures could enter now, but more than enough had already managed to cross over.

Lann sobbed as he neared the dying body of his aunt. Blood poured from the dreadful wounds she'd suffered, her clothes already soaked through with the stuff. His head was filled with a tumult of sound: the screeching, gibbering, moaning cacophony of the monstrous horde was matched by the Dreadblade's screams as it demanded to be about its work. Over and above all this was his own bellowed cry of anguish as he threw his head back and cursed the gods.

Then Astrid was there. Falling to her knees beside his aunt, she looked first at Lann and then at the horrifying host massed behind him.

'Go!' she said, her eyes already full of tears. 'I am with her. Go and do what you must!'

With one last look at Fleya, he turned towards that terrifying horde. Then, driven by rage and grief, he snatched up the sword and ran into it.

To anyone watching that day, it would have appeared that the boy and the dark blade he wielded were a force of nature. Wild, vicious and merciless, they set about the malevolent mass of creatures. Slashing and stabbing, cutting and hacking left and right, they were as relentless as they were ruthless. Limbs were severed, terrible wounds opened up, and blood flowed in torrents from the shrieking, howling things that had dared to come through the portal. Many ran or flew away before this onslaught, seeking to get as far away from the black blade as they could. Others tried to resist, and these were the first to fall, scythed down by the young man and his sword.

The Dreadblade sang in his hand and head. It drank deep that day, doing what it was forged to do. Wild with the bloodlust, Lann had no idea how long the slaughter went on for; time no longer had any meaning to the boy or the blade as they stabbed and slashed and cut. Everything was death and destruction.

When the killing was finally over, the blade fell silent, and both sword and wielder collapsed to the ground amidst the dead.

* * *

325

Astrid felt the silence too. She had been kneeling at Fleya's side, cradling the woman in her arms as the last breath left her body. Now she lifted her head and saw Lann stagger and fall.

Reluctant to leave her charge, she gently placed Fleya back down on the earth and went to him. Lann was on his hands and knees, surrounded by the bodies of his victims. Astrid's first thought was that he must be mortally wounded. He was a thing of red in a sea of the same colour; a sea made up of limbs and wings, heads and corpses. It was only his eyes that weren't the colour of the death about him, and they now stared sightlessly out from a gruesome crimson mask.

'Lann? Lann, it's me … Astrid.' Dropping down beside him, she frowned when he didn't respond. 'Lann. Let me help you up. Please.' She reached out a hand to him, and when he eventually put his own in hers, she gently pulled him to his feet. Somehow the sword still remained grasped in his other hand, and she gingerly reached out and took it, returning it to the scabbard by his side.

'Are you hurt?' she asked.

Staring out into nothingness, he answered her question with a small, almost imperceptible shake of his head.

'Fleya?' he said, looking at her for the first time. He waited, then nodded when he saw the answer in her eyes. When he spoke again, his voice was little more than a whisper. 'She knew. She knew she would not leave this place. And yet she still came.'

'She thought she could stop Kelewulf. She had to try.'

At the mention of the necromancer, Lann turned to look in the direction of where he'd last seen the young man. But the circle was empty.

'He's gone,' Astrid said.

'I couldn't reach that creature in time. I tried, but I couldn't. And then –' he stifled a sob – 'then … I left her to die alone.'

Astrid shook her head and let out a shuddering sigh. 'She was not alone. I was with her and spoke to her before she died. She somehow managed to hold on long enough for me to do that. She knew you could not be with her, Lann. She told me she had seen what would happen here today in a vision.' Astrid paused and gathered herself. 'She told me to tell you that she loved you, and that she was proud to have been a part of your life in this world.'

He looked down at his bloody hands, slowly turning them as if trying to grasp how they could have come to look like this. 'I let myself be taken over by anger, and by the needs of the blade. I should have been at her side—'

'No, Lann. You did what you had to do – what you were fated to do. Come. Come and say goodbye to her.'

Unable to speak, Lann could only nod. Tears fell, making pale tracks down through the blood that covered his face.

Astrid took his hand and led him over to his aunt's unmoving body. The majik that had sustained her for all of her long years in this world was gone now, and the woman he looked down on was elderly and frail, beautiful and at peace.

'I am sorry for your loss, Lannigon Gudbrandr.'

The pair spun around at the sound of a man's voice.

He was dressed in rags, like a beggar, and he had a long silver beard, but Lann immediately recognised the golden eyes.

Rakur.

'Your aunt was a good woman who used her majik for the betterment of the people around her. She was much admired and will be missed in this world.'

Lann looked stonily at the god. 'She wasn't a fan of yours.'

'No. Then again, few people are.' The god turned his attention to the girl at Lann's side, giving her a nod. 'Astrid Rivengeld.'

'You have me at a disadvantage. You are?'

'I have many names, in different places. But to your people I am known as Rakur.'

The girl nodded, and he raised an eyebrow.

'Usually the arrival of an old god is met with more deference.'

'You are not the first god I have met in recent times.'

She stared out at the bloody field. 'What I find hard to understand is why the gods who have ignored our prayers and worship for centuries have suddenly decided to come among us again?'

Rakur, too, looked about him at the carnage before turning back to them both. 'Ah, but these are not ordinary times, are they? And neither of you are ordinary people.'

'And yet my aunt still had to die,' Lann said, the anger in his words clear to hear.

'You would have had me meddle with fate and save her?'

'Yes.'

'And if I had, would your rage have been so great when you saw her struck down like that? Your fury sustained you here today in a way that no other emotion could. How many of these foul creatures did you kill, fuelled by that same rage?'

'Not enough. Many escaped.'

'Yes. And this world and the people of these lands will suffer because of that. But their suffering would have been far greater had it not been for you.' The god gave a little shake of his head. 'She had to die. It was written. We interfere with the fates of you humans at great risk.'

'Yet you interfered with *my* fate. You gave me the dark sword, knowing I would never be the same again.'

'Ah, but did I? Maybe I just facilitated something that was meant to be.'

'What are you saying?' Lann said, frowning. 'That I was … *destined* to wield the weapon?'

'Who else?'

Lann waited for the god to continue, shaking his head when the deity stared back at him blankly. 'It's true what they say about you. You speak only in riddles. Half-truths and words designed to trick us. My aunt knew this. She warned me never to trust you.'

Rakur smiled, but there was no humour in his look. 'Then let me speak plainly to you, Lannigon Gudbrandr. Your aunt told you many things, but she withheld something crucial. When we first met, you asked me whether I was your father. Do you remember?'

Lann nodded.

'You also asked me what happened to the gods when people stopped believing in them.' He hesitated as if weighing up how best to go on. 'Who was the sword forged for?'

'Trogir.' Lann remembered his time in the catacombs. 'He who banished the dark god Lorgukk. And after he'd saved the world from the dark god, you and the other gods tried to kill him.'

Rakur nodded. 'He was insane. The fight against Lorgukk had taken his senses. Power can corrupt the purest heart. He wanted to rule over this human world on his own. If that had happened, we would simply have been swapping one tyrannical monster for another. But we were unsuccessful. He escaped. Trogir wandered this world for hundreds of years, half mad, and unaware of who he was.' He lifted his extraordinary eyes and looked at Lann. 'He found peace when he finally found love.'

Realisation dawned on Lann. 'My mother … She fell in love with the god Trogir?'

Rakur nodded. 'By then he was neither god nor man. He fell in love with Lette every bit as much as she loved him. You were a result of that happiness.'

Lann felt the sword stir at his side.

'The Dreadblade. Nobody else can wield it, can they?'

'No. Not while you live.' The god studied the boy for a moment. 'Now do you understand what I meant when I told you I have not interfered with your fate?' He made a gesture that took in the carnage behind them. 'This *is* your fate, Lannigon Gudbrandr. Yours too, Astrid Rivengeld. And your journey together has only just begun. Your destinies, and that of the young necromancer Kelewulf, are like intertwined ropes stretching out before you all. Your aunt knew this. She gave her life so you might know it too.'

He glanced behind him, as though called by a voice only he could hear. 'I must leave you now.'

Lann took a step towards him. 'Wait. You say we have a path to walk together – what do we do now?'

But the god had turned his back on them and was slowly

walking away. He called back over his shoulder, his voice coming to them faintly. 'First, you and the Dreadblade must rid these lands of the vile creatures that escaped you today. Make these lands safe again.'

'And then? What about Kelewulf?'

'Hasz. That is where you must journey if you wish to stop the necromancer. Today was merely a test of his new-found powers. To bring Lorgukk back to this world, he needs the dark god's heart. And that is in Hasz. But beware. The Hasz'een have no love for the Volken people. You will have to be brave, little demigod.' He laughed at this, the mocking sound carried away on the wind and disappearing just as he himself did.

The rush of wings made Lann turn. A crow flew past him, so close he could feel air on his face. Looking to where Fleya's body had been, he saw that only the clothes she'd been wearing remained.

He looked past the garments towards the two crows perched on a large lichen-covered rock. The creatures seemed to be intently watching him and Astrid.

'Lette and Fleya. They are together again,' Astrid said softly.

'Yes. My aunt will be happy. She missed her sister very much.' He swallowed, his mind a jumbled mix of feelings and emotions. He knew Fleya had faced Kelewulf with full knowledge of what would happen. He also somehow knew that she was happy now, and free. But he felt desolate without her.

'And they will always be with you, Lann. You know that, don't you?'

'With *us*,' he said, glancing at her. 'I cannot do this alone, Astrid. I would not be standing here now if you had not come along with me.' He remembered an expression his aunt had been fond of, the memory making him smile, despite everything. 'We are leaves being blown around on the breath of the gods. Will you allow yourself to sail on those winds with me a little longer?'

The grin she gave him in return made his heart lift for the first time since they'd arrived in Vissergott. 'I would like that.'

As one, the crows cawed – a triumphant sound. Then, unfurling their wings, they leaped into the sky and flew off towards the sea – towards the West and the land of the Hasz'een.

Lann had no choice but to follow.

At least he would not do so alone.

Acknowledgements

I did something I said I'd never do with this book – I pitched the idea to my editor while I was in the middle of writing another book. And when I did, I was a little taken back by her reaction: 'Write *that* book. That's the book you should write next.' Her enthusiasm for the idea was such that I took her advice and started work on it straight away.

Dark Blade was a long time in the making. Some of that was down to me and some of it wasn't, but the fact that it exists at all is thanks to a group of people who have believed in me throughout my writing career, even when I'd lost my own faith.

Thanks to everyone at Bloomsbury Children's for their hard work on *Dark Blade*, but in particular: Rebecca McNally for that initial encouragement; Callum Kenny for his enthusiasm and for being not just a flipping great editor, but for 'getting it'; Fliss Stevens for spotting my errors and stopping me from looking like a fool; Ian Lamb, Emily Moran and the marketing team. And thank you to all the other wonderful people working behind the scenes who helped make the majik happen.

I also have to thank my agent, Catherine Pellegrino, who has been with me through thick and thin, good times and bad. You picked me out of the slush pile and have been a great source of encouragement when I need an ear to bend or someone to moan to.

Thank you also to the ridiculously talented Francesca Baerald, who turned my inept scribble into the fabulous map of Strom and its surrounding kingdoms. And ZhiHui Su for devising and creating such a wonderful cover.

Finally I'd like to thank my family for everything they have had to put up with. Zoe, Hope and Kyran – I love you, and this book is as much yours as it is mine. x

About the Author

Steve Feasey lives in Hertfordshire with his wife and children. He says he didn't learn much at school, but he was always a voracious reader. He started writing fiction in his thirties, inspired by his own favourite writers: Stephen King, Elmore Leonard and Charles Dickens. His first book, *Changeling,* was shortlisted for the Waterstones Prize and became a successful series. He is also the author of the acclaimed Mutant City series. This is his first novel set in the world of Stromgard.

@stevefeasey

Fifty years ago the world was almost destroyed by a chemical war. Now the world is divided into the mutants and the pure.

Thirteen years ago a covert government facility was shut down and its residents killed. The secrets it held died with them. But five extraordinary kids survived …

Everything changed when Rush discovered that he
wasn't the only mutant with incredible powers.
Now he and his friends have a deadly mission
that means more than their own survival.

Together they're the ultimate weapon – but
someone will stop at nothing to break them up.